Merry Christmas and a Happy END OF THE WORLD

After encountering a peculiar creature deep in the woods, Bennie and his friends are whisked away on a fantastical adventure that carries them to bizarre, far-flung places and exposes them to a terrifying enemy.

To rescue Christmas and the planet, Bennie and his friends must coax Earth's most reclusive hero from retirement.

Jump into the blue and join Bennie and his friends on a whirlwind adventure this Yuletide—a fun, festive story for all the family!

Books by Iestyn Long

The Timothy Williams Saga

Book One: Demon Hunter
Book Two: The Infernal Shadow

Demon Hunters

The Black Knight
The Chronicles of Cassius
Zen Lee & The Yellow Emperor

Other Stories

Merry Christmas and a Happy End of the World

Merry Christmas and a Happy

END OF THE WORLD

By Iestyn Long

https://www.demon-hunter.co.uk
https://www.demonhuntersupplies.co.uk

ISBN: 978-1-7384182-0-6

For Reuben

This one's for the kids!
And thanks to the real Alice and Mabel

1

Poor Old Farmer Grindle

The fire crackled, and the radio hummed quietly with Christmas carols. In an armchair beside the hearth, Farmer Grindle dozed contentedly. That's what happens after a hard day's work at the ripe old age of seventy-one, especially after scoffing an overloaded plateful of pie and mash, a tankard of best stout, three glasses of mulled wine, and an obscenely large dollop of treacle tart drowned in custard.

And what do seventy-one-year-olds dream about after succumbing to the land of nod in front of the hearth? Well, more often than not, they dream of their lost youth. In Farmer Grindle's case, a youth spent playing in his grandfather's apple orchards.

Transformed into a smaller, skinnier, and far happier former version of himself, the freckled, short-trousered Farmer Grindle of yesteryear cavorted merrily through his grandfather's orchards mounted atop Gertrude—a particularly plump yet surprisingly dexterous sow.

However, as dreams have a tendency to do and usually without warning or consideration for the mental turmoil unleashed on their hosts, the episode rapidly developed a fanciful theme. Not that riding a pig like a jousting warhorse at Camelot was anything less than farfetched, of course.

Gertrude promptly sprouted a pair of magnificent pink wings, and now young Farmer Grindle wasn't charging through the trees like Sir Lancelot; he was swooping between their knotted trunks and sprawling branches like an RAF fighter ace on a daring mission behind enemy lines. He dived and rolled, dodging blossom flak and apple bombs with gung-ho gallantry.

Then, following another abrupt and disorientating change to proceedings, Farmer Grindle found himself waiting patiently at the dinner table while his mother happily carved the Sunday roast: plump winged sow.

'Mmmmmm... GERTRUDE,' Farmer Grindle moaned, licking his lips, his weathered face twitching as he dreamed. Despite Farmer Grindle's full stomach, it was all too evident that poor Gertrude tasted rather lovely.

Curled by her master's feet, Mr and Mrs Grindle's pet dog snored abominably. She was a black and white border collie. Actually, she was all black except for a white nose and four paws. It looked like she had stuck her snout into a tin of emulsion before knocking it over and jumping gleefully in the resulting puddle. Her name was Maggie. Well, Farmer Grindle called her Maggie. Mrs Grindle allowed no such lapse in etiquette. She was Lady Thatcher or, very occasionally, in moments of weakness, Margaret.

Not only was Mrs Grindle a Thatcherite—and no, not a dastardly splinter faction spouting imperialism in a science fiction movie, although some will inevitably identify similarities, but a devout yet dwindling army of elderly, middle-classed women who smell of lavender, like the colour blue, and pine for the return of public hangings, the abolition of the welfare system, and an outright ban on denim—she was also a fervent royalist.

The walls of Mr and Mrs Grindle's farm cottage were smothered with past and present portraits of royals and conservative leaders. And it was these pictures that began shaking first.

Immediately, Maggie's black ears pricked up. Raising her head, she sniffed the air with suspicion.

The rumbling grew.

Suddenly, Princess Beatrice was launched from above the fireplace, quickly followed by Boris Johnson, Prince Albert, and Lord Lucan. Then—and thank goodness Mrs Grindle wasn't home to witness the tragedy—Queen Victoria herself plummeted to the floorboards with an almighty crash. It was this final tragic royal suicide that stirred Farmer Grindle from his happy slumber.

'What's goin' on?' the farmer blurted, lurching forward in his chair. He grabbed the armrests with his bony hands and held on for dear life as the room shook around him. 'An EARTHQUAKE in LARKBRIDGE! WELL, I NEVER!'

The lights flickered, and the patterned lampshade above his balding head swung like a pendulum. The radio made a terrible high-pitched squealing before perishing in a puff of smoke. Then Farmer Grindle heard a loud fizzing noise from outside, like a supercharged pylon about to explode.

Maggie began whimpering.

As the rumbling reached a crescendo, a bright light flashed through the windows. Farmer Grindle jumped in shock as the remaining royals and prime ministers joined their fallen head of state by simultaneously leaping from the walls and dashing themselves at the farmer's slippered feet.

'CAWD A HELL!'

Just as quickly as the incident started, it stopped.

Farmer Grindle winced at the damage. *I'll need to put this lot right before Her Majesty gets home.* He was, of course, referring to his beloved wife.

Mrs Grindle was out at a Christmas party with friends. It never ceased to amaze Farmer Grindle how his wife had any friends at all. There were trout in the River Orwell with infinitely more warmth and social charm. *They're not friends; they're ruddy subjects,* he mused, a slight smirk twitching his thin lips. Farmer Grindle suspected they were simply too scared to tell her how they really felt. *Just like I am,* he thought, eyeing the woman's collection of broken portraits with dread. *Well, they'll have to wait.*

Opposite the hearth and miraculously unscathed by the disturbance stood Mr and Mrs Grindle's Christmas tree. It was a stiff plastic thing, six feet tall and perfectly symmetrical. 'The same tree as last year,' Farmer Grindle muttered, shaking his head. *And the year before then.* And every year for as long as he could remember.

Farmer Grindle much preferred a real tree, like the ones his father brought home for the holidays when he was a nipper. He wasn't a fan of the fake offering Mrs

Grindle insisted he haul down from the attic each December.

It was the aroma Farmer Grindle missed the most. 'Cat's wee,' he said with fondness. 'That's what them conifers smell like.' *The scent of Christmas.* He wouldn't have it any other way. Well, he wouldn't if he and not his wife were in charge.

Farmer Grindle stared disapprovingly at the tree with its regimented blue baubles dangling exactly ten centimetres apart. *Damn plastic don't smell of nuth'n.* It didn't have any lights either. Mrs Grindle said they were a waste of electricity. And worse than that, the tree's crowning glory wasn't a star or an angel or even Father Christmas; it was Mrs Grindle's idol.

Perched atop the tree, casting her beady gaze over one and all was Baroness Thatcher herself, the matriarch of all Thatcherites, complete with power suit, blue-rinsed perm, and a wagging battery-powered index finger. The fact that dear old Mrs Thatcher had passed away some years ago had seemingly not diminished Mrs Grindle's loyalty.

God knows where the wife found the ruddy thing. Farmer Grindle was fairly certain high street stores didn't stock ex-prime minister dolls. *Mind you,* he thought wryly, *there's undoubtedly a market for usin' 'em as target practice.*

Pushing himself to his feet, Farmer Grindle grabbed his flat cap from beside the hearth and made his way to the hall where the peculiar rumbling had brought more pictures and ornaments tumbling from their positions.

Cursing his arthritic joints and bad back, the farmer claimed his green wax jacket from the tiles where it had fallen. Slowly straightening, he slipped his arms into the coat before zipping himself in nice and tight. In Farmer Grindle's opinion, there was no such thing as bad weather, only the wrong sort of clothing.

'Come on, Maggie. Let's check on them turkeys,' he said, unhooking a torch beside the back door.

The dog stared wide-eyed from the kitchen doorway, trembling with fright.

'Don't be daft, Maggie. It's just a bit of bad weather, that's all. What do you think is out there? MONSTERS?'

Tentatively, Maggie crept to her master's side.

Switching on the torch, Farmer Grindle braced himself against the expected storm and opened the door. 'That's a rum ol' do.'

There wasn't a breath of wind. The night air was bitterly cold, and the farmer's breath misted in front of his face, rising like smoke into the sky.

'The weather must've moved on,' he muttered with a shrug. 'Jigger me, Maggie. It's brass monkeys out here.'

The old man pointed the torch at the farm buildings. 'I can't see nuth'n amiss.'

Suddenly, there was a crash from the turkey barn. Farmer Grindle heard the birds inside gibbering in alarm. 'FOXES!' he cursed, hurrying across the yard.

Another bright flash illuminated the night.

Undeterred, he shouldered open the wooden doors and burst into the barn. Inside, the light had vanished—and so had his birds.

In a panic, Farmer Grindle shined the torch into every nook and cranny, but there wasn't a single turkey to be seen. 'WE'VE BEEN ROBBED!'

He flicked the barn's lights on… but nothing happened.

The storm must've knocked out the power, he mused, repeatedly turning the switches on and off.

Maggie bared her teeth and growled. She stared into the shadows with hackles raised. Something had spooked her.

'What is it, girl?' The farmer directed his light deeper into the barn's black depths. 'WHO'S OUT THERE?'

All of a sudden, Maggie turned tail and promptly bolted through the doors and out into the night.

'Maggie, where you goin'? So much for man's best friend!'

Something moved in the darkness.

Farmer Grindle couldn't see anything, but he could sense a presence. His breath caught in his throat. *There's somethin' in here with me.* He wanted to run like the dog, but he couldn't seem to move. He was frozen to the spot. Fear numbed his limbs. The farmer's trembling hand gripped the torch so hard his fingers turned white.

'What… do you… want?'

There was no answer.

'Where are my turkeys?' he demanded, sounding braver than he felt.

'*Your turkeys?*' came a voice from the darkness, the speech scarcely decipherable. It was a strange guttural gibbering.

'You sound awful peculiar. Where you from… **GRIMBSY?**'

A tall figure emerged into the torchlight.

'I'LL BE… YOU'RE A RUM-LOOKING FELLA!'

Farmer Grindle shuddered. Surely, not even folk from Grimsby looked as odd or as scary as this chap. *Norwich, maybe?*

Cold dread seized the farmer's heart, and as the strange intruder crept closer, the torch slipped from his grasp, clattering to the ground.

2

Sausage Fight

Mr Markles didn't like parties. The bespectacled headteacher of Larkbridge Primary School was a stern, disciplined man who secretly wished he could whip dawdling students into classrooms and electrocute troublemakers during lessons. He was a stickler for rules, obedience, and good manners.

Scowling from the sidelines like a human gargoyle, he wondered whose idea *this* was? It certainly hadn't been his. Mr Markles liked things quiet, orderly, and just so. Christmas parties were none of those things.

He eyed his staff with suspicion, searching for the culprit responsible.

Mr Shabley was DJ for the afternoon and never had a balding sixty-year-old looked more uncomfortable or out of place. Mr Markles cringed. Any respect the children once had for the teacher had been crushed into oblivion.

You can't retain discipline without respect. And you don't earn respect by cavorting to Mel and Kim's "Rockin' Around the Christmas Tree" from behind a toy microphone and a pitiful collection of feeble disco lights wearing a moth-eaten Santa Clause beard and an 'I Love Snowmen' cardigan.

Discounting Mr Shabley from his inquiry, the headteacher's vulture-like gaze homed in on Mrs Scrange's skeletally thin frame. He smiled. The dinner lady had organised the party food, and once again, she had demonstrated an excellent aptitude for saving money. Yesterday's leftovers became today's party treats: cabbage and carrot sausages, chocolate-dipped Brussels sprouts, mashed potato ice creams, and pea-green smoothies.

Mr Markles nodded with approval. No, Mrs Scrange wasn't to blame. Her inventiveness saved the school hundreds of pounds every year. Money that could be spent elsewhere. *Rome or Las Vegas this Christmas?* Mr Markles couldn't decide.

Next, the headteacher found Mrs Crispwhistle. Now, here was a proper teacher. No nonsense, no backchat, no quarter given. She was in charge of the party games.

Using canes and whips to thrash gifts from Rudolph's bottom, '*Flog The Reindeer*' was a variation of Pinata, the popular Mexican game. The best bit was that the gifts beaten from Rudolph's insides were unclaimed items of lost property.

'*Stuff It In Your Face*' entailed cramming as many marshmallows into a child's mouth as possible without choking them to death, but of course, there weren't any marshmallows, only Mrs Scrange's mushy chocolate sprouts. Unsurprisingly, the game produced numerous puddles of brown and green coloured vomit all over the dancefloor.

'*The Christmas Wrapping Game*' or, more accurately, '*The Wrap A Child Until They Can No Longer Move Christmas Game*' was Mr Markle's favourite. Executed properly, the child in question could neither move nor talk—the perfect combination.

Mr Markles narrowed his beady eyes. *Is Mrs Spleen-Weasel actually having fun?* Of all his teachers, she was the most likely to have organised this fiasco. *The impertinence of youth.* She was joking, laughing and… *dancing* with her pupils. Talk about fraternising with the enemy. Nothing good ever came from being *nice* to the children. *She's only making a rod for her own back.* They weren't at school to have fun or make friends; they were there to learn and develop life skills—i.e., to do as they were told.

Mr Markles shook his head disapprovingly. *I should have sent her away like I did her husband.* Well, they couldn't have two Spleen-Weasels at the school, now could they.

Miss Spleen had married Mr Weasel, the newlyweds opting for a fashionable double-barrelled surname. An unsatisfactory outcome for all concerned. Before Mr Markles knew it, a pair of Spleen-Weasels were roaming Larkbridge Primary School's corridors. The couple had toyed with the idea of becoming Weasel-Spleens. However, being associated with the internal organs of small carnivorous mammals was a step too far, even for animal lovers.

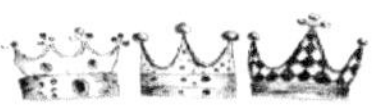

Mr Markles glanced at his watch. *Thank goodness, there's only another half an hour to endure.* He was already dreaming of lounging beside the pool under the hot sun with a cold drink in one hand and a good book in the other. The British weather was always dreary in December. Today was a perfect example. It hadn't stopped snowing, not for a second. Mr Markles hated snow nearly as much as he hated chattering children…

and chattering children in the snow really didn't bear thinking about.

Mr Markles had drifted away on his holidays again when something soft, wet, and squishy struck him between the eyes. Brutally torn from a personal tour of Rome's Colosseum courtesy of Pope Francis and esteemed Italian goalkeeper Gianluigi Buffon, he stared down to see a half-chewed cabbage and carrot sausage splodged all over his right shoe. And when he glanced up, the hall erupted into a warzone.

'HAVE MERCY! A FOOD FIGHT!'

Bennie Perkins grabbed a handful of sticky Brussels sprouts from a mountainous heap stacked on the buffet table. 'One for Veronica Whitehead,' he yelled, flinging a bio-hazardous vegetable through the chaos. 'One for Barry Slapham, one for Rory Brannigan, one for Ricky Kittens—and two for Mr Shabley for being a *LOSER!*'

Bennie wasn't a bad kid, but he wasn't exactly a good one, either. It wasn't his fault. Well, not entirely. His parents had raised him to stand his ground, instilling a stubborn refusal to back down, turn a blind eye to something wrong, or take a cabbage and carrot sausage in the face without exacting revenge. If Bennie thought he was in the right, there was no surrendering. It simply wasn't in his DNA. Admittedly, this trait got him into all sorts of bother.

It was a Perkins thing. He remembered his grandad sitting him down and telling him that it was his solemn duty to uphold the Perkins family values. 'Injustice needs to be confronted, no matter the cost,' he had said. 'My daddy fought in the war. He did his duty by standing up against wrongdoers. Now it's your turn, my boy. Whether it's saying no to a megalomaniac with a silly moustache or a school bully with a mean streak.'

Bennie was only five years old at the time, but he never forgot his grandad's words, especially the bit about school bullies.

'I'll pound you for that, PERKINS!' Ricky Kittens growled, scraping liquified sprout from his eyes.

He wasn't the only one promising retribution. Amidst the carnage, Bennie's enemies gathered. Rory Brannigan, Barry Slapham, and Veronica Whitehead joined Ricky Kittens, each with their grubby little hands loaded with mutated sweet and savoury projectiles plundered from the buffet table.

Larkbridge Primary School's teachers screamed for calm through a storm of inedible party food. Mr Shabley was mercilessly peppered until he was knocked flat, his mangy beard and snowman jumper stained a lurid green.

Mrs Crispwhistle was beside herself with worry. How had she lost control of her students on such a scale? What must Mr Markles be thinking? She hoped the headteacher wouldn't hold this disaster of a Christmas party against her when it came to her end-of-year appraisal?

Abruptly, the music stopped, and the children froze. Mr Markles glowered menacingly over the scene, looking for someone to blame for the atrocity.

'*HE* started it, sir,' Ricky Kittens said, nodding at Bennie, who, with a handful of thawing potato ice cream dripping between his fingers and his arms suspended mid-throw, appeared guilty as sin.

'No, I didn't,' Bennie protested heatedly. '*HE DID!*'

'DON'T LIE, BOY!' Mrs Crispwhistle snapped, her hands firmly planted on her hips.

'It wasn't Bennie, Mrs Crispwhistle. It was Ricky,' Mabel Jane said. She noticed her friend's eyes narrowing with anger. No one called Bennie a liar and got away with it, not even a teacher. It was like a red rag to a bull.

'HOW DARE YOU LOOK AT ME IN THAT TONE OF VOICE, MISS JANE!!!'

'It's true, Mrs Crispwhistle,' Alice Bean added defiantly. '*They* started it.' She temporally unfroze a limb to jab an accusing finger at Ricky Kittens and his motley brood of accomplices.

Despite Alice and Mabel not having much in common—Alice wore her hair in braids and pigtails, Mabel liked hers wild and free; Alice had blue eyes, Mabel green; Alice loved skipping and animals, Mabel adored war games and blowing stuff up—they were inseparable, defending each other to the hilt.

Mrs Crispwhistle thrust her mean, pointy face toward the alleged instigators of this travesty. 'None of you will be going home for Christmas until this mess is cleaned up. DO I MAKE MYSELF *CLEAR?*'

Through gritted teeth, Ricky and his gang chorused, 'Yes, *miss*,' but all the while, they were shooting daggers with their eyes at Bennie Perkins and his do-gooding friends.

'You're in for it now,' Boris Griggs whispered into Bennie's left ear.

'Don't you mean WE'RE in for it now?' Ravi Singh corrected from where he was hiding behind Boris. His friend made for a surprisingly impressive human shield. 'Haven't you heard of being guilty by association?'

Boris thought long and hard before answering. 'No,' he said with a frown. 'But Mrs Spleen-Weasel says I'm guilty of procrastination. Is that the same thing?'

Ravi shook his head despairingly.

'SILENCE!' Mrs Crispwhistle shrieked. 'I WILL HAVE ORDER!!!' Suddenly, the teacher's face was splattered by a generous dollop of thawed mash. All eyes swivelled to stare at the culprit. Whoever it was, they were in big trouble.

Mr Markles stood grinning like a naughty schoolboy. Everyone in the hall gawped open-mouthed, and no one gawped more than Mrs Crispwhistle.

The headteacher shrugged his shoulders. 'What can I say? I never could resist a food fight. Let's get those party tunes back on, shall we, Mr Shabley? I feel like dancing. Merry Christmas, boys and girls!'

Falling to her knees, Mrs Crispwhistle was caught in a savage crossfire of deadly Christmas leftovers.

3

Ambushed

'That was the best school disco *EVER!*' Alice declared happily, leaping from the school with the enthusiasm of a frolicking fawn.

Outside, the snow was tumbling, and within seconds of seeing everything glistening pure white, children were diving headfirst into drifts and hurling snowballs as eagerly as if they were chocolate-covered Brussels sprouts.

'Who would have thought Mr Markles could breakdance to Cliff Richard,' Bennie said, genuinely impressed by their headteacher's moves. He had certainly put Mrs Spleen-Weasel to shame. She had knocked out poor Mrs Scrange with a flailing arm before rupturing her lower bowel trying to re-enact a scene from Dirty Dancing.

'Who would have thought ANYONE could breakdance to Cliff Richard,' Mabel replied, shaking her head. She couldn't seem to banish the disturbing image from her mind. *Why are teachers so embarrassing?*

'Who's CLIFF RICHARD?' Ravi asked, but his friends were already crossing the road to the park. Pulling his beanie hat over his head, he scurried through the snow to catch them.

None of them could explain Mr Markles' dramatic U-turn. Perhaps the sausage strike to the forehead had contributed to a sudden realisation that there was more to life than obeying rules—at least at Christmas parties. And having fun, especially at someone else's expense, was actually good for the soul and not a crime. To be honest, with school out until New Year, no one cared. It was Christmas, and it was snowing!

The Larkbridge schoolkids began going their separate ways, eager to get home as fast as possible so they could start the holidays. Bennie and his friends lived on the same estate on the other side of the park, Norbert's Way, which is named after the local church of Saint Norbert and situated in the town square. Legend says he spent his short life helping injured animals. Ironically, he perished after being crushed to death by a rather amorous three-legged bullock.

'Shake a leg, people,' Bennie said. 'Or we'll be heading for a showdown with the Ricky Kittens Gang.'

They passed the town's Christmas tree. It was everything Larkbridge Primary School's wasn't: tall, shapely, twinkling with lights—and not dead.

'I don't see them,' Mabel said, checking behind as they entered the park. The path cut between two football pitches that were buried a good six inches beneath the snow. 'I hate to say it, but I've got the horrible feeling they're setting us up for an ambush. They must have jumped us at the school gates.'

'Oh, no,' Ravi groaned. 'It's all right for you lot. You can run. I'm just not fast enough. You remember what they did to me last time we had snow, right?'

Bennie and Boris cringed. Alice and Mabel sniggered.

'Take it from me; there are places where snow shouldn't go.'

'You're not the only one they picked on, Rav. They tied my hands together and buried me alive in a snowdrift. I literally had to eat myself free.'

Ravi eyed Boris up and down. 'It wasn't a problem for you, though, was it.'

Boris scowled. 'I'm big-boned, that's all.'

It was true. Boris' bones *were* big.

The leaden sky, thick with swirling snow, began to darken. The children passed between the white-crusted football pitches, eying the dense cluster of pine trees ahead with trepidation. The path twisted through their dark domain before re-emerging onto Bishop's Road on the other side. But with streetlamps few and far between and enough hiding places to conceal a small army, they knew it was perfect ambush territory. If Ricky Kittens was waiting for them, they wouldn't know it until it was too late.

'Why didn't we go around?' Boris moaned, peering anxiously toward the trees.

'Because it takes another twenty minutes, that's why,' Bennie said. 'And besides, we were too busy nattering to evaluate the situation.' He really hoped they wouldn't live to regret their lack of judgment.

The treeline loomed closer, and the day grew darker. By the time the five friends entered the wood, they were practically in each other's pockets. Wide-eyed, they searched the shadowy places beneath the trees for signs of the enemy.

'Where are they?' Bennie whispered.

The wood was eerily quiet, the snow-laden branches muffling any sound. Nonetheless, the further the children marched without incident, the more relaxed they became. Yet, as every ambusher worth their salt knows, success is determined by surprise.

Ravi had no idea what hit him. One minute, he was following in Boris' huge footprints, and the next, he was lying flat on his back, staring into the sky, half-buried in the snow.

'MAN DOWN! MEDIC!' Alice cried.

Mabel was immediately on the scene. Crouching beside Ravi, she pulled her battlefield medi-kit from her camouflaged rucksack and got to work. Mabel didn't go anywhere without a bag stuffed with battlefield accessories and survival aids.

Blinding Ravi with torchlight, Mabel whipped off his hat. Then, grabbing his head between her hands, she hauled it from side to side before yanking open his mouth and checking his teeth.

'Is this entirely necessary?'

Mabel ignored Ravi. 'The patient has sustained a shallow two-inch laceration to the scalp. There's no sign of concussion, but there is *SIGNIFICANT* blood loss. Administering first-aid now.'

'BLOOD LOSS!' Ravi exclaimed, panic-stricken. 'How bad is it?'

'It's really nothing to worry about,' Mabel replied matter-of-factly, winding a ridiculously long bandage around the boy's head. 'A typical eleven-year-old holds nine pints of blood inside their body...' She paused to re-evaluate her patient. He wasn't a typical eleven-year-old—not physically, anyway. There were zombies in haunted graveyards with more meat on their bones. 'Probably nearer eight in your case, so losing a few won't hurt *TOO* much.'

'But I'm *TEN!*'

'Are you?' Mabel made a sad face. 'Oh, that is a shame. I'm *SO* sorry.'

'OH MY GOD, I'M BLEEDING OUT!'

Alice started giggling. 'She's kidding, you donkey. I've seen more blood squished out of an ant.'

Boris piped up. 'Actually, ants don't have blood, not really. Not like us, at any rate. They have greenish, yellowish stuff called—'

'INCOMING!' Bennie yelled, cutting off Boris mid-flow. 'GET DOWN!'

A storm of snowballs bombarded their position. The silent missiles pelted them from either side of the path, zipping through the falling snow like cannonballs. The kids hunkered down, cradling their heads in their hands.

'We're too exposed here,' Mabel yelled. 'We need to get into the trees.'

'Yeah, we're sitting ducks,' Bennie agreed, *ducking* just in time to avoid a direct hit.

Meanwhile, wedged behind Boris, Ravi seized the chance to inspect the enemy's ammunition. There was something odd about them. They whistled through the air like bullets.

'AH, HA! I KNEW IT!' Ravi declared after breaking open and examining a snowball. A deadly collection of icicles lurked beneath its fluffy white exterior, and at the centre, he found a lump of solid ice hard enough to smash teeth and crack skulls. These weren't just any old snowballs; these were weaponised snowballs designed to hurt… a lot.

'This isn't a snowball fight,' Ravi stated grimly. 'THIS IS ATTEMPTED MURDER!!'

Frantically, the gang dug themselves into the snow as the lethal projectiles continued raining down on their heads. It felt like they were under fire from a battery of howitzers.

'Sometimes the best form of defence is attack,' Mabel said, displaying an impish grin. She loved to attack things, and this seemed the perfect opportunity.

'As much as I hate the idea of charging straight into the line of fire, I think G I Jane has a point,' Ravi said.

G I Jane was what everyone at school called Mabel. She wasn't happy unless she was running through the woods like a loon dressed head to toe in camouflage and plastered in face paint.

'If we stay here, we'll get pummelled,' Ravi concluded unhappily.

Bennie nodded. 'We'll need cover as we retreat, though. Something large and well-padded.' He looked at Boris.

Boris narrowed his eyes. 'I'm not sure I like where this is headed.'

Bennie smiled. 'Don't worry, we'll be right behind you.'

'I bet you will be,' Boris snorted.

Ravi studied the enemy's pattern of fire. 'They're stronger on the right than the left. Three to two. If we're going to do this, we should attack the left.'

'Agreed,' Mabel replied, coming to the same conclusion. 'We smash their weaker flank, establish a firing position, and then HAMMER THEM TO KINGDOM COME UNTIL THEY RUN CRYING TO THEIR MUMMIES IN A WORLD OF PAIN!!!'

They all stared open-mouthed at Mabel.

'Calm down,' Bennie said. 'We're not SAS; we're Larkbridge school kids.' It was fair to say she was getting a bit carried away.

Mabel looked disappointed.

'Secure your bobble hats. We're going in,' Bennie said, pulling his woolly Father Christmas beanie firmly into position.

Boris didn't look happy. 'I can't believe I'm doing this.' Despite being twice the size of any of his friends, Boris wasn't one for heroics. In fact, he was something of a pacifist and finding himself the focal point of a full-scale military offensive didn't sit well with him, even if it was only a snowball fight.

'Ready, big man?'

Boris sucked in a deep breath and burst from the snow, roaring like a grizzly bear. Actually, he sounded more like an adolescent badger with a throat infection.

Boris thundered toward the trees, an unstoppable human snowplough. A barrage of high-velocity snowballs thumped against the boy's beer-barrel chest. Boris grunted with each blow, but his puffer jacket was so well-padded it was as good as a suit of armour.

Boris charged beneath the pine trees like the Abominable Snowman—admittedly, a bright green abominable snowman with a Rudolph the Reindeer bobble hat complete with flashing antlers.

Veronica Whitehead and Jimmy Weiner—and yes, he loved hotdogs—disappeared screaming into the woods. But then, from the opposite side of the path, came the defiant shouts of Ricky Kittens, Rory Brannigan, and Barry Slapham.

'Change of plan,' Bennie announced. 'WE LEG IT!'

There were no arguments. Together, they scarpered deeper into the trees. Mabel led the way. No one knew Larkbridge Park better than she did. Hurtling beneath the branches, they ran until they couldn't run any longer—except for Alice, who could happily run all day and night if she wanted.

'WAIT!' Ravi called pleadingly from deep in the growing gloom. As the least capable at cross-country—or climbing, jumping, throwing, or anything that required coordination or physical aptitude—he had predictably dropped behind during the gang's *strategic withdrawal.*

'Can we rest for a bit, *PLEASE?*' he begged, stumbling straight into a snowdrift.

While the others rescued Ravi, Mabel secured a headtorch to her festive camo beanie. The wind picked up, and as the children caught their breath resting against tree trunks, the snow thickened, quickly becoming a swirling blizzard.

They marched on, fighting through the storm, guided by Mabel and her torch. Larkbridge Park wasn't huge. If they continued in the same direction for long enough, they would find civilisation sooner or later.

Following Mabel over a frozen stream, the children scrambled up a shallow bank before wading through a snow-covered clearing dotted with picnic tables. Halfway across, a ferocious gust of ice-cold wind knocked them onto their backsides.

'OUCH!' Ravi cried. Everyone else had managed to land in the snow, but Boris had landed on Ravi. 'BORIS! I CAN'T BREATHE!'

Directly ahead, highlighted by Mabel's torch, the frigid air shimmered, the snow turning to rain.

'What's going on?' Bennie said, pushing his hat from his eyes.

Then, with a fizzing crackle, a hole appeared from nowhere, like an open doorway in the sky. Through this door, they could see somewhere else—a village in the mountains. They heard screams, and everything there was on fire.

The door disappeared, but not before something hurtled through from the other side. Ravi had only just shoved Boris away when the unidentifiable *something* crashed straight into him, driving him back into the snow.

'GET IT OFF ME!' Ravi yelled, desperately trying to disentangle himself from whatever *it* was.

Screaming all at the same time, the children scrambled to their feet, hopping hysterically from foot to foot like they were performing a crazy yet highly intricate tap dance.

'What is *IT?*' Mabel whispered, blasting the thing with torchlight.

It was small and childlike—but like no child they had ever seen.

'What's wrong with its eyes?' Boris cried.

Alice clamped a gloved hand over her shocked face. 'Look at its ears!'

'IT'S A GOBLIN!' Ravi blurted, finally freeing himself. Usually, Ravi wasn't one for hysterical outbursts of a fantastical nature, but the situation had gotten the better of him.

The creature stood no more than three feet tall, and with pointed ears, weird spikey hair, alien-like features, and unnaturally bright violet irises that gleamed in the dark like cat's eyes, it really didn't look right.

'Who wears a cloak?' Alice whispered.

Its other garments were no less strange. It was dressed in green and brown woollens with what appeared to be chunks of tree bark woven into the fabric, making the creature look like it was encased in a suit of wooden armour.

'Do you think it's from MIDDLE EARTH?' Bennie said. 'You know, a hobbit or something?'

'Or SHERWOOD FOREST,' Mabel added, admiring the outlandish outfit. The creature's blend of colour and materials was inspiring. It was the best camouflage scheme she had ever seen.

'Where did it come from?'

'Did you hear the crackling before the hole opened?'

'What was happening on the other side?'

Despite looking weird, the children decided it wasn't going to eat them. They crowded around the creature, pointing and gesticulating excitedly. They hadn't seen anything like this before. This was something new.

Boris came to his senses first. 'STOP, YOU'RE SCARING IT!' he shouted, pushing his friends away. 'How would you like it if you were frightened and alone, surrounded by strangers making fun of you?'

'Boris is right,' Bennie said. 'Give the thing space.'

The appearance of this odd woodland *thing* amazed them so much they hadn't thought about how it might be feeling. They backed off at once.

The creature was shaking like a leaf.

'Look,' Alice said to the others, 'it's hurt.' It held its left arm awkwardly as if in discomfort. 'Are you okay?' she asked softly, creeping forward cautiously. Alice held her hands out to show she meant no harm. 'What's your name?'

It didn't answer. It just continued to shake.

'My name's ALICE,' Alice said, pointing to herself. 'ALICE,' she repeated slowly.

One by one, the others introduced themselves.

'Now it's your turn, little friend,' Bennie said after saying hello. 'What's your name?'

The creature relaxed. At least enough to stop trembling. It studied the children, its strange violet eyes glowing in the deepening dark.

Like a lost puppy, it looked rather sorry for itself. Then its tiny face lit up, and the creature jabbed a long, slender finger at Bennie's Santa hat before blurting out an indecipherable string of sentences that baffled the children almost as much as Mr Shabley during algebra.

It pointed to its chest, just like Alice had done. 'I AM ELF,' it said in a small, almost musical voice. 'I CALLED ZATHERINA-RARMATAIN-NIMTHRUSH-NURBLE-NOO-GERBLEFUZZ-VARKEITH.'

4

Keith

'KEITH FOR SHORT, THEN?' Bennie said. There was no way in a million years that he or any of his friends would remember the elf's full name, never mind pronounce it.

Alice and Mabel stared at Bennie like he was something nasty they had scraped off the bottom of their shoes.

'It's a GIRL elf,' Alice said in disgust. 'You can't call her KEITH!' Why were boys so maddeningly idiotic? 'ARE YOU BLIND OR STUPID OR BOTH?'

'A girl? Are you sure? How can you tell?'

'She's beautiful, in a weird sort of way. You know, like llamas. Much too beautiful to be a boy anyway,' Mabel replied, making snake eyes and sneering for good measure. 'And, well, you know, she's got boobies.'

'So has Boris, and he's not a girl,' Bennie said.

'HEY! I haven't got…' Boris couldn't bring himself to say the word. In his house, boobies and bottoms were never ever mentioned. 'They're pectoral muscles, thank you very much! They just need a bit of toning up, that's all.' Boris subconsciously covered his chest with his hands.

Ravi couldn't care less if it was a boy or a girl. He was more interested in how the thing got here. He wondered what other secrets the government kept to themselves: mind control, super strength, indestructible undergarments? The possibilities were endless.

'Aren't any of you in the least bit thrilled to have witnessed an interdimensional warp teleporter in action?' A real-life elf standing right in front of him was neither here nor there.

'An inter—WHAT?' Boris asked half-heartedly. In fact, he only responded out of politeness. The existence of fairytale creatures was infinitely more interesting than whatever spewed out of Ravi's boring face.

'INTERDIMENSIONAL WARP TELEPORTER!' Ravi snapped irritably. 'Mind you, that's probably not what it's really called. It'll have a codename or something. You know, like *LIGHTNING STRIKE* or *ROARING THUNDER*.'

Ravi sighed. He realised no one was listening to him, nor had they been for quite some time. It was a common occurrence whenever he opened his mouth.

'Jump sickness,' Keith suddenly announced. She screwed up her face and began twirling an index finger around her right ear as if suggesting she had gone cuckoo.

Even though Keith remembered her name and a few choice words in English, she was severely disoriented. Passing through the portal unprepared had scrambled her brain like eggs, and until she recovered, she was dangerously vulnerable.

'HELP *KEITH*,' she said to the children, her tone pleading, her violet eyes wide and doleful. She cradled her wounded arm, wincing pitifully as if the limb were on fire. It was a theatrical performance worthy of a BAFTA. Although mentally underdeveloped and doubtlessly inept, the children were the elf's best bet at keeping her safe until her wits were restored.

There was something deep inside Keith's head nagging her. She felt it trying to wriggle through the sticky spiderweb-like fuzz clogging her brain. Her neurons were misfiring like a trillion out-of-control pinball machines. She was supposed to be doing something important, wasn't she?

'What are we going to do with her?' Bennie said. 'It's dark, and we really should start heading home before our parents send out a search party.'

None of them moved. They just stood in the snow, staring gormlessly at the creature. The simple truth was that none of them wanted to turn their backs and walk away. Who could abandon such a sad face?

'Well, we can't leave her here. She'll freeze to death for a start,' Mabel said, scanning the cold dark woods with concern.

'And goodness knows what would happen if Ricky Kittens and his losers found her,' Alice added, shuddering at the thought. She had once watched the bullies torture a frog in biology. Admittedly, the amphibian was already dead, but that didn't make it any less horrible to witness.

Bennie nodded. 'It's decided then. Keith will come and stay with me until she's better.'

It was the only logical option. Alice and Mabel lived with older siblings who wouldn't think twice about grassing on them. Boris shared a room with his younger brother, who was scared of his own shadow and would almost certainly freak out seeing a fairytale creature in his bedroom. And as for Ravi, he would be hard-pushed to look after a tray of watercress.

Cocooning Keith in the middle of their ranks, the children began marching home, and they didn't stop talking for the whole journey. What a start to the holidays! This was going to be the best Christmas ever!

The gang agreed that Keith was going to be their little secret. They couldn't wait to learn about elves and whether other fanciful creatures like pixies, unicorns, and Furbies existed.

Emerging from beneath the trees, the children waited to cross Bishop's Road. The traffic struggled to traverse the snow-covered tarmac, slipping and sliding all over the place. Keith yelped each time a horrible metal monster roared past, belching black smoke like a dragon.

'How are you going to keep her hidden from your mum?' Boris asked, watching a car career in circles like a robotic ballet dancer.

'I'll stash her in my bedroom. Mum hardly ever comes in.'

Alice scowled. 'STASH HER? Keith's not a dodgy toy you've pinched from Larkbridge market. She's a living, breathing person—well, elf person—and should be treated respectfully.' What were they thinking? A *boy* wasn't a suitable candidate for nursing a vulnerable elf back to health.

'It was only a figure of speech, Alice. Keith will be provided with every luxury. I'll even give up my bed for her.'

Mabel narrowed her eyes. 'See that you do,' she warned. 'Because if you don't, you'll wish you had never been born. Do I make myself clear?'

Blimey, I can't believe how protective they are. It was like Keith was their little elf sister or something. Well, Bennie had looked after things before, and they nearly always survived. How hard could looking after an elf be? Surely, it wasn't much different than looking after a cat or a dog.

Crossing the road, they entered Norbert's Way. The housing estate was undisturbed by tyre tracks and glistened white beneath a thick blanket of pristine snow.

Keith peeked between the children, marvelling at the pretty Christmas lights decorating the gardens and houses. They sparkled and flashed in vibrant colours. The sight ignited something deep inside her, something magical. She couldn't remember what exactly, but she knew it was important to her.

The gang crept along the path behind the estate, keeping to the shadows. Reaching the back of Bennie's house, they shouldered open the gate, but it got stuck in the snow halfway. The gang slipped through the gap into the garden and hid themselves behind the shed.

'Okay. We go in hard and fast. If my parents intercept us before we reach the stairs, I'll do the talking.' Bennie stuck his head around the side of the shed. 'It looks like my mum is in the kitchen. Dad's probably still at work. Remember, don't stop for anything. Only once Keith is secured in my bedroom can we relax.'

They wrapped the frightened elf in Boris' puffer jacket and bundled her through the thick snow toward the house. They couldn't afford any slip-ups. There would be consequences if Keith was discovered, even if it was only by Bennie's mum and dad.

Bennie yanked his Christmas beanie from his head and rammed it over the elf's spikey hair, pulling it down so it covered her pointy ears. Spikey hair and pointed ears were a dead giveaway. *So are weird glowing eyes and looking like an extra-terrestrial.* He just hoped his parents wouldn't notice.

Slowly, Bennie opened the door. As quiet as thieves, the gang stepped inside… but then Boris tripped over his feet and bellyflopped like a walrus.

CRASH!!!

The gang froze on the spot.

'Is that you, Bennie?' Mrs Perkins called from the kitchen.

'Yes, Mum.' Bennie couldn't decide whether to dash for the stairs or retreat back into the garden. 'Is it okay if my friends stay for a bit?' he said instead, frantically signalling for the others to continue down the hallway.

They nearly reached the stairs when Bennie's mother answered, 'Okay, but shoes and coats off at the door, please. I don't want puddles of melted snow all over the house.'

Cursing under his breath, Bennie marched his friends back the other way, where they obediently kicked off their sodden footwear on the doormat.

Suddenly, Mrs Perkins appeared in the hallway, blocking their route to the stairs. 'Oh, you're *ALL* here. Well, I hope you've let your parents know where you are?'

'Yes, Mrs P,' they all lied simultaneously, trying to keep Keith out of sight.

Mrs Perkins smiled warmly. 'Did you have fun at the school disco?'

The gang nodded. 'Yes, Mrs P.'

'How's your mum, Boris?'

Bennie rolled his eyes. This wasn't going to plan.

'Much better now, thank you, Mrs P.'

Mrs Griggs had contracted a nasty case of the runs after being poisoned by Boris' father. It was accidental, of course. Mr Griggs had used leftovers from the deep, dark depths of the refrigerator to create an exciting concoction for date night—or so he had thought. The only problem was the ingredients were so out of date that they had grown arms and legs and developed conscious thought.

'Oh, that's good,' Mrs Perkins replied before focusing on Alice and Mabel. 'Hello, girls. Say hi to your mums for me.'

'Will do, Mrs P,' they chimed sweetly as if butter wouldn't melt in their mouths. It was a far cry from screaming like banshees while hurling snowballs at Veronica Whitehead and Jimmy Weiner.

Bennie began to panic. His mum was working her way through them all, and soon, she would discover Keith. He had to do something quickly.

Bennie opted for drastic action. Leaping forward, he slung his arms around his mother's waist and bear-hugged her back into the kitchen, allowing the gang to scurry past with Keith.

'Aww, how sweet,' Mrs Perkins said. 'A cuddle for your mummy AND in front of your friends.'

Bennie's embarrassment knew no bounds, but it was a price worth paying to keep Keith a secret.

'Can I make you boys and girls a hot chocolate?' she called after them.

'No thanks, Mrs P,' they answered in unison.

'Or how about a nice warmed-up mince pie with a dollop of cream?'

'We're fine, thanks, Mum,' Bennie said, desperately trying to extract himself from his mother's embrace. No matter how hard he tried, he couldn't escape. She just squeezed him tighter and tighter. 'MUM!'

Boris' substantial frame materialised in the kitchen doorway. 'A mince pie sounds wonderful, Mrs P,' he said, grinning like a Cheshire cat. 'With cream, please.'

Why does my mother feel the need to force-feed anyone who comes through the front door equipped with a rucksack? He wondered if this was common practice or were his parents the only ones afflicted with the urge to fatten other people's offspring? *I've only got to look at the biscuit tin before she glares at me like Medusa.* He was sure she would turn him to stone if she caught him pinching a chocolate Hobnob, but as soon as she clapped eyes on one of his friends, she was shoving biscuits and cakes down their throats as if their lives depended on it.

'He doesn't want a mince pie, Mum. He's just being polite. AREN'T YOU, Boris?'

Boris frowned. 'Yeah, that's right,' he confirmed, finally noting Bennie's less-than-satisfied expression. 'I had a big lunch. Way too big. Thanks anyway, Mrs P. Perhaps next time.'

'Okay, dear. If you change your mind, you know where to find me,' Mrs Perkins said, finally releasing her son. 'Off you go then. Have fun!'

Bennie ushered Boris along the hall and up the stairs, checking over his shoulder for signs of his mother the whole way before shoving him into his bedroom. Bennie shut the door behind them and let out an enormous sigh. 'Where's Keith?' he said after turning around. Then he noticed two violet orbs glowing under his bed. The others sat on the carpet, staring at Bennie's odd guest like she was a new pet.

'Poor little thing,' Alice said. 'She's all alone. I bet she's missing her family.'

Bennie felt bad for Keith. If what they saw through the magic door in the woods was her home, it was burning. *Alice is right,* he thought sombrely. *Poor Keith.* Bennie couldn't imagine what she was going through. He wondered what the elf had escaped from. *Something awful.*

Keith tentatively reappeared from beneath Bennie's bed, her big, wide eyes flicking suspiciously from boy to girl.

Mabel carefully undraped Boris' puffer jacket from around Keith's slender shoulders. 'Let me look at that wound,' she said, reaching for her arm.

The elf recoiled, scurrying back under the bed.

'What's THAT?' Ravi said.

Something had fallen out of the elf's pockets. It looked like a TV remote with lots of flashing buttons but with a screen like a mobile phone.

Edging from under the bed again, Keith shrugged as if she didn't have a clue what the thing was. Ravi made a grab for it, but Keith pounced, hissing like a cat. The gang had never seen Ravi move so fast. He shuffled backwards across the bedroom like his feet were on fire. It was a wonder he didn't burn a hole in his pants.

Boris smirked. 'I think you better leave Keith's toys alone, Rav.'

Ravi was intrigued by the device but less so by the elf's rather disturbing reaction. 'Fascinating,' he said, eyeing the gadget with longing. 'I bet it's how the creature opened the warp gate. I'd love to study it.'

'There's no chance of that happening any time soon, not unless you want to have your arms gnawed off at the elbow,' Bennie said.

Alice glowered at Bennie for suggesting such a thing, and then she glowered at Ravi for being an idiot. 'She's not a creature; SHE'S AN ELF!'

Meanwhile, Mabel had miraculously coaxed Keith into her care and was already examining her injured arm.

'How did you do that?' Boris asked.

'I have a gift.'

As well as being really good at war games and plotting imaginary military invasions, Mabel had a way with animals. Not that Keith was an animal, of course, but in her disorientated state, she was close enough.

'This is a nasty burn. The skin has blistered. It must be very painful.' Mabel snatched up her rucksack before rummaging inside for her medi-kit.

'That burn wasn't caused by fire,' Ravi said, studying the elf's wound with interest. 'It's too precise. See, the affected area is perfectly symmetrical.'

'What caused it then, EINSTEIN?' Alice replied wryly, folding her arms across her chest.

Mabel smeared a soothing ointment into Keith's arm before wrapping the injury with a bandage. 'There, much better.'

Ravi pondered Alice's question. 'If I had to guess, I'd say the creature's injury was caused by a ray gun.'

The others burst out laughing. Even Keith joined in, although she hadn't a clue what she was laughing at.

'A RAY GUN!' Bennie exclaimed. 'I think you've been watching too much science fiction, Rav.'

5

The Sleep Over

Before long, it was time for Bennie's friends to go home. They didn't want to leave and promised an early return in the morning. Alice and Mabel were still unconvinced by the quality of Bennie's elf care.

'It's just you and me now, Keith.'

The elf tilted her head. Perhaps staring really hard at the strange organism from a different angle would help her remember what it was supposed to be. Whatever it was, it didn't look very inspiring. No matter how hard she scrunched up her little face in concentration, the answer wouldn't come. Shrugging her shoulders, she gave up and jumped on the bed instead. Keith crossed her legs and began observing her new surroundings, her strange violet eyes flashing from one poster to another.

Bennie wasn't sure what she thought of Premiership footballers and Formula One racing cars. By the look on her face, not a lot.

'BOY!' Keith suddenly yelled, wagging a finger at Bennie. 'YOU ARE BOY!'

'SSSSHHHH!' Bennie clamped a hand over Keith's mouth. 'Yes, I'm a boy, but please keep your voice down.'

Bennie picked up the elf's peculiar gadget from the carpet before sitting beside her on the bed. 'What does this do, Keith?' he asked, looking the device over.

'Pretty,' Keith said, mesmerised by the gadget's flashing lights.

'Yes, but what is it?' Bennie was tempted to see what would happen if he pressed all the buttons at once, but something told him it would be a very bad idea.

Keith shrugged her shoulders again. 'Elf hungry.'

Bennie sighed. 'Yeah, me too, Keith.' He could smell the dinner cooking downstairs, and evidently, so could she. Bennie began wondering what elves ate. *Probably the same as us*, he concluded, after discounting cat biscuits and dog meat.

Right on cue, his mother's voice squawked from the kitchen. 'TEA IS READY!'

Bennie bounced to his feet. 'I'll see what I can scavenge. You stay here.'

Opening his bedroom door, he glanced over his shoulder to make sure the elf wasn't freaking out at the thought of being left alone. She wasn't. She was standing right behind him.

Bennie closed the door again. 'Keith stays here, REMEMBER?' he said very slowly and very deliberately, pointing at the bed.

Keith didn't say anything. She just stared up at him with her weird violet eyes.

Bennie strode across his room, shaking his head. Keith followed. Bennie slumped onto his bed again and beckoned the elf to join him on his blue and white Ipswich Town FC duvet cover, his favourite team.

Obligingly, Keith scrambled up and perched herself beside him.

'Good girl,' Bennie said. 'Now, let's try this again, shall we. YOU STAY HERE, and I'll find something for us to eat. OKAY?'

Grinning like a loon, Keith nodded enthusiastically.

'Alright then,' Bennie said, slowly moving away. 'Remember to STAY HERE!'

Regardless of what Bennie said, the elf was on his heels again by the time he reached the door. 'FOR GOODNESS SAKE, KEITH!' It was worse than looking after a toddler, or so he imagined. It definitely couldn't be any better.

Bennie grabbed a skinny wrist and marched the elf back to the bed.

I need a distraction, Bennie mused, searching his bedroom for ideas. *Of course! I'll do exactly what all sleep-deprived parents do when they're at their wit's end and need five minutes to themselves—I'll plonk her in front of the telly.*

He encouraged Keith up onto the mattress again before switching on a random station. She was immediately captivated. *Meerkat Makeover* wasn't the most orthodox or indeed ethical wildlife programme Bennie had ever seen, but if it kept the elf quiet, all well and good.

Surprisingly, the show didn't focus on the day-to-day trials and tribulations of the animals but on their transformation into celebrity lookalikes. Teams of contestants were tasked with changing meerkats into famous faces before taking turns guessing who they were. *It's shocking what lengths TV bosses go to these days.* Still, he would rather watch a meerkat dressed as the Archbishop of Canterbury than random wannabes and desperate has-beens confined in a jungle with nothing to do except talk nonsense and eat kangaroos' naughty bits all day long.

Happy his guest was sufficiently entertained, Bennie crept from his bedroom, leaving Keith chortling inanely at the sight of a meerkat parading as Ed Sheeran, complete with guitar and ginger wig.

'Oh, there you are,' Bennie's mum said when he finally appeared in the kitchen. She was busy dishing up fish and chips for dinner. Bennie persuaded her to let him eat his tea in his bedroom. 'A last day at school treat,' he called it. His mother called it something else, but Bennie didn't hear because he was already halfway up the stairs carrying his prize.

Knowing he had an elf stashed in his bedroom was a strange feeling. He had taken in wounded animals before, but nothing like this. Bennie remembered young Sebastian with fondness. He found him in the garden before school one spring morning. He was a poor little sparrow with a broken wing. Bennie had made Sebastian a nest in an old shoebox. He collected bugs and worms for him, nurturing him for weeks, keeping him safe until he was strong enough to be released back into the wild. One day, Bennie returned home from school to find his bedroom strewn with feathers and his pet cat, Miss Fluff-Face, licking her lips. *Poor Sebastian.*

At least this time, Bennie didn't need to worry about the cat devouring Keith. In truth, he was more worried about Keith eating Miss Fluff-Face.

Balancing his dinner tray one-handed, Bennie shouldered open his bedroom door. Inside, there was no sign of the elf.

'KEITH?'

Meerkat Makeover was finished, and now the evening news was doing its best to bury Christmas cheer under an avalanche of doom and gloom.

Bennie peered under the bed. 'What are you doing under there?' he whispered, although he had a fair idea. The news was scary for impressionable minds. *It's usually a hundred times more disturbing than anything at the cinema. It should have an age-appropriate certificate like films and video games.*

Laying on his belly, Bennie stretched out a hand toward the elf. 'It's alright. There's nothing to fear. Look, I've brought food.'

On hearing the word 'food', Keith shot from beneath the bed and attacked Bennie's dinner tray like a wild animal. She shovelled handfuls of chips into her mouth as if they were going out of fashion. 'WHAT

THIS?' she asked, her cheeks so stuffed with potato she looked like a chipmunk.

'Chips,' Bennie said, grinning at the elf's behaviour. Not even Boris ate as quickly as this, and he loved food more than he loved his mum and dad.

'AND THIS?' Keith asked, ramming the battered cod in with the chips.

'Fish.'

Suddenly, potato mush and half-chewed cod exploded from Keith's lips straight into Bennie's face.

'UURRGGGHHH! DISGUSTING!' she spluttered. 'WHY YOU MURDER FISH AND GIVE TO KEITH? IS BOY SICK IN HEAD?'

Bennie feared the elf was about to regurgitate the contents of her stomach all over his bedroom carpet.

'Chip animal, too?'

'No, chips are vegetables,' Bennie explained, picking chunks of cod from his hair. 'I'm sorry about the fish. I didn't know you were a vegetarian.'

Keith didn't look happy. 'Why you eat poor little fishies?'

Bennie was taken aback by the question. 'I don't really know. I just always have.'

Actually, he hadn't given it a second thought. Of course, he knew some people didn't eat fish or meat, and some didn't eat eggs or drink milk. Bennie didn't much like the idea of cucumber sandwiches every day of the week for the rest of his life. He would miss burgers and hotdogs and roast beef… and, well, tons of dead stuff.

His dad called vegans *vegilantes* and said that if everybody stopped eating meat or drinking milk, there would be no need to keep animals at all. You would only see them in zoos or weird people's gardens, and eventually, they would become extinct like dinosaurs.

Bennie started fantasising. *Mmmmmmm... chicken nuggets dipped in barbeque sauce.* Then, a familiar location on the telly distracted him. 'Look, Keith, Larkbridge is on the news!'

There had been another turkey raid, the fifth in East Anglia this week, sparking fears of a turkey shortage come Christmas. The odd thing about it all was that it wasn't only the birds disappearing, but their owners, too.

A teary-eyed Mrs Grindle, the missing farmer's wife, was being interviewed:

'I returned home having spent a wonderful evening at Hog Hut, a super little restaurant specialising in pork recipes. If you go, I recommend Sow Seven Ways... Oh, and the snout smeared in a mustard reduction wrapped in a floury bap is simply sublime! You really must try it.'

'Yes, it sounds heavenly, but what happened when you arrived home, Mrs Grindle?' the reporter pressed impatiently.

'Well, I came home to find my beautiful cottage RAVAGED, my precious portraits SMASHED, and all my beloved birds STOLEN!'

'And your husband was missing, too. Is that correct, Mrs Grindle?'

'What? Oh, yes. No sign of him either. Terrible news. Without him, who's going to clean up the mess?'

Poor old Farmer Grindle, Bennie thought sadly. Why would turkey hustlers kidnap people, too? Perhaps the thieves needed them to look after the birds? It was all very odd.

Keith was glued to the TV screen, enthralled by the news bulletin. No, she wasn't enthralled; she was horrified. She couldn't focus her mind; the jump sickness befuddled her thoughts. Why were the pictures inside the box so important to her?

Mum will be panicking, Bennie mused. *If there's not a roasted turkey perched on the dinner table come Christmas Day, Dad will be filing for divorce come Boxing Day morning.*

Suddenly, there was a sharp gasp behind Bennie. 'WHAT ON EARTH happened to your dinner?' his mum squawked over his shoulder.

Bennie very nearly jumped out of his skin. His mother had literally materialised from thin air! She had a habit of doing that. Bennie half suspected she was a witch. *She certainly looks like one.* And then Bennie remembered the elf sitting on his bed. *Keith!* He spun around so fast it was a wonder he didn't give himself whiplash.

Keith was gone.

'WELL?' Bennie's mum demanded, hands on hips, face like a disgruntled Rottweiler.

Bennie racked his brain for an answer. 'Erm… I'm sick,' he replied, adding a pathetic cough for good measure. To be fair, because of his Mach 3 head spin, he had momentarily turned green, which definitely aided his cause.

Feigning illness is every kid's get-out-of-jail-free card. Used sparingly, the tactic guaranteed exemption from almost all known engagements and situations, including going to school, the dentist, weddings, funerals, your creepy uncle's house or, in Bennie's case, the desecration of a perfectly good meal.

'Oh, dear,' Bennie's mum said, making a sad face. 'I expect it was all the party food at school.'

That much is true, Bennie mused. Mrs Scrange's chocolate Brussels sprouts could kill. As for her sausages, they posed an unparalleled biological threat to all life on Earth.

'I think it best you get an early night. A good sleep will put you right.'

Excellent! I'll be left alone. Bennie nodded feebly.

'Is there anything I can get you, love?' she asked, bending to retrieve her son's defiled dinner tray, which was swimming in semi-digested fish and chips. It looked like liquified roadkill.

'No thanks, Mum. I'll go straight to bed,' he replied miserably, playing the get-out-of-jail-free card to perfection.

'Okay, love. Oh, you have some visitors.'

Miss Fluff-Face, the cat, closely followed by Hedgehog, the dog, squeezed past Mrs Perkins and bolted straight under Bennie's bed.

Oh, no! That's where Keith is hiding!

The instant Bennie's mum shut his bedroom door behind her, he heard growling and hissing. He prayed it wasn't going to be another *Sebastian* incident. Five seconds later, Hedgehog and Miss Fluff-Face slunk from beneath the bed, whimpering with their tales between their legs.

Keith scrambled out behind them. 'Keith teach hairy monsters lesson,' she explained, grinning impishly.

That night, Bennie had nightmares. He couldn't stop dreaming about Keith's village. The fire spread through the magic door, and before Bennie knew it, Larkbridge was burning, and there was nothing anyone could do to douse the flames.

Bennie awoke in a panic, his heart hammering inside his ribcage like a woodpecker on candyfloss. Once he realised it was only a dream, he relaxed. 'BLIMEY,' he gasped, gulping down big lungfuls of air, 'that was a bit toasty.' The experience was enough to put him off Bonfire Night for life.

Bennie tried going back to sleep but soon became aware of flashing lights. At first, he thought it was police cars or fire engines whizzing past his window, but he soon realised they were coming from inside his room.

Bennie sat bolt upright inside his sleeping bag. 'Keith's gizmo thingy,' he whispered. And there it was, lying on his desk, lit up like a fruit machine having a nervous breakdown. Accompanying its psychedelic light display, it was making noises, too, a steady, continuous

BEEPING.

Unable to extract himself from his sack quickly enough, Bennie slithered across his bedroom floor like a snake until finally bumping into his computer desk. Reaching up, he grabbed the contraption from beside his keyboard. A red blip pulsed over a street map on the thing's display screen. 'Is that Larkbridge?'

Bennie glanced at Keith. The elf was fast asleep, cuddled up in Bennie's bed with Miss Fluff-Face and Hedgehog for company. He thought about waking her but decided whatever it was, it could wait until morning. The elf needed her rest.

Placing the device back on his desk, Bennie slithered across the floor again and tried to get some sleep of his own. But sleep wouldn't come. He was restless with thoughts. They buzzed inside his head like a swarm of killer bees. Why was Keith's village on fire? Was she an alien from another planet, like Ravi said? Why did Brussels sprouts taste so terrible, even smothered in chocolate? And if elves existed, was it possible, however ridiculous it seemed, that so too did Father Christmas?

Eventually, Bennie drifted into a deep sleep.

'WAKE UP, BOY!'

Bennie's eyes shot open. 'NO, YOU CAN'T SNIFF MY DAD'S CHEESE!'

Keith raised a curious eyebrow before shaking Bennie by the shoulders even harder.

'What is it? What's happening?'

'WAKE, SILLY BOY!'

'Alright, alright! I'm awake,' he cried. 'Now get off me.' The elf was straddled across his chest, and even though she was only three feet tall, she was heavier than she looked.

Hedgehog's ears pricked up, and he raised his head to see what was going on.

'KEITH REMEMBER!' the elf blurted excitedly. No, she wasn't excited; she was frantic.

'What do you remember?' Bennie mumbled drowsily.

The dog's interest waned, and he went back to sleep.

'EVERYTHING!' Leaping off Bennie, Keith grabbed her flashing gadget from the computer desk. 'WE MUST GO!'

'Go? Now?'

'YES, NOW!'

Bennie glanced at his alarm clock and groaned. 'But it's only five in the morning.'

'WE MUST FIND BEARDED ONE!' Keith explained, and she wasn't calming down.

'Who?'

'ELF FATHER, SILLY BOY!'

6

The Bearded One

Earlier, late the night before…

'Wide of girth?' *Well, perhaps a little.*

'Massive white beard?' *Ha, ha! Why, of course!*

'Obese? Senile? A washed-out has-been?' *Blooming heck, but that's below the belt!*

'Who's he talking to, Brett?' Sid asked.

Best mates Brett and Sid swigged from beer bottles at the head of a back alley, watching the large, bearded man with curiosity. Why the old fool was wearing nothing except an enormous red dressing gown barely big enough to contain his wobbly parts and a pair of giant fluffy fluorescent-pink slippers that glowed in the dark like a pair of alien monsters was a mystery, albeit a highly amusing mystery.

'Himself, I *THINK?*' Brett said with a hiccup.

Brett and Sid were on their way home after being booted out of the Jolly Roger—the least hospitable and most notorious public house in Larkbridge, where looking mean and having a sinister limp were necessary entry requirements.

Sid sniggered drunkenly, mesmerised by the heated conversation the bearded man was having with himself—well, his own shadow cast on the alley wall, to be precise.

'I reckon the old-timer's had more BOOZE than we have, Brett.'

Abruptly, the bearded man spun around. 'WHO'S THERE?'

'Look, Sid, it's Grandad Crimble!' Brett chortled, enthusiastically pointing his half-empty beer bottle at the deranged pensioner. The round belly, the big beard, the red gown... What else was Brett going to think a week before Christmas?

'What are you doing in LARKBRIDGE?' Brett slurred contemptuously. 'Shouldn't you be at the NORTH POLE with all your little ELF FRIENDS making pressies for the kiddies?'

'ELVES?' the bearded man said with interest, blundering toward the pair like an intoxicated hippopotamus. Elves sounded awfully familiar. If only he could remember.

'Tell me more about these ELVES!'

Sid laughed so much he sicked up over his suede shoes. 'On your bike, GRANDAD! You don't want to be late for your big day,' he hollered, wiping his vomit-smeared lips on a beer-stained sleeve.

Scoffing, the two men staggered away through the snow, singing something about jingling their bells in the back of a one-horse open sleigh.

My big day? the bearded man mused, hunching his bushy white eyebrows. He had absolutely no idea what the idiot was talking about. Maybe the big, wobbly chap he had been speaking to in the alley was right? *Maybe I am going senile?* He peered down to see a bulging belly and a pair of bloated tree-trunk legs. He shook his head. 'I'm well past my best. I'll be lucky to get the sleigh off the ground at this rate.' *Sleigh? What am I prattling on about?* He hadn't a clue.

The bearded man decided he needed to find elves. He didn't know why. In fact, he didn't even recall what *elves* looked like. And if not elves, a sleigh… No, a pub. A pub and a substantial meal. Yes, that would clear his head. His belly rumbled so violently it caused his whole body to shudder. *To be honest, I don't look like I need another meal.* But how could he deny his belly when his cravings were so intense they loosened his teeth and rattled his brain?

The bearded man stumbled from the alley and began wandering the white streets of Larkbridge. The night was bitter, the air thick with snowflakes. He pulled his dressing gown tight. Didn't he usually wear more clothes than this? Shrugging his broad shoulders, he ambled aimlessly, the snow freezing his exposed ankles with each step.

The bearded man gazed at the endless lights shimmering in people's windows and gardens. There were blues, greens, and reds, but most sparkled a beautiful golden yellow. Some flashed, others cascaded, and a few pulsed like distant stars. The more he stared, the more they began to merge.

'So many colours,' the bearded man muttered, struggling to separate them. They swirled in front of his eyes like a kaleidoscope of psychedelic fireflies having a good old knees up. He could hardly see anything else. He certainly couldn't think about anything else. It was like having a really bad migraine during a seventies disco.

'MUST… REMAIN… IN… CONTROL!!'

But he couldn't. His mind began unravelling. Everything around him took on a life of its own. It was as if he existed within an alternate reality. Nothing appeared or behaved as it should, at least it didn't inside his brain.

Houses became castles with spires towering into the night sky. Trees became monsters, streetlamps exploding fireballs, cars grazing wildebeest, and the falling snowflakes blood-sucking moths with razor-sharp teeth. And then, through the swirling swarms of vampire insects and beyond the metallic herds grazing flesh on the side of the street, he saw it. 'Blooming heck! A demon!'

Of course, what he was actually seeing was a harmless ten-foot conifer adorned with twinkling red lights in Mrs Foster's front garden. And in no way did the tree resemble a fearsome satanic monstrosity from the Underworld.

'Fear not, brave folk of Larkbridge! I will send this diabolical creature **BACK TO HELL!**'

Above the fiendish tree, Mrs Foster's bedroom light flickered on, and then an old, wrinkled face appeared at the window.

Blimey, the poor princess is trapped in the demon's tower. I must vanquish the thing and rescue her at once.

There's nothing quite so disturbing as seeing an obese, half-dressed elderly gentleman rugby tackle a Christmas tree. Mrs Foster could vouch for that. Her traumatised face was proof.

Remarkably, the bearded man's shoulder charge snapped the conifer like a twig, sending the tree crashing to the ground, obliterating Mrs Foster's prize-winning Hydrangea in the process. Mrs Foster's screams could be heard three streets away despite her bedroom's triple-glazed windows.

The felling of Satan's tree didn't end the bearded man's crusade—far from it. Convinced the wildebeest had fallen under an evil spell, he bellowed like a Viking berserker—well, more like a giant demented yak—and launched himself at the cars lining the pavements, starting predictably with poor Mrs Foster's Nissan Micra.

Befuddled by the warped world of his dream state, the bearded man had little notion of his own strength. Wheels, bumpers, bonnets, and doors were torn from vehicles and hurled into people's gardens. The whining of car alarms only fuelled his deranged crime spree. The death toll would have been unimaginable if his victims had been real wildebeest and not inanimate lumps of metal and hardened plastic.

The bearded man's episode finally passed, the fantasy inside his head receding, revealing the cold reality of his exploits. Once more, exploding fireballs became streetlamps and the scattered limbs of wildebeest broken bits of automobiles.

'Oh, dear.' His memory hadn't fully returned, but he knew enough to realise he had made rather a mess.

The bearded man winced. *Well, I suppose it might have been worse. My dressing gown could have popped open during proceedings.* He shuddered at the thought. *No one wants to see my rear end on a cold winter's night.* Witnessing something like that could ruin someone's life.

He glanced up to see Mrs Foster glaring at him from her bedroom window, snarling and shaking her fists. *Fair do's, I suppose.* 'Sorry!' he mouthed apologetically. Mrs Foster rewarded him with a two-fingered salute. *Charming, I'm sure.*

Blue lights flashed at the end of the street. The bearded man tensed, fearing another demon, but as the lights drew nearer, weaving between the broken bits of vehicle littering the road, he realised he wasn't hallucinating anymore.

'Oh, no. It's the fuzz.'

Suddenly, the bearded man's brain fog lifted, enough at any rate to reveal his identity. It felt like being zapped by an invisible lightning bolt after having a bucket of icy cold water chucked in the face.

I remember who I am! His name came as a real surprise because, like so many boys and girls these days, he honestly didn't think he existed. *Well, fancy that. I am real, after all. Would you Adam and Eve it!*

The police car finally crunched to a halt outside Mrs Foster's house, and a pair of uniformed officers stepped from the flashing vehicle into the snow. Neither of the men appeared especially happy to meet him. *I just don't seem to command the same respect as I used to.* What did he expect? He had been pensioned off more than fifty years ago and now resembled something that wallowed in a swamp with a long white beard.

'Good evening, officers. What seems to be the trouble?' The bearded man said, displaying his best smile.

The policemen glanced at one another and then at the carnage surrounding them in the snow. It looked like a war zone. The policemen raised their eyebrows.

'What's your name, please, sir?' the older of the two officers asked. He was a stern-looking fellow who reminded the bearded man of a grey day in Skegness.

'Which one?'

The officer frowned. 'What do you mean, WHICH ONE?'

'Well, I've got more than one name.'

The younger officer began dutifully jotting notes into a little black book. If the older policeman was a grey day in Skegness, he was a wet weekend in Hull.

The younger officer stopped his scribbling and looked up. 'Are you telling us you have multiple aliases, sir?'

'HOW DARE YOU! I've never been so insulted!' And then the bearded man remembered what the word *alias* meant. 'Ah, yes. If you mean NAMES, then I've got loads of them. In fact, I can't keep track of them all, if I'm perfectly honest.'

The older officer sighed. 'What's your REAL name, sir? And please don't waste police time.'

'My real name? Blimey, let me think… It's been so long since I last used it. Nick… Nicholas? No, that was later… or was it? KRIS, *THAT'S IT!* No, it isn't. Noel? No. Gwiazdor? Mikulas? ANTHEA! No, that was my wife's name. Bless her.'

The older officer sighed again, but much heavier and with more feeling this time.

'No, it's no good. I can't remember.'

The younger officer pursed his lips thoughtfully for a moment before resuming his scribbling.

'Okay, sir. Let's try again, shall we?' the older officer continued, speaking slowly as if to a very small child who had only learnt to talk the day before yesterday. 'Which of your MANY NAMES are you best known by?'

'Erm… It depends on which country I'm visiting.'

The older officer was losing his patience and was beginning to look like a dark, stormy night in Clapham.

'You're in ENGLAND, for goodness sake, man! Tell me your name before I taser you for AGGRAVATED VERBAL ABUSE!!'

'*Aggravated verbal abuse,*' the younger officer repeated as he recorded the offence in his notebook. He had never heard of that one before and wondered if Trevor was making them up as he went along again. It was becoming a habit. Indecent staring, perverting the course of placing an order at a drive-through, looking a bit shifty without intent, disturbing a picnic, breathing under the influence… The list was growing by the day.

'BLIMEY! Yes, of course. I wouldn't want that. It sounds downright blooming awful. Let me think… England… Erm…'

'Last chance before I zap your brains out.'

'*Zap your brains out,*' repeated the younger officer.

'GORDON BENNETT, JONNY! You don't have to write down everything I say.'

'I'VE GOT IT!' the bearded man blurted.

'Have you, Sir,' the older officer replied wryly.

'YES! I'M FATHER BLOOMING CHRISTMAS! It's a bit of a mouthful, so Santa's just fine.'

The older officer shook his head. 'And I'm Mary Poppins, I suppose.'

'Mary Poppins, you say?' Santa scratched at his beard, eyeing the policeman up and down. 'Well, to be perfectly honest, I was expecting a dress. At the very least, a magical umbrella.'

'It looks like we've got ourselves a comedian, Jonny.'

The younger officer nodded solemnly. 'I don't see Mrs Foster laughing, guv.'

'No, Jonny, and do you know why Mrs Foster isn't laughing?'

'Yes, guv. Because Santa has smashed up her car and parked what's left of it on her lawn beside her murdered tree.'

'That's right, Jonny.'

The younger officer looked pleased with himself and quickly penned the exchange into his notebook, adding an asterisk and a smiley face.

The older officer glared at Santa. 'I don't care if you're SIR CLIFF RICHARD, the KING OF SPAIN, or FATHER BLEEDING CHRISTMAS!! No one goes on the rampage in Womble Street and gets away with it!'

The younger officer looked confused. 'Why's that, guv?' In his admittedly limited experience, most criminals *did* get away with it—Womble Street or not.

'Because, JONNY, my dear old mum lives at number thirty-two, that's why. And I'll not allow her neighbourhood to get wrecked by a crazy old man wearing nothing but a BATHROBE AND A PAIR OF GIANT FLUFFY SLIPPERS THAT GLOW IN THE DARK!!!'

The older officer grinned sadistically at Santa. 'You're nicked, my old mucker!'

Santa stuck up his hands. 'No need to be hasty, officer,' he said, protesting his innocence. 'To tell you the truth, I can't remember a thing. I had a funny turn, you see.'

The older officer unhooked his handcuffs from his belt. 'That's convenient, sir,' he said, reaching for Santa's hands. 'Now, let's not make a scene, shall we?'

'It's the truth,' Santa said, backing away through the snow. Well, it was true enough. 'You can't seriously believe a man of my, well, dotage—'

'And physique,' the younger officer added, after subjecting Santa to a once over, which, in hindsight, he rather wished he hadn't started. Flesh oozed between gaps in the man's robes like something from an X-rated horror movie.

'And PHYSIQUE,' Santa repeated grudgingly, 'can knock down trees and throw cars, do you? I've never heard anything so ludicrous in all my years.'

The older officer paused. 'Now you mention it, it does sound all very farfetched. Be that as it may, you're our only suspect.'

'If we don't bring someone—anyone—in for questioning, our boss gets tetchy,' the younger officer added. 'And we don't get any doughnuts for a week. I like doughnuts, especially the iced ones with sprinkles on top.'

The older officer glowered. 'Alright, Jonny. Keep the information to a minimum. Remember who you're talking to, son. You're not in the station canteen now.'

The younger officer closed his notebook and stared at his feet. 'Yes, guv. Sorry, guv.'

Santa's stomach growled again. 'If I come quietly, will I get fed?' A hot meal and a night in a warm cell didn't sound too bad, and until his memory was fully restored, there wasn't much he could do.

'You'll get fed. We aren't living in the Dark Ages.' Although having seen the size of the old man's stomach, he wondered if the station canteen was sufficiently stocked to cope.

'What about finding me some clothes?'

The older officer shrugged. 'I expect so. If we can find some that *FIT*.'

Santa's smile returned. 'Blooming marvellous,' he said, offering his hands for cuffing. 'I'M RUDDY WELL STARVING!'

7

Weird Science

'We track down Elf Father QUICKLY!' Keith said, stomping ahead at a furious pace.

Keith was impatient. She had already been made to wait for Bennie's friends before leaving, and now they meandered like cattle cropping grass. 'Day gone by time we find Elf Father,' Keith fumed, stamping her feet.

The late departure did at least give the elf a much-needed rest, and Bennie had fixed her some breakfast, too. Bennie's mum had been shocked after he turned down a bacon sandwich in favour of a bowl of fruit and muesli. She assumed he still wasn't feeling himself after yesterday.

The gang had marched halfway across Larkbridge since breakfast. Goodness only knew where they would be by lunchtime. The snowstorm had passed, and the sun shone, but the pavements were thick with snow, and hiking through the stuff was tough going. Even so, they managed a good pace, even if the elf didn't agree. 'Faster, silly humans.'

Bennie had dressed Keith in one of his old coats, and with a woolly hat pulled down over her pointy ears and a pair of sunglasses hiding her peculiar eyes, she almost looked normal. Well, as normal as a fairytale creature wrapped in ill-fitting winter clothes can be.

'Who is this Elf Father, and what's he doing in Larkbridge?' Ravi asked, fascinated by this latest turn of events. Not only had they discovered an elf, but now they were on their way to meet her leader.

'He is ELF FATHER, the BEARDED ONE,' Keith stated, shrugging irritably. She couldn't understand how they hadn't heard of him before. Surely every boy and girl knew of the Elf Father? 'You know, FAT MAN who gives children SURPRISES?'

Ravi frowned. To be perfectly honest, that didn't sound like anyone he wanted to meet any time soon. He didn't like surprises, especially ones dished out by large, bearded strangers.

'He not always so round and decrepit. Many winters ago, he young and strong,' Keith recalled wistfully. 'A HERO.'

Bennie could tell Keith was fiercely proud of her Elf Father.

'Now he sad and older than ever.'

What an odd thing to say, Bennie mused. *Older than ever?* He wondered what she meant by it.

The elf's moment of gloom passed, and she concentrated on the red dot flashing on the screen of her gadget. 'And he in Larkbridge because Keith send him accidentally,' she explained, answering Ravi's question.

'What do you mean ACCIDENTALLY?' Mabel asked. In her experience, spilling a glass of milk was an accident. Inadvertently teleporting someone to an entirely different country was something else entirely.

'We should have come through VJP together, but VTM run out of power before Keith follow—'

'HOLD YOUR HORSES! VJP? VTM? What do you mean?' Ravi interrupted, waving his hands about.

'She sounds like an IT consultant,' Boris added. And the only reason he said it was because his dad *was* an IT consultant, and that was precisely how he talked all the time. *FWD this, R&D that, DM me ASAP*. Boris didn't even know what *IT* meant. Most of the time, he didn't have the foggiest idea what his dad was going on about.

'It simple: VJP—VORTEX JUMP PORTAL!' Keith snapped. Then she noted the children's vacant eyes staring back at her. She sighed. 'Magic door in sky Keith fall through.'

Their faces lightened with understanding. 'Oh, that!'

'VTM,' she said, acknowledging the device held in her hand. 'VORTEX TIME MANIPULATOR.'

Ravi almost stopped breathing. 'INCREDIBLE!' he mouthed in awe. 'I was right, wasn't I? It IS how you got here.'

'Yes,' Keith replied, 'but it capable of more than boy's PRIMITIVE brain can POSSIBLY IMAGINE.'

'It doesn't manipulate time by any chance, does it?' Ravi replied sarcastically, adding, 'DUH!' to emphasise just how obvious the answer was.

Keith growled. 'Time manipulation single greatest invention in planet's history and not subject of FLIPPANT REMARKS!!! You not comprehend brilliance involved in creating device.'

'Sorry,' Ravi whimpered with a gulp. Keith was scary when she was angry. 'I'm hugely impressed, honest.'

And he was. In fact, he would go as far as saying this was the best day of his life. Bearing witness to technology so advanced it made the boffins at NASA look like primary school physics teachers was beyond his wildest dreams. He just couldn't help making flippant remarks; it was in his genes.

'With what poor Keith has been through, you should be ashamed of yourself, Ravi,' Alice retorted, frantically rubbing her gloved hands together in the hope of stimulating her seemingly deceased circulation. 'Don't you have feelings?'

In such situations, Ravi had learned it was best to do and say nothing because whatever you did do or say would inevitably be wrong. However, Alice was mistaken; he did have feelings. Ravi stared at the VTM device with excitement bubbling in his belly like a hotpot on the hob. He couldn't wait to see it in action.

'I'm glad you're feeling better, Keith,' Alice said, draping a friendly arm around the elf's slender shoulders. 'And I hope we find your friend.'

Every muscle in Keith's body tensed. Contrary to popular belief, elves aren't an exceptionally touchy-feely race.

Keith bit her lip and endured the uncomfortable sensation without resulting to extreme violence. She realised Alice was the caring type, and the elf didn't want to upset the girl by rejecting her act of kindness. At least not until they had found the Elf Father. After that, she wouldn't need the children's help any longer, and Keith wouldn't need to contain her emotions.

'What was wrong with you yesterday?' Mabel inquired, walking on the other side of the elf. 'Were you POISONED?'

'It called JUMP SICKNESS,' Keith answered. 'Keith pass through VJP without preparation. Elf Father suffer same fate.'

Bennie grimaced. He dreaded to think what might have happened to the Elf Father if he reacted even half as badly as Keith had.

'Keith not ready to jump… none of us ready,' Keith continued, her small musical voice sounding happier than she looked. 'There no time to programme accurate coordinates. Bearded One might have found self in Pacific Ocean or on Everest. We lucky.'

Boris sniggered. 'I wouldn't call ending up in Larkbridge lucky.'

Alice glared at Boris. This was not the time for stupid jokes. 'It sounds awful,' Alice said to Keith, her face a picture of concern. 'Poor you.'

Beneath her sunglasses, the elf rolled her eyes. Human children were so sentimental it made her want to retch.

'Are you from the future?' Bennie asked excitedly. 'Did you *TIME TRAVEL HERE?* After all, wasn't that what time manipulation was for?

The elf shook her head. 'Time travel FORBIDDEN. If past altered, even by smallest detail, consequences CATASTROPHIC!!!'

Bennie felt immediately deflated. He so wanted to meet a time traveller. 'So what is the thing used for if not time travel?' Bennie really couldn't see the point in it otherwise. He couldn't think of another way in which time might be manipulated.

'It difficult to explain,' Keith said. 'Especially to BRAINLESS LITTLE CHILDREN.'

Mabel scowled. 'You do know that we're all a lot taller than you, don't you?'

'And we're smarter than we look,' Boris said tartly.

Ravi glanced at Boris and snorted. 'Most of us are.'

'Okay, SMART boys and girls, try comprehend. Additional to opening vortex portals—wormholes through space and time—elves use VTM to create TIME BUBBLES. Within bubble, time slow, so hardly ticks at all.'

'SHUT THE FRONT DOOR!' Ravi blurted, repeating a phrase frequently used by his father. 'SERIOUSLY?' He had never heard of anything so unbelievably fantastic.

'My head is hurting,' Mabel declared, rubbing her temples.

'Why would you need to slow time?' Bennie asked. Like Mabel, his brain was in danger of exploding inside his skull.

Keith shook her head crossly. 'ENOUGH!' she shrieked. 'Keith answer no more idiotic questions. My people's secrets not be shared with OUTSIDERS!'

Blimey, she'd do well as a teacher at school, Bennie thought. He was convinced very loud shouting was mandatory for all Larkbridge Primary School teaching posts.

The children trudged through the snow with heads down, following the elf and her flashing VTM in silence. No one on the streets of Larkbridge paid them the slightest bit of notice. Mind you, Larkbridge folk were renowned for keeping themselves to themselves:

'If you don't poke your snout in other people's business, they won't poke theirs in yours.'

Bennie suspected the policy would be severely tested if Keith was exposed. It was almost tempting to de-robe her just to see their reaction.

Keeping their tongues in check was proving to be a challenge, particularly for Ravi, who was bursting to ask questions. He desperately wanted to learn all there was to know about time manipulation and vortex portals. He couldn't understand how Keith and her fellow elves resisted the urge to time travel. If he owned a time machine, there was no way on Earth he would be able to stop himself from playing with the thing. He also didn't understand why it was forbidden. If you were really careful, it would be alright, wouldn't it? Surely, a quick peek at some dinosaurs couldn't hurt. It seemed such a waste.

The red dot on the VTM's screen began flashing with greater enthusiasm. 'We close,' Keith said, taking them down a snow-chocked side alley before emerging onto the main road heading out of town.

'I'm wondering,' Alice began tentatively, risking a telling off, 'if you've had the Elf Father chipped? You know, like a cat or a dog? We chipped Daisy in case she wanders off. Does the Elf Father wander off? Is that how you're tracking him?' Alice regretted opening her mouth. The words didn't sound quite so dumb inside her head.

'No, he not CHIPPED. After passing through VJP, DNA signature stored on VTM.'

Alice quickly glazed over again.

Ravi, on the other hand, gleefully danced a jig on the ice beneath his feet, unable to contain his excitement. 'So you can track anyone who has jumped before?' Science was so amazing! Why his friends didn't share his enthusiasm was a mystery. What was wrong with them?

'Yes,' Keith confirmed. 'Anyone who jumps using device.'

'Are there more?'

'Yes,' Keith chirped, coming to a halt. 'NOW SHUT UP.'

She glanced at the VTM and scowled. 'We here but no Elf Father.'

When nothing happened, she started banging the device against her knee.

'WORK WRETCHED THING!!!'

Hissing like a cat, Keith threw the VTM into the drifted snow beside the footpath, where the gadget promptly burst into song and dance, flashing and trumpeting a fanfare: 'You have reached your destination!'

The elf growled. 'Keith switch audio OFF!' she said, retrieving the device from its icy tomb. 'Why infuriating woman STILL TALKING?'

The children winced. They preferred yesterday's elf.

A building loomed before them. It was old and intimidating—like a university lecturer—and not the sort of place any of them wanted to go.

'The Elf Father is in THERE?' Alice questioned, eyeing their destination as if it were the entrance to the Underworld.

Keith checked the VTM. 'Affirmative.'

Their eyes were drawn to a sign above the door.

Framed in snow and dripping icicles, it showed a red sun sinking below the leafless branches of an autumn tree. Beside the picture, worked in a bright lurid orange, were the words: 'Sunset Rest'.

'Sunset Rest? What's he doing in an old people's home?' Bennie said.

'ASSISTED LIVING RETIREMENT FACILITY,' Boris corrected with a tut. 'Saying OLD PEOPLE'S HOME is upsetting.'

Bennie frowned. Upsetting to who? He was pretty sure the residents didn't care. What was wrong with calling them old people's homes? They were homes with old people in them—go figure. It couldn't be any more self-explanatory if it tried. Where was the insult?

Keith removed her sunglasses and handed them to Bennie. 'Thank you for help, silly boy. Keith take it from here.'

The gang exhibited mixed emotions. It was true; they didn't want to set foot inside an old people's home—especially one that looked like it belonged in a particularly scary ghost story—but neither did they want to go home without seeing the Elf Father or finding out what was really going on.

'That's it, then, *IS IT?*' Bennie said grumpily. 'After all we've done for you, we don't even get to meet the Elf Father. We at least deserve that much, don't we?'

Bennie didn't want to walk away. He firmly believed in fate, and something told him this adventure and his part in the story had only just begun.

Keith opened her mouth to speak but hesitated. Instead, she scrunched up her tiny features and studied the children. Finally, the elf nodded her bobble-hatted head.

'There something you must know,' she said. 'If help, you will be in GRAVE DANGER!'

8

Sunset Rest

'WE'LL BE IN GRAVE DANGER?' Bennie had the feeling Fate was about to reveal her hand. Destiny was calling him, and for better or worse—or something utterly absurd in between—he couldn't wait for the adventure to begin.

Bennie hadn't bargained for such a dramatic start to the holidays. Yes, he had met an elf, which certainly was dramatic, but to be told his life would be at risk if he faced his calling was like being offered the chance to play football for England, knowing the Wembley pitch was a minefield. It was a bittersweet situation.

Keith glanced at the care home and then at the children.

Bennie grimaced. It looked like she was weighing up the odds of their survival.

'Once you meet Elf Father, there no going back,' Keith said. 'Not because you cannot but because you not want to. Bearded One infectious, especially to children—and not like disease. He has way with little humans. You will see. Before you choose whether help or not, Keith tell you what happened in Hasseldorf, my home.'

Here it comes, Bennie thought. *The smell after the fart.* The dire warning after the promise of adventure, the free ride on the world's scariest rollercoaster without a seatbelt. He didn't care about health and safety warnings; he wanted excitement no matter the danger. *Bring it on! Whatever it is, I can take it.*

'Do you think we can get on with it? Only I can't feel my toes anymore,' Alice asked politely, stamping her feet.

'Keith see what attacked Hasseldorf,' Keith began ominously.

'Don't you mean WHO attacked Hasseldorf?' Ravi interrupted smugly. He liked nothing more than correcting other people's mistakes.

Keith glared at Ravi. 'EIGHT FEET TALL, SOULLESS BLACK EYES, RAZOR-SHARP

BEAKS, AND CLAWS LIKE MEAT HOOKS. What you call them?'

Ravi's eyes bulged. 'I stand corrected,' he said with a gulp.

The others were no less disturbed by the elf's description. Boris literally shook with fright. So did Alice; mind you, she had an excuse: she was suffering from the onset of hypothermia.

'What ARE THEY?' Bennie asked eagerly. This was getting better and better! First mythical creatures and now horrible monsters. *This is going to be a proper adventure, like in stories.*

'I not know. They like giant turkeys.'

'*TURKEYS?*' Mabel had never heard of anything so ridiculous.

'Keith only tells you what she saw,' the elf replied testily, folding her arms and scrunching up her face. 'It like they had VTMs, too. They jump from nowhere, shooting us with ray guns.'

Ravi squealed. 'See, I told you! Keith's burn WAS caused by a ray gun. I KNEW IT! They're aliens, aren't they?'

'Let's not get carried away,' Bennie warned. Although it was difficult not to with mutant ray-gun-toting turkeys on the loose.

'Before we can work out their end game, we need to establish what they were after in Hasseldorf,' Mabel advised, wagging a finger.

'Where *IS* Hasseldorf?' Alice whispered to Mabel.

Mabel shrugged. 'BELGIUM?'

Keith jerked a hand toward Sunset Rest. 'They want Elf Father.'

'But why?'

'Elf Father Earth's last hero.'

Keith's answer wasn't what they had been expecting. All manner of fantastical scenarios sprung to life inside the children's minds.

'Earth's last hero,' Bennie whispered, picturing King Arthur in shimmering armour slaying giant rampaging turkeys from horseback with a gigantic gleaming magical sword.

Mabel imagined a flame-haired, spear-throwing Queen Boudica thundering into battle in a chariot. Alice conjured a young Serena Williams wielding tennis rackets like Nunchucks. And Boris, a Lycra-clad Sir David Attenborough in a Spiderman costume, bouncing to Kylie Minogue while rescuing butterflies with a net.

Sir David Attenborough was Boris' favourite hero. In his opinion, saving wildlife was the most heroic thing anyone could do—and who doesn't like boogying to Kylie?

'I wasn't aware Earth HAD heroes,' Ravi announced sceptically. He didn't have an imagination, at least not for anything unrelated to science fiction or mathematical algorithms. 'Is he like Flash Gordon?'

In all honesty, Sunset Rest wasn't the sort of place where you would expect to find a hero. Perhaps he was undercover? Perhaps he was visiting a relative? *Or,* Bennie thought gloomily, *maybe he is just really, really old.* His heart sank. Adventuring with a pensioner didn't sound half so appealing as with a hero. Could the Elf Father be a pensioner *and* a hero? He hoped so.

'So what you're saying is, if we help, there's a good chance we'll be hunted down by EIGHT-FOOT TURKEY SOLDIERS armed with RAY GUNS?' Bennie said to Keith.

Keith nodded.

'Well, I don't know about anyone else, but a few overgrown CHICKENS aren't going to stop me from helping a REAL HERO. I've waited my whole life for adventure. Now's my chance. We eat turkeys for breakfast… Well, for Christmas dinner. They don't scare us.'

'Speak for yourself. They sound ABSOLUTELY TERRIFYING!' Boris declared with a shudder. 'The thought of turkey men OR WOMEN scares me half to death!'

Discriminating against one gender or another without knowing the facts was prudent in the company of such headstrong individuals, i.e., Alice and Mabel—and probably Keith, too. Boris was ever mindful of people's feelings. Upsetting someone unintentionally was a constant worry. It was the reason Boris took so long to answer questions. Everyone assumed he was a bit thick, but he wasn't. He was simply vetting multiple replies inside his head all at the same time before choosing the one which offended the least.

'BUT,' Boris continued, shaking his head as if he couldn't quite believe what was about to spill out of his mouth, 'helping those in need, ESPECIALLY heroes, is the right thing to do.'

'I'm in,' Ravi chirped eagerly. Admittedly, he didn't give a monkey's backside about helping heroes. However, having been exposed to the technological secrets of a lifetime, there was no way—monster turkeys or no monster turkeys—that he wasn't going to sign up. Vortex time manipulators, jump portals, ray guns… What was next? He couldn't wait to find out.

'Me, too,' Mabel declared firmly. She was right into heroes, adventures, and anything to do with war zones.

'What about you, Alice?' Bennie asked. She was the only one undecided.

Alice pursed her lips thoughtfully. 'I'm not entirely sure we should be getting involved with something like this,' she said. 'But if we don't, who else will ensure these turkey people ARE GIVEN THE RIGHTS THEY DESERVE?'

Alice supported human rights, animal rights, insect rights, vegetable rights and just about any rights anyone could possibly think of. 'What harm have they done?' she added passionately.

'They SHOT Keith in the arm and BURNT her village to the GROUND!' Mabel answered crossly. 'As far as I'm concerned, THAT MEANS WAR!!'

Bennie grinned. 'It looks like we're all going on an adventure.'

'So be it,' the elf said with a smile. Well, the children took it for a smile, but it might have easily been a sneer. 'Come, now we meet Elf Father.'

The first thing to hit them inside Sunset Rest was the smell.

'Why does it always STINK OF CABBAGE in these places?' Boris complained, pinching his nose. He only wished he had a clothes peg to hand.

'Because they cook a lot of cabbage,' Ravi replied.

On this occasion, he wasn't trying to be funny. In fact, Ravi rarely dabbled in humour. When he did, it was always by accident. His brain was wired differently from other people's, in a matter-of-factly sort of way. Life experiences were managed logically in a computer-like process—unless science fiction was involved, in which case, logic went straight out the window.

Boris' grandmother had ended up at Crinkly Haven, a home on the other side of town. He didn't visit her as much as he should. Assisted living retirement facilities unnerved him. He wasn't sure why. Perhaps it was because they made him feel sad. Ending your life alone in these places seemed terribly unfair. Then again, it was probably the awful cabbage smell.

The second thing to hit them inside Sunset Rest was the way-over-the-top, obscenely extravagant festive decorations. Gaudy was an understatement. Bennie had never seen such an offensively garish collection of trimmings and trinkets. Multicoloured baubles of all shapes and sizes dangled from the ceilings, and everything in sight was buried beneath heaps of glittering tinsel.

'Don't they realise that stuff is BAD for the environment?' Alice said with a disapproving scowl. The decorations in her house were made from bits of cardboard, old sweet wrappers, and recycled toilet paper. Admittedly, Christmas didn't smell an awful lot better in the Bean household than it did at Sunset Rest.

Bennie cringed. *Please, no one say a word.* Plastic pollution was the foremost of Alice's bugbears. Once she got started on the topic, there was no stopping her.

Boris couldn't help himself. 'Yeah,' he said, agreeing with Alice, 'every time I see anything like this, I imagine it STRANGLING A DOLPHIN or something.'

Although Boris wasn't as clued up as Alice on such issues—he thought Greta Thunberg was a brand of Icelandic yoghurt—he shared her loathing for pollution and its damaging effects on wildlife.

Boris adored animals and regularly wept at the sight of roadkill. When he was seven, he missed school for a whole week when his dad accidentally splattered a pheasant with his car—and then Boris missed a further week after discovering the poor thing wrapped up in the freezer.

The third thing to hit them inside Sunset Rest—and in doing so, mercifully distracting Alice from erupting into having a full-blown rant at anyone within a five-yard radius—was a barrage of boiled eggs hurled by an old lady called Shirley.

Like a bedraggled witch, Shirley guarded the resident's lounge as if her life depended on it. Bent but defiant, she stood beneath the arched entrance, daring anyone to challenge her.

'Go no further, I WARN YOU!' she crowed, aiming a second batch of eggs at the intruders. 'I am a servant of the secret nest! NONE SHALL PASS!!!'

Sunset Rest's duty nurse intervened. Extracting her ample frame from behind the reception desk, she waddled across to the gang like a giant penguin.

'Take no notice of our Shirley. She likes to re-enact movie scenes, bless her,' she said, tutting playfully. 'It's

THE LORD OF THE RINGS today by the look of it. We had the ambulance out for her last week. Everyone thought she'd snapped a hip, silly thing.'

'What movie was she re-enacting?' Bennie asked, intrigued by the old woman's antics. It was precisely the kind of thing he could aspire to when he was her age.

'THE KARATE KID,'

she said, demonstrating a selection of kung-fu chops. She stopped short of attempting the Crane Kick when she saw the children's baffled faces. 'Before your time, I suppose, my lovelies.'

Bennie winced. *No wonder Shirley nearly busted a hip*, he thought, watching her fight imaginary goblins with a walking stick in one hand and a handful of eggs in the other.

Eventually, the old woman-cum-witch shuffled down a corridor, searching for a new audience to intimidate.

'There she goes, our very own Keira Knightly,' the nurse said, smiling fondly.

Blimey, Keira's really let herself go, Bennie mused with a grin.

'Now, my lovelies, who are you here to see?'

Keith shoved between the children and presented herself before the nurse. 'We must see ELF FATHER!' she insisted, fixing the woman with a stern stare.

The nurse peered down at the elf and smiled again. 'Big chap, LOVELY BEARD, likes to sing carols and gorge on mince pies?'

Keith bobbed her head up and down so fast it was a wonder she didn't give herself brain damage. 'Yes, Elf Father.'

The nurse raised her eyebrows. 'Well, aren't you a funny little THING? You've got the STRANGEST EYES.' She thought it best not to mention the girl's other oddities. She didn't want to upset her.

'Your eyes nice too, BIG LADY,' Keith replied with a shrug. 'Like DIRTY PUDDLES in a MUDDY FIELD.'

The gang cringed. They were fast learning that elves didn't mince their words and, contrary to popular belief, they didn't have a poetic bone in their bodies.

'Sorry about our friend,' Alice said, smiling apologetically. 'She was hit by a… DOUBLE-DECKER BUS… IN THE FACE… EVER SO HARD!' It was the first thing that popped into her head.

The elf glared at Alice. 'Hit by bus in face? What nonsense is this?'

Alice giggled nervously. 'The accident is much too stressful for her to talk about, so she blocks it from her mind. It's her way of dealing with it all.'

'Oh, poor thing,' the nurse murmured soothingly. 'Oh, bless her. I completely understand.'

Keith narrowed her violet eyes and growled. 'ELF FATHER, NOW, PLEASE,' she demanded in a very deep, disconcerting voice.

The nurse did her best to ignore the elf's peculiar behaviour. She leaned in close to Alice. 'Who is this *ELF FATHER* to the little girl?' she asked quietly like she thought Keith couldn't hear, even though the elf was standing right next to her. 'Nobody here knows his real name. The police dropped him off early this morning without saying so much as a word.'

'He's her GRANDPA!' Mabel blurted, seeing Alice struggling to find a suitable answer. 'And his real name is… BRIAN!'

While his friends slowly talked themselves into a deep dark hole, Bennie was experiencing an epiphany.

Older than ever, he mused, scrutinising the evidence again. Its meaning implied that the Elf Father had always been old or had been for a very long time. What else had Keith said? *The fat man who gives children surprises.* And surely now the nurse had confirmed his suspicions? *Big chap, lovely beard, likes singing carols and gorging on mince pies.*

Bennie's jaw dropped open. *It can't be, can it?* Realisation struck him like—well, yes—a double-decker bus in the face ever so hard.

Bennie felt as if he was having an out-of-body experience. He floated above the scene like a spirit in the sky, gazing down on proceedings as they unfolded beneath him. In a bewildering daze, he stumbled after his friends as they followed the nurse into the resident's lounge.

Bathed in winter sunshine that streamed like liquid gold through the room's big rectangular windows sat a man on a throne. His lush, wavy hair cascaded to his broad shoulders like a lion's mane, and his thick, bushy beard gleamed as white as the driven snow.

Bennie's imagination was broken when a dark cloud passed over the sun, plunging the lounge into shadow.

'OH,' he said, seeing the truth.

In no way did this man meet Bennie's expectations.

Dressed in a less-than-pleasant, too-tight gravy-stained shirt with rolls of belly fat oozing between the buttons was the Elf Father, who slouched in a rocking chair snoring like a bloated walrus.

'I'll leave you to it, my lovelies. By the sound of it, Shirley's making a nuisance of herself again. Oh, I do hope it's not another rendition of JURASSIC PARK! My ears have only just recovered from last week's ROARING and SCREECHING,' the nurse said before bustling away in a fluster.

'Earth's last *HERO?* He looks more like a retired sumo wrestler,' Ravi stated. He had never been more disappointed at the sight of another human being in his entire life.

'He's not even an ELF!' Mabel announced, scowling like a cat who had been served sour milk. 'How can he be called the ELF FATHER if he's not an *ELF?*'

Bennie began laughing. It wasn't a normal laugh. It was a weird, hysterical giggle that immediately drew the attention of his friends.

'What's the matter with *YOU?*' Alice asked, looking at him as if he belonged in Shirley's next movie re-enactment.

Bennie pointed a finger at the dishevelled old man slumped pitifully in his chair like a giant sack of potatoes. '*THAT'S* FATHER CHRISTMAS!!'

9

Saint Nicholas

Bennie's friends stared at him like his brain had dissolved into mush.

'Are you feeling okay, Bennie?' Mabel asked, studying him with worry. He had a strange glint in his eyes.

'If that's FATHER CHRISTMAS, I'm MAHATMA GANDHI!' Ravi declared.

'He's dead, isn't he?' Boris said.

'PRECISELY.'

'Why didn't you say he was SANTA?' Bennie demanded of Keith, unable to unglue his eyes from the scruffy lump dribbling into his beard sprawled before him.

'ELF FATHER, BEARDED ONE, SANTA CLAUS... they all same obese man. Elf Father has many, many names. Keith cannot remember them all. Keith tells STUPID BOY who Elf Father is. Keith tells STUPID BOY about presents. It not Keith's fault BOY slow in head like PIGEON.'

'You can't seriously believe THIS... THIS...' Alice couldn't find the words to accurately describe whatever *this* was.

'Brian,' Mabel intervened.

'Yes, this BRIAN is Father Christmas?'

Boris was beyond confused. 'Will someone tell me what's going on? Why does Bennie think Brian is Father Christmas?'

'Who's BRIAN?'

'ELF FATHER SPEAKS!' Keith proclaimed.

All eyes swivelled to peer at the old man. Expectations were renewed, and excitement reignited.

Smacking his lips together, the old man scratched at his bulbous nose with a fleshy hand. Then, shifting his bulk ever so slightly to the left, he broke wind like a warthog before dozing off once more.

'There's that stench of cabbage again,' Boris said, looking like he was about to retch up his breakfast. He wasn't the only one suffering. The foul aroma brought a tear to Alice's left eye.

'Some hero,' Ravi scoffed. 'He couldn't—'

'SILENCE!' the elf hissed. 'THE BEARDED ONE AWAKENS!!'

Gradually, the old man's eyes opened. It took a while for his vision to clear, but when it did, a huge smile cracked his rosy-cheeked face from ear to ear. 'KEITH!' he bellowed joyously. 'It's so good to see you!'

Bennie beamed. The old man's smile was infectious. 'You call her KEITH, TOO!'

The old man focused on Bennie, his bushy white brows hunched low over his eyes. 'Well, of course I blooming-well do. Elf names are INFURIATINGLY UNPRONOUNCEABLE!'

Manoeuvring himself in the rocking chair, the old man leaned forward to better study his visitors.

'Children,' he mumbled after a good hard look. 'Why have you brought me *CHILDREN*, Keith? Wait, don't bother to explain. I know why, but it won't work, ELF!'

He slumped again, seemingly unimpressed by the sight of his guests.

Keith sighed. 'Not this again,' she muttered under her breath. 'They come to help, Elf Father. Something bad happening, REMEMBER?'

'PAH! I'm not interested,' he said, turning his face away like a petulant child. 'GO AWAY; I'M RETIRED!'

Poor Keith appeared crestfallen. Her little face sagged with rejection. 'But home gone. Elves lost, many dead. Elf Father not safe here. Monsters hunt Elf Father.'

'POPPYCOCK! Why would anyone bother with me? I'm finished, a has-been. Even the police don't want me. Leave me in peace.'

It was hard not to be moved by the old man's hopelessness. Whoever he was, it seemed life had little meaning for him anymore. Bennie couldn't imagine feeling so miserable.

'I like it here,' the old man mumbled. 'The food's good—lovely big portions—and there's bingo and music, and everyone's so nice.' He pointed to a wrinkly old lady asleep in the chair opposite. 'That's Marjory. She likes to impersonate howler monkeys. Not in the slightest bit ANNOYING,' he joked, rolling his eyes theatrically.

'And there's Jim,' he said, giving the man a wave. Jim sat next to Marjory, watching the telly. 'Jim's a bright spark. He speaks six languages—all at the same time, mind and never in the right order. GOOD OLD JIM! Mick, on the other hand, doesn't speak one bit, but boy, CAN HE SING! On the hour, every hour, we're treated to a right old knees-up. Usually, it's FRANK SINATRA or ROY ORBISON, but when I arrived this morning, he was belting out MEAT LOAF!'

Mabel was impressed. 'You've only been here half a day, and you already know everything there is to know about everyone.'

'I told you, ELF FATHER has way with people,' Keith retorted sharply.

The old man shrugged. 'A gift, that's all.'

Bennie couldn't help wondering why the Elf Father had given up on life. How had he become content with living *here?* 'Why won't you help us?' Bennie asked.

The old man blew out his cheeks. 'You know, it's funny, but ending up here at Sunset Rest after all these years has finally made me realise I'm ready to call it a day. When you can barely walk to the privy on your own steam, it's time. I'm old, boy. And I mean REALLY OLD. I'm not long for this world. I just want to live out my remaining days in peace. Is that too much to ask?'

Ravi wholeheartedly agreed with the old man's self-diagnosis. He didn't have anything against him, but it was all too evident that his glory days were well and truly behind him. And, in Ravi's opinion, venturing any further than the care home's *privy* was a heart attack waiting to happen.

'I beg you, Elf Father, HELP US!' Keith implored.

'Look,' she said, jabbing a slender finger at the telly. 'GIANT TURKEYS attack HASSELDORF, and now little turkeys go missing here.'

Keith was right. Another case of turkey rustling had made the news.

'Monster turkeys not care about ELVES, only want ELF FATHER,' Keith said.

The old man chuckled. 'Why would they want me?'

'BECAUSE YOU LAST HERO!'

'Do I LOOK like a hero to you? Goodness gracious me, those days are long gone.'

Bennie's friends couldn't agree more. The old man couldn't look less capable if he had been dead for a week.

'Why does Keith call you the last hero?' Boris asked the old man.

'Blooming heck, what is this? TWENTY QUESTIONS? MASTERMIND? I'm too old for interrogations. It's in the Geneva Convention. You can check if you want.'

'Why, are you the LAST hero?' Alice pressed, ignoring the old man's immaturity. She didn't believe any of this hero nonsense, not for a second, but there was something intriguing about him. Something that compelled her to want to learn more.

'Because all the others are as DEAD AS DODOS! THERE, HAPPY?'

Alice folded her arms grumpily and joined her friends in watching the news report.

'How many farms is that now?' Bennie whispered.

'Nine,' Ravi said.

'Do you really think there's a connection between Keith's turkeys and the missing ones?' Alice asked the others, uncrossing her arms.

Mabel nodded. 'I bet there is,' she said, 'and in any case, it's a good place to start our investigations.'

'INVESTIGATIONS?' Boris said. 'We're not REALLY going to help, ARE WE?'

Alice and Mabel shot Boris daggers with their eyes.

'We said we would, DIDN'T WE?' Alice snapped. 'Or DON'T YOU KEEP your promises?'

A squeaking trolley trundled into the resident's lounge, pushed by a dark-haired nurse. 'Tea or coffee?' she asked pleasantly.

'Tea, please, dear,' the old man requested with another beaming grin.

'Of course you can, sweetie,' the nurse said, pouring steaming water into a white porcelain cup. 'One lump or two?'

'Seven, please.'

The nurse looked to the heavens before shaking her head playfully. 'You'll rot your teeth, BRIAN!'

The old man laughed, and it wasn't your standard run-of-the-mill laugh; it was a full-blown belly wobbler.

'Me and sugar go way back,' he chortled, flashing her his gleaming gnashers. 'They're all my own, you know.'

Giggling like a schoolgirl, she pushed her trolley over to Jim, who asked for a coffee in Russian, Swahili and Mandarin before requesting two lumps of sugar in Welsh—backwards.

'AGAIN with this BRIAN chap. WHO THE BLEEDING HECK IS HE?' the old man exclaimed once the nurse was out of earshot. He shrugged his shoulders and brought the cup to his lips. 'Lovely lady is Carrol,' he said, slurping down the hot beverage with all the manners of a toothless goat sucking soup through a straw. 'Now, where were we? Ah, yes, INVESTIGATIONS! That sounds like an AWFUL LOT OF FUN!'

Dumbfounded, the children glanced at each other. Where had the old man's sudden enthusiasm come from? One minute, gloom was gushing from his every pore and the next, he looked ready to compete in the British Fell Running Championships.

'It sugar,' Keith whispered. 'But not last long.'

'We should go to Mr Grindle's farm,' Mabel said, striking while the iron was hot. 'It's on the outskirts of town.' She was really trying her best to prick the old man's interest. She even forced her face into a smile, which she rarely managed, not for teachers, relatives or even friends.

As the elf feared, the old man's sugar count took an abrupt nosedive. 'Leave Sunset Rest? Leave my ROCKING CHAIR? Not on your nelly, LITTLE LADY!'

Mabel snorted like a disgruntled horse. 'Suit yourself,' she huffed. 'We can help Keith by ourselves, can't we?'

'I suppose,' Boris mumbled dejectedly. He thought they should call the whole thing off and go home, but he didn't have the nerve to say so.

Disheartened, the gang stared at the floor with hands in their pockets. But Bennie glimpsed something in the Elf Father's sapphire eyes to give him hope. There was a faint twinkle, like a glowing ember in the ashes of a spent fire.

The old man saw the disappointment on the children's faces. And if there was one thing in all the world to weaken his resolve, it was disappointed children. It was like a stake through the heart. The sole purpose of his existence was and always had been to make children happy.

'I appreciate what you're trying to do,' he whispered softly, becoming curiously profound as he gazed absently through the big windows. 'But you must understand, it's not like how it was in the old days. The magic has gone. Yes, I know we have science, thanks to the elves, but it's not the same. I don't belong in this new age.'

Suddenly, he thumped his chest. 'I WAS SAINT NICHOLAS!' he boomed. 'And at my side were my brethren: SAINT GEORGE, SAINT BENEDICT, SAINT JOAN, SAINT EDMUND, AND SAINT RALPH! No, hang on a minute. That's not right. Ralph was my gardener at Hasseldorf, wasn't he? Yes, that's it. An expert vegetable grower, particularly good with marrows...

Where was I? Oh, yes, my saintly friends, of which there were many. We fought EVIL wherever it raised its ugly head, helping the peoples of Earth live in peace. It was a full-time job. We couldn't rest. Evil has a way of sprouting from thin air like SHADOWS!

The Christmas gift-giving was my idea,' he said proudly, the twinkle in his old eyes glowing brighter. 'Well, I might have borrowed it from the THREE WISE MEN, so MUM'S the word, GOT IT? It was a ray of sunshine in dark times, a tiny sliver of hope for the children and all those trying to find their faith.' The old man faced the gang once more. 'Did you know that just a *GLIMPSE* of festive magic, of the *UNBELIEVABLE*, is enough to reinvigorate the spirit? The gift-giving thing just got out of hand, that's all. I never imagined it to catch on quite as well as it did.'

The spark in the Elf Father's eyes gradually faded, and he looked like the old man again. 'I don't know why I'm telling you any of this. Nobody cares; no one believes anymore.'

The children were left speechless.

'You *ARE* Father Christmas, AREN'T YOU?' Alice whispered.

'We believe in you,' Bennie said, now convinced more than ever that the old man WAS Father

Christmas, albeit a retired senile version with gout and flatulence.

'No, you don't. You're just saying that to make me help. Well, I won't.'

Bennie wouldn't be put off. 'When I was younger, my friends said you weren't real, but I didn't believe them. That was until I saw my dad filling my stocking with presents.'

'Schoolboy error,' the old man said, retaking an interest. 'I bet he didn't use the old PTB TEST, did he, hey? It never fails.'

'What's with you lot and ABBREVIATIONS?' Boris asked, exasperated. 'What does PTB stand for?'

'PULSE, TEMPERATURE, BREATHING,' Keith explained. 'Elf instrument to make sure children sleeping.'

The old man sighed. 'In the good old days, I didn't need gadgets. I had a sixth sense, a kind of magic. I could tell who was sleeping and the rascals who weren't.'

'The point is,' Bennie continued, doggedly undeterred by the interruptions, 'believing in something you haven't seen with your own two eyes takes faith. I was distraught when I caught my dad pretending to be you, but deep down, despite the fact I'd never seen you before, I STILL believed.

Somehow, I just knew you WERE REAL, and now I have proof.'

The old man raised his bushy white eyebrows, and his blue eyes narrowed with thought. 'So what you're saying is, the younger boys and girls BELIEVE, and the older ones DON'T, but secretly, they still DO, even though I'm NOT the one DOING the job anymore?'

'Erm… Yeah, something like that.' Bennie gestured to his friends, pleading for support.

'Yes, that's right,' Mabel said. 'We never doubted you for a second.'

'I BELIEVE!' Alice stated firmly.

Boris nodded. 'I BELIEVE.'

'Okay, okay. I BELIEVE, TOO,' Ravi admitted.

'Well, why didn't you say any of this earlier?' The old man suddenly burst to his feet. 'Call me SANTA! Father Christmas is such a blooming mouthful,' he said. 'RIGHT, LET'S GET OUT OF THIS DUMP. WE HAVE MISSING TURKEYS TO FIND!'

10

Keith's Short-Cut

Extracting Santa from Sunset Rest proved relatively straightforward. Shirley's timely heart-wrenching re-enactment of *Watership Down*, accompanied by Mick's poignant rendition of the movie's soundtrack 'Bright Eyes', eased their passage. The residents and staff were too busy blubbing into their handkerchiefs to notice *Brian* being ushered past them and out the front door.

On the icy pavement outside, Santa cast the retirement home a final farewell. 'I'll miss the old place,' he muttered into his massive beard. 'So many fond memories.'

Mabel looked to the heavens. 'You were only there for a morning, for goodness sake,' she said, shaking her head. 'You make it sound like you've lived at Sunset Rest FOR YEARS!'

Santa's face crumpled like a screwed-up fish and chips wrapper. 'Do you want me to HELP OR NOT?' he barked cantankerously. 'I don't even know why I agreed to this. Actually, you know what, I THINK I'LL GO BACK INSIDE!'

Alice tutted disapprovingly. 'Well done, Mabel. Now look what you've done.' She quickly grabbed Santa's arm just as he started for the entrance. 'Please, don't go.'

Santa gazed into Alice's pleading puppy-dog eyes and sighed. 'Oh, alright,' he conceded grumpily. 'But we're only going to have a nose around. Nothing more than that.'

Alice nodded. 'Of course, only a snout about, that's all.'

'This isn't an adventure, got it?'

'NOT AN ADVENTURE,' she repeated obediently. 'Yes, we've got it, haven't we, gang?' Alice glanced at the others for confirmation and was answered with an enthusiastic head-bobbing display.

'Now that's sorted; where is this turkey farm, Mabel?' Bennie asked, keen to leave Sunset Rest and its temptations behind. 'The farm is on the outskirts, right? We're on the road out of town, so it can't be much further.'

Mabel grimaced. 'Actually, it's on the other side of Larkbridge.' The location of Mr Grindle's farm was hardly her fault, but the way her friends stared at her, they obviously thought that it was.

'We can't walk all that way; WE'LL FREEZE,' Boris protested glumly.

Alice agreed. She had only just thawed out from the walk earlier.

'We'll DRIVE,' Santa announced merrily.

'Drive WHAT?' Ravi queried.

'An automobile, of course. What else?'

'But we haven't got a car,' Bennie said. 'Have we?'

'No, but we'll borrow one.'

Santa's willingness to break the law surprised the children. As far as Bennie understood, car theft was a serious felony which nearly always involved a high-speed police chase and a nasty crash. At least, that's what happened on YouTube. Bennie didn't much like the idea of being subjected to a police chase, let alone a nasty crash.

Mabel, on the other hand, was already eyeing potential targets parked alongside the street. Yes, crime was wrong, but it was a necessary evil in the circumstances. And, after all, this was supposed to be an adventure, wasn't it? Even if Santa said otherwise.

Mabel discreetly dipped her bobble hat toward a silver-coloured people carrier. 'What about that MPV?'

The Volkswagen was perfect for their needs: four-wheel drive to tackle the winter weather, plenty of room to accommodate all shapes and sizes—including extra-large heroes—and tinted windows so nobody could see the thieves in action.

Like the wings of a startled dove, Santa's white eyebrows nearly took flight. 'We can't *BORROW* without ASKING, little lady,' he said sternly. 'Keith, remind me to put this one on my NAUGHTY LIST!'

'Yes, Elf Father,' Keith replied, grinning impishly.

Mabel shrugged like she didn't care, but the others could tell she was more than a little uncomfortable. Getting told off by parents or teachers was one thing, but by Father Christmas was quite another.

'Do you really have a *NAUGHTY LIST?*' Boris asked excitedly. If there was a list, he bet Ricky Kittens and his gang were on it.

'NOPE. Never have and never will,' Santa replied. 'BLOOMING HECK, it's not my place to judge. It's down to parents to raise their offspring in the right way. And in any case, Christmas is a time for forgiving, ISN'T IT? I'm hardly going to contradict the whole RUDDY ethos by punishing every juvenile who's ever told a white lie or nicked their sister's lipstick, am I? What sort of message does that send? Forgiveness all year round but NOT AT CHRISTMAS? Utter nonsense fabricated by the ruling classes and by mothers and fathers who can't control their young. A BLOOMING TRAVESTY IF YOU ASK ME!'

Crikey, Boris has hit a nerve, Bennie thought. Who knew you could get away with murder and still find a bulging sack from Santa Claus under your Christmas tree? *Well, probably not murder, but definitely wiping the odd bogey behind the sofa.*

While the children mulled over the ramifications of a non-existent naughty list and the lengths governments stooped to maintain order amongst the adolescent population, Santa was striding out into the road.

'WHAT'S HE DOING!' Bennie cried. Santa was about to meet his end squashed under the number forty-seven bus to Biddington.

'He doing what Elf Father does best,' Keith said proudly.

'And what's that? Getting RUN OVER?' Ravi replied, grimacing as the bus swerved around the old man at the last second.

'Making friends.'

Ignoring the number forty-seven's rather rude-sounding horn, Santa stepped right into the path of a red Mini Metro. The car skidded to a halt mere inches from Santa's prodigious belly.

'Is Santa about to commit GRAND THEFT AUTO?' Mabel said, smirking mischievously.

Keith scowled. 'Of course not, SILLY GIRL. He ASK nice lady for car.'

'She's hardly going to agree, is she?' Bennie said. If anything, he expected to see her calling the police on her mobile any second.

Keith grunted. 'Watch, and you see, STUPID BOY.'

To Bennie's amazement, Keith was right. In no time at all, the Mini's owner was standing in the middle of the road, and Santa was wedged behind the wheel, ready to go.

Santa wound down the window. 'What are you lot waiting for? COME ON, WE'VE GOT A MYSTERY TO SOLVE!!'

Bennie smiled. Santa's twinkle was back.

Keith led the schoolchildren to the car. Bennie presented the bemused driver with an awkward smile as he strode past her.

'We'll never fit in THAT!' Ravi whined. It was the smallest car he had ever seen. How Santa had squeezed himself into the driver's seat was a miracle.

'You'll be surprised how much you can CRAM into small boxes,' Santa said. 'In you hop. Yes, that's it. YOU THREE in the back, the BIG BOY in the front next to me, KEITH in the footwell, and the SKINNY ONE WITH THE HUGE EARS in the boot.'

'I'm not getting in the BOOT!' Ravi protested, subconsciously feeling his ears.

'It's the boot or someone's lap?'

'Fine.' Ravi scrambled over Alice into the back.

'Can you even drive?' Bennie asked, squished between the two girls.

'If I can drive a sleigh, I can drive a car,' Santa declared, ramming the Mini Metro into first gear and jamming his foot hard on the accelerator. 'How hard can it be?'

Stomachs lurched, and heads snapped backwards as the car sped away, wheel-spinning down the icy road.

'WRONG WAY, SANTA!' Mabel screamed.

'OOPS! MY BAD.' Yanking the handbrake up, Santa spun the car around in a drifting arc before snaking side to side along the road the other way. 'Sunset Rest does a lovely cuppa, MRS QUACKENSNATCH!' he hollered out the open window, hammering past the car's bewildered owner.

Boris fumbled with his seatbelt, frantically trying to secure the thing before Santa crashed, but every time he aligned the buckle with the slot, the Mini thumped over a bump. It was like controlling a mechanical claw from the amusement arcades while riding a rollercoaster.

'STRAIGHT over the roundabout, SANTA!' Mabel shouted.

And *straight over* was precisely how Santa negotiated the junction. Boris fastened his seatbelt just as the car launched skyward.

Ravi wasn't so lucky. The boy bounced about in the boot like a beachball. 'Remind me NEVER to get in a sleigh with YOU!' he yelled.

Screaming the length of St Bernard's Road, a second roundabout loomed ahead.

'LEFT, SANTA! LEFT!' Mabel cried.

Santa heaved the steering wheel hard over.

'HOLD ON!'

The Mini Metro hurtled around the corner sideways, its rear end threatening to overtake the front and send them spinning. Santa wrestled the car straight—but not before forcing another driver off the road.

'Oh dear,' Boris said, watching the car bury itself into a huge snowdrift. 'I think that was Mr Markles.'

Alice flung herself across Bennie and Mabel to see for herself. 'Do you think he saw us?' she questioned anxiously, staring out the window.

'If he did, we'll be in trouble next term,' Bennie said, wincing painfully as Alice's elbows dug into his ribs.

Sliding into Lark Street, they passed the school in a blur. Bennie couldn't see how fast they were travelling, but he guessed it was well above the speed limit. He grinned. This *was* an adventure, no matter what Santa said.

Suddenly, the elf emerged from between Boris' legs. 'Keith knows SHORTCUT,' she announced, pointing at the town's big Christmas tree ahead. 'Past tree and across park.'

'NO!' the children yelled all at once, but they were too late. Santa was already sending the Mini careering across the road.

The car mounted the curb with a juddering bump, crashed over the pavement, and hammered straight into the snow.

CRUNCH!

They missed the Christmas tree by a hair's breadth, causing the giant Scandinavian conifer to sway like it had been watered with mulled wine for the last two weeks. They kept on going, smashing across the park like a snowplough.

'WATCH OUT!' Mabel shrieked.

'OH, HO! I SEE THEM!' Santa dodged hardcore winter joggers, dog walkers, and an army of snowmen endowed with varying lengths of carrot noses as he raced over the football pitches toward the woods.

Boris closed his eyes as the Mini squeezed between the trees, their branches scratching against the car's bodywork and windows like fingernails raking a blackboard.

Miraculously unscathed—although caked in snow, pine needles and a collection of sparrow nests—the car burst from the foliage onto Bishop's Road.

'What were you THINKING?' Alice reprimanded through clenched teeth. 'YOU'RE INSANE!'

'Loosen up, girl. You sound like your MOTHER,' Santa answered childishly.

'WE MIGHT HAVE KILLED SOMEBODY!'

'PAH, POPPYCOCK! I had everything under control.'

Bennie was pretty sure Santa didn't. Even so, it was the single most exciting thing he had ever experienced. His heart was thumping like a galloping horse. *Actually, make that two horses*, he thought.

Larkbridge swiftly disappeared behind them. Soon after, on the left-hand side of the road, Boris spotted a sign: *Grindle's Turkeys.* Actually, half-submerged in drifted snow, it read: *Grin...keys.* Which, when put together, sounded just like the sort of word Bennie's dad conjured from thin air when playing Scrabble.

Santa swung off the road and followed a meandering track toward a pretty, thatched farm cottage. He parked up behind a derelict barn hidden from view.

'This will do nicely,' Santa announced, cutting the Mini's engine.

Although concealed from the cottage, they could still see most of the farm buildings and the main road at the bottom of the track.

'Now then, before we go any further, I need to know who's who?'

Boris frowned. 'I don't mean to be rude, but I thought it was your job to KNOW?'

Santa snorted. 'You seriously expect me to remember every child's name ON THE PLANET? I can barely remember the names of my elves. Isn't that right, Keith?'

Keith's approving thumb appeared from the footwell, where she lay curled up like a cat on Boris' feet. Boris didn't mind. She was keeping him nice and warm.

Santa stared at Boris. 'Let's start with you, shall we?'

Boris gulped. It was surprisingly unnerving having Father Christmas stare at him. 'I'm Balthazar-Bartholomew Boris Griggs.'

Boris' friends sniggered. They always did when Boris shared his full name.

Santa nodded sagely. 'I see,' he said. 'And why do people call you Boris?'

Boris couldn't help thinking it was a trick question. 'Erm... Because having an unusual double-barrelled first name is a bit of a mouthful?'

'EXACTLY!' Santa said. 'Parents seldom consider the practicality of their child's name in day-to-day situations. It's all very well being called BALTHAZAR-

BARTHOLOMEW, but if no one can ruddy well pronounce it, what good is it? What's wrong with DAVE or SHARAN or SOMETHING NORMAL?'

Santa glared accusingly at Keith. 'The elves are the worst, of course. They deliberately create names they know I can't get my lips around just to spite me. PESKY LITTLE BLIGHTERS!'

Ravi's head popped up from behind the back seat. 'I'm Ravi Singh,' he announced as if he expected Santa to have heard of him.

'Oh, yes, the SKINNY BOY with ELEPHANT EARS,' Santa said, manoeuvring his substantial frame so he could see behind. 'And can you?'

Ravi looked confused. 'Can I what?'

'SING!'

'NO!'

'Shame. I do enjoy a good sing-song. Who's next?'

'Alice Bean,' Alice said proudly.

'And do you like beans, Alice?'

Alice hesitated. 'Erm… I suppose so.'

'EXCELLENT! And what about you?' he said, gazing at Mabel.

'Mabel Jane, sir.'

'G I JANE more like,' Ravi added. 'She thinks she's a soldier.'

'SHUT UP, SPIT FACE!!'

'Now, now, children. There's nothing wrong with adopting the military code to live by. Although I'm not so keen on all the SHOUTING and BLOWING STUFF-UP! You'll learn discipline, self-sufficiency, and how to survive in the harshest of Earth's environments: Christmas markets, late-night shopping centres, and Santa's grotto. HA, HO! ONLY JOKING! I wouldn't miss any of it for the world! Except for the grotto in King's Lynn… Blooming tough crowd, I can tell you.'

Next, Santa turned his attention to Bennie. 'And your name is Bennie, isn't it?'

'How did you know?'

'Oh, I overheard, that's all,' Santa replied with a wink.

Bennie's eyes widened. *He did know our names. Even before we told him.* Bennie couldn't help wondering if Santa was playing games with them.

'What now?' Ravi asked.

'Now we wait for the cover of darkness,' Santa said, wriggling his vast posterior to find a more comfortable position.

Mabel checked her camo-green army watch. 'But that's another TWO HOURS AWAY!'

Santa scratched at his beard. 'Who likes CHRISTMAS CAROLS?'

11

Grindle's Turkeys

Blaring sirens and flashing blue lights had the gang twisting in their seats to see. At the bottom of the farm track, four police cars zoomed past on the main road heading for Larkbridge.

The spectacle was a welcome distraction from playing endless games of I Spy and Guess What I've Got In My Metaphorical Bag while waiting for the sun to clear off. In truth, Santa had spent most of the time snoring his head off like an asthmatic mule.

Bennie hadn't imagined adventuring was going to be quite so dull. He supposed it couldn't be care home rescues and off-road rallying all of the time. *More's the pity,* he thought with a sigh.

'I really hope that hasn't got ANYTHING to do with us,' Alice said quietly. She had never seen so many police cars in Larkbridge before. Not even when Mrs Trotter ran off with a side of pork from the local butchers: Head, Knees & Toes.

Santa switched on the radio. 'Let's find out what's going on.'

'747FM,' Mabel said. 'It's the local station.'

'Good work, Mabel.' Santa began dialling the Mini's radio to the frequency, a loud crackling accompanying the search. Santa locked onto 747FM, and…

BOOOOOOM!!!

The speakers exploded with music—a roaring audio assault on the eardrums. If the deafening sound wasn't bad enough, the music blasting over the airwaves was Santa's least favourite in the history of music: *pop*. What was wrong with a nice Christmas carol or a good old Gregorian chant?

Partially incapacitated by the awful din, Santa prodded at the radio's controls in a desperate attempt to make it stop. 'Please, no more… I CAN'T TAKE IT!' Mercifully, he jabbed the off button a millisecond before his brain imploded.

'Oh, thank goodness,' Santa gasped. 'It seems Mrs Quackensnatch likes her music rather loud—or she's INCREDIBLY DEAF.'

Mabel used her sleeve to wipe the condensation from the car window and scanned the farm for signs of life. 'The cottage and surrounding area are secure,' she declared with an affirmative nod. *The farmer's wife must be hard of hearing, too,* she mused.

'Blimey, we mustn't attract Mrs Grindle's ATTENTION!' Santa warned anxiously. 'Before she married, she was a Thatchcock. And the THATCHCOCKS HOLD A GRUDGE, I CAN TELL YOU. They've got it in for me; have done for years.'

'Why?' Boris asked.

'They took offence when I parked my sleigh on the roof back in sixty-five. Mrs Grindle's grandmother—BIG BARB, they called her, teeth like TOMBSTONES and arms like TREE TRUNKS—came charging out blasting at me with a

RUDDY SHOTGUN! And to think I was delivering the woman's granddaughter a present. It's downright rude if you ask me. Mind you, the daft old bat missed by a country mile!'

Another police car flashed past on the road, its siren screaming like an owl giving birth. The blue lights jerked Santa's thoughts back to the present.

'Have you got your mobile phones with you?' he asked. 'You can check the local news on them, can't you? Keith is forever badgering me about them, "YOU SHOULD GET ONE, ELF FATHER. YOU NEED

ONE, ELF FATHER. WHY HAVEN'T YOU GOT ONE, ELF FATHER?" BLAH, BLAH, BLAH!!'

Keith had explained the usefulness of a mobile phone to Santa umpteen times. Of course, most of what she said sailed over his head and disappeared into the stratosphere like an unpleasant smell. Pairing Santa with technology was a long, winding road beset with potholes, gravel traps, and land mines.

'No, we're not allowed to use them outside,' Alice said, answering for her friends. 'You know, in case we lose them.'

'What's the point of having a mobile phone if you're not going to use them WHILE MOBILE?'

'Haven't you heard of social media?'

Santa thought long and hard. 'NOPE.'

'He has. Keith tells him,' the elf said sleepily. She had been having a lovely snooze before being rudely awoken by the racket on the radio—banging drums and boys shouting—shrieking directly into her right ear from the speaker housed in the Mini's door.

'I've got mine,' Ravi stated nonchalantly.

'BRAVO, BIG EARS!' Santa exclaimed happily. 'I'm glad one of you has an inkling of sense.'

Ravi looked smug.

Alice looked ready to commit grievous bodily harm.

'Come on then, Dumbo. Use the ruddy thing before I DIE OF OLD AGE!' Santa said, sighing impatiently.

Fishing his mobile from a coat pocket, Ravi began hammering the device with a finger. The Nokia's bright screen shone into the boy's face, illuminating him in an unearthly glow in the growing darkness.

'You're not going to believe this,' he said. 'Apparently, we've all been abducted by, and I quote, "*A deranged Father Christmas impersonator called Brian, who, after absconding from a local nursing home, has caused havoc in Larkbridge.*"'

'But that's not what happened AT ALL! If anything, we kidnapped you, Santa,' Alice said, tugging on her pigtails crossly.

'The police say the PERPETRATOR—whatever that means—is wanted for abduction, car theft, dangerous driving, criminal damage, and STEALING ONE HUNDRED AND THIRTY-SEVEN SUGAR CUBES!'

Santa puffed indignantly. 'It was one hundred and thirty-six, actually.'

'I hope Mr Markles is okay,' Boris said, wincing at the memory of their headteacher being run off the road.

'He's fine,' Bennie replied. 'It'll take more than crashing into a pile of snow to put him out of action.'

Bennie pictured the headteacher bursting triumphantly from the snowdrift like a superhero. Well, perhaps not a superhero, more a supervillain. Either way, he was pretty sure he had survived the incident unscathed.

'There's going to be an organised search for us tonight,' Ravi announced, scrolling through the posts on his phone. 'SOCIAL'S GONE BALLISTIC!'

Santa wasn't at all pleased. 'Didn't any of you think to let your parents know what you were up to?'

The children looked sheepish. Actually, they looked decidedly fawnish, which is as contrite as anyone can look, with the exception of looking hedgehogish—the ultimate in bashfulness.

'OH,' Ravi said. 'It seems I've missed FIFTY-SEVEN messages and SEVENTY-TWO calls.' He fingered his earlobes nervously. 'I could have sworn I switched vibrate on.'

Santa shook his head. 'Right, that's it. I'm taking you all home.'

Disappointed groans filled the Mini Metro.

Shifting his substantial backside—a challenging undertaking in such a small seat—Santa peered at the children, his expression dour. 'You've only got yourselves to blame,' he said, speaking in that all too familiar tone perfected by parents and teachers and nearly always delivered with stern faces and crossed arms.

Then, ever so slowly, Santa's lips began curling upwards until he was grinning like a clown. 'ONLY JOKING! I'll take you home AFTER a good snoop around. How does that sound, hey?' Rummaging about in his trousers, he produced a paper bag. 'Sugar cube?'

'I bet I know where you got those from,' Bennie said, relieved the adventure was back on.

'A souvenir from Sunset Rest. I'm sure they won't miss a few; they've got mountains of them piled about the place.' Santa rustled the bag in front of their faces. 'Come on, you must be hungry?'

'Yeah, for BURGER AND CHIPS,' Boris said, his belly rumbling at the thought.

'Well, I haven't got anything else, so it's these or nothing.'

Alice turned up her nose at the sight of them. 'I'm not a horse,' she snorted, 'and eating too much sugar isn't healthy.' But even as she said it, her stomach growled louder than Boris'.

Alice extracted a cube from the bag. 'In the circumstances, one won't hurt, I suppose,' she said before shrugging and shoving it eagerly into her mouth.

The others weren't so fussy. Mabel took three, Bennie and Ravi four, and Boris half a dozen. 'WHAT?' he said when his friends stared accusingly. 'I'm starving.' Boris crunched his way through the sugary lumps like they were pork scratchings procured from the Dog and Rat on Bishop's Road.

'ENERGISED? EXCELLENT! Let's get to it then, shall we?'

Santa clicked open the driver's door, gently pushing it wide. A high-pitched squeal, not too dissimilar to a very happy piglet, pierced the cold, crisp, and, up until then, quiet early evening air. 'I bet the poor old girl hasn't had a good service for years,' Santa mumbled, chuckling into his beard. 'THE CAR! Not Mrs Quakensnatch.'

Untangling themselves, the others squeezed out of their seats and fell into the snow.

Bennie scrambled to his feet. *She'll need more than a service*, he thought wryly, brushing himself down. Ravi had highlighted a significant number of new defects with his phone's torch. The little red Mini Metro looked ready for the scrapyard.

The gang gathered beside the car, awaiting instructions. Keith switched on the VTM, which, like Ravi's mobile, was equipped with a torch function but infinitely more powerful—at least it would have been if not for being dangerously low on juice.

'A nice warm glow, please, Keith,' Santa requested. 'Nothing too garish. We don't want that AWFUL WOMAN to chase us with her grandmother's shotgun.' By 'that awful woman', Santa was, of course, referring to Mrs Grindle.

'Aren't you cold, Santa?' Mabel asked. She was wrapped in a coat, hat, and boots and was still shivering. Santa was dressed in what the staff at Sunset Rest had found him earlier that morning: a red and white striped shirt, enormous khaki slacks secured over his shoulders with black braces, and a pair of brown suede shoes so worn they were practically slippers.

Santa tried not to think about where the outfit had come from—or, more accurately, *who* they had come from. Wearing the clothes of a deceased Sunset Rest resident wasn't an especially nice thought.

'I don't feel the cold, little lady. Well, that's not strictly true, but a few degrees below freezing is POSITIVELY BALMY compared to the temperatures at the North Pole. The Alps can get rather nippy too.' Thinking about it, why hadn't he retired somewhere warm like the Caribbean? He blamed the elves.

Keith tugged at Santa's braces.

'FOR GOODNESS SAKE, what is it now, Keith? Can't we just get on and investigate without you interrupting every five minutes?'

Keith ignored Santa's prattling. She was used to his Grinch-like temperament. 'VTM showing signs of vortex activity here.'

Santa fondled his beard thoughtfully. 'That's very interesting.' He stared toward the farm's largest barns.

Shrouded in darkness, the ramshackle buildings resembled hulking great shadow monsters from a grim fairytale. After seeing them, the children didn't seem quite so enthusiastic to explore the site as before.

'Tell me, Keith, besides the elves, does anyone else have vortex manipulation technology?'

'No.'

'This is a dilemma, make no mistake,' Santa mumbled, molesting his beard more vigorously.

'What if the plans were stolen and sold to the highest bidder?' Ravi said. 'It happens all the time. It's called ESPIONAGE.'

Keith shook her head vehemently. 'IMPOSSIBLE. No plans to steal,' she said. 'And unlike HUMANS, elves loyal.'

'OUCH!' Bennie remarked. 'That's one in the eye for humanity!'

'SSSSHHH!' Mabel hissed. 'Keep your voices down. We're supposed to be investigating, remember?'

Santa put a finger to his furry lips. 'Mabel is right,' he whispered. 'We need to be professional. Try pretending we're famous detectives on a case.'

Bennie raised an eyebrow. 'Famous detectives?' He could only think of Scooby-Doo, which didn't bode well.

'We'll cross the yard and start with the biggest barn,' Santa whispered.

The barn in question was sandwiched between a higgledy-piggledy arrangement of lesser barns. Even in the dark, these smaller buildings appeared dilapidated—their roofs sagging like cow udders and timber walls leaning like pensioners tackling a stiff breeze.

'Right then, off we go, quickly and quietly,' Santa instructed, tiptoeing through the snow. He looked like an elephant doing ballet.

The cottage overlooked the yard, and as the gang ventured into the open, they felt uncomfortably exposed. If Mrs Grindle was anything like her grandmother, they really didn't want to be discovered.

The clear skies had frozen the snow blanketing the farmyard, and no matter how carefully they placed their feet, each step across its lake-like surface crunched louder than Boris munching sugar cubes.

Keith led them further into no man's land, lighting their way with the VTM.

Bennie gulped. They were now in full view of the cottage. And then, halfway across…

CLATTER! BANG! CRASH!

Keith thrust a hand into the air, and the gang froze mid-stride like statues. It was like they were playing

Grandma's Footsteps—but in this particular case, Grandma was a shotgun-wielding psycho.

The elf pointed toward the cottage where one of Mrs Grindle's bins had fallen, spilling its smelly contents into the icy snow.

'Most likely a fox,' Boris whispered. *And definitely NOT a giant mutant turkey man... turkey woman... or turkey other*, he mused, sniggering nervously.

'I thought I SAW SOMETHING!' Mabel hissed, her cold breath trailing into the darkness. 'I'm not sure what, but it was WAY BIGGER than a fox.'

Then disaster! A light shone through a downstairs window in the cottage.

'FORGET THE FOX! It's Mrs Grindle and her shotgun we need to worry about,' Bennie said, praying she wouldn't spot them.

'Stay completely still,' Santa whispered loudly—well, at least as loudly as possible before it was no longer deemed a whisper.

It was difficult to remain *completely still* while balancing on one foot. 'I can't stay like this for much longer,' Bennie stated, tottering precariously. 'I'M NOT A FLAMINGO!'

After another minute, the light blinked out.

'Oh, thank goodness!' Santa said.

Keith decided that *quickly* was now preferable to *quietly,* and she scampered the rest of the way as fast as she could. The gang came next, eager to cross the frozen forecourt or, as Mabel called it, *the killing zone,* without getting blasted to pieces. Even Santa put in a spirited burst through the snow, fearing Mrs Grindle's wrath.

Once safely assembled outside the big barn, they all sighed in relief—puffing lungfuls of cold air into the night sky.

'That was close,' Mabel said, checking back toward the cottage to make sure the farmer's wife wasn't sneaking up on them.

'What are you waiting for, Keith?' Santa said, giving the elf a persuasive nudge. 'Get in there before SHE comes out and catches us.' He shuddered at the thought.

Keith hissed at Santa like a feral cat, her violet eyes gleaming in the dark.

Santa flinched and decided it would be best for his health—and the length of his beard—if he pushed open the door himself.

'Oh, no,' Boris groaned, following the others inside. It smells worse in here than it did at Sunset Rest.'

'I think we can risk a little more light now we're inside,' Santa declared. 'If you would be so kind, Keith?' he asked nicely, not wanting to upset her further.

The elf spun a dial on the VTM until the device shone brightly.

'YUCK!' Alice shrieked. 'I've stood in something HORRID!'

Although there was no sign of the turkeys, there was no shortage of evidence highlighting their recent presence. This came in the form of sticky green heaps dolloped all over the ground.

'I've never seen so much poo,' Bennie muttered.

'Poo and feathers,' Mabel added.

'How many birds lived here?' Alice asked, desperately trying to scrape the turkey muck from her boots.

'Thousands, I shouldn't wonder,' Santa answered, peering into the barn's extremities for signs of anything unusual.

'So many?' Boris said. 'Poor things, all crammed together like sardines.'

'Don't get sentimental, Boris,' Ravi said. 'The giant versions burnt Keith's home to the ground, REMEMBER?'

Although the turkey barn was far from an ideal home for the birds, Farmer Grindle had installed a number of extras to ensure their stay was less awful than it otherwise might have been. Running the length of the walls, wooden shelters with high, flat roofs permitted the birds to roost off the ground like they did in the wild. Also, the barn was exposed to the elements, allowing fresh air and natural light to stream inside via large, open windows.

The gang moved deeper into the barn, hoping to find something to link the giant turkeys to what happened at the farm.

'Anything showing up on the VTM, Keith?' Santa questioned, struggling to find a clue that might help their inquiries.

'Strong vortex activity here, Elf Father,' she replied, holding the device at arm's length as they searched. 'Keith thinks it—'

Suddenly, the air directly ahead crackled with arcing blue electricity. It was as if a mini lightning storm had materialised from nowhere. The flashing energy intensified, pulsing brighter and brighter until the area became a shimmering blue wall like the surface of a mountain pool rippling with lightning.

'HIDE!' Santa bellowed.

12

Maggie

The gang split left and right, seeking the safety of the turkey shelters. While Keith, Ravi, and Mabel leapt into one, Santa, Bennie, Alice, and Boris flung themselves into another.

'Boris, remove your foot from my BACKSIDE!' Bennie moaned. How the four of them had squeezed inside a single shelter was almost as impressive as all seven of them cramming inside the Mini.

Smeared in turkey poo, Alice was squidged underneath Santa's left armpit and was much too traumatised to speak. On the other side, Bennie and

Boris were a jumble of legs and arms twisted together like eels in a barrel. And lodged between them all was Santa, frantically gesturing toward the opposite shelter. 'BIG EARS, SWITCH OFF YOUR BLOOMING TORCH!' he mouthed, wagging a sausage-like finger at Ravi.

Ravi didn't need telling, but his Nokia had frozen. 'It's NEVER DONE this before!' No matter how hard he poked the buttons or how often he swiped a finger across the screen, he couldn't make the phone obey. Ravi resorted to the only logical solution left open to him, the tried and tested tactic of beating technology into submission. 'TURN OFF!' he cried, thrashing the device against the side of the shelter.

'Vortex energy interference,' Keith stated.

The portal's surface quivered in the centre of the barn, precisely between the separated investigators. It was like the thing was made from jelly and had just been given a stiff poke by an inquisitive child at a birthday party.

A dark shape appeared in the portal, undefined and indistinct, like a menacing shadow at the end of a blue tunnel. And even though it didn't seem to be moving, somehow it grew bigger and bigger, traversing the magical passage as if floating through the air.

The gang stared aghast as the shape of a seven-foot-tall monstrosity loomed from the shimmering pool in front of them.

'A TURKEY MAN!' Bennie whispered in dread.

Just before the creature emerged from the vortex portal into Farmer Grindle's turkey barn, Ravi's Nokia slipped from his fingers, striking the floor with a sharp

CRACK!

The torch winked out in the nick of time.

'OH... MY... GOD!' Alice mouthed. She had never seen anything so revolting, not even Santa's armpit.

Illuminated blue by the portal's light, the monster was revealed in all its hideousness. Hairless cats didn't come close to its grotesqueness. It certainly wasn't how the children had envisaged them inside their heads.

Regular turkeys were stumpy-looking feathered creatures with flappy wings. This thing was wolf-like—tall, lean, and mean. It looked like it couldn't wait to peck them to death with its cruel-looking curved beak. It had arms, not wings, and its fingers were unusually long with pointy black talons

at the ends. It was dressed in something resembling black leather. *Like armour,* Bennie thought, studying the monster through the cage.

'It isn't wearing SHOES!' Alice thought this was highly unhygienic—especially considering the state of the floor. Its feet looked as tough as its armour and were finished with the same lethal talons as the thing's fingers.

'Why doesn't it have more feathers?' Alice mumbled into Santa's armpit. The only ones she could see protruded like a multi-coloured frill from behind its peculiar-shaped purple and blue head. The plumage grew from the base of its absurdly long neck that bent and twisted from side to side as the creature surveyed its surroundings with black beady eyes.

'And what's that REVOLTING WARTY-LOOKING red sack dangling from its chin?' Whatever it was, it made her stomach turn.

That has got to be the scariest thing ever, Bennie mused. Not even an angry Mrs Crispwhistle looked as terrifying. Yet more disturbing than anything else was what it cradled in its arms. 'A RAY GUN!'

The giant turkey soldier lurched forward, its talons scraping horribly against the concrete floor. It strode to the far end of the barn, taking up a position overlooking the portal.

Moments later, a second giant turkey materialised from the blue light. It was taller, meaner, and endowed with a bigger, brighter frill, not to mention a much larger, wartier sack drooping from beneath its beak.

Bennie was drawn to what the creature clutched within its purple-fingered grasp. Not a ray gun like the soldier, but a rod. Bennie thought it looked like a royal sceptre. He had seen something similar during a trip to the Tower of London. This one had a shaft of twisted gold, topped with a glittering jewel—probably a diamond, although he wasn't sure. Bennie wondered what it was for. This second creature promptly moved aside, allowing room for another arrival. Again, the portal flared, yet this time, the pulsing blue light disgorged not one turkey but an army. However, they weren't the giant monster turkeys like the first two. They were the standard everyday roast-in-the-oven Christmas types.

Side by side, rank by rank, the animals streamed from the vortex portal in perfect unison. Once they filled the barn, the giant turkey with the sceptre started shouting gibberish at its companion. Bennie thought it sounded a bit like German.

After responding with a sharp salute—a weird pecking action that caused the creature's grotesque chin sack to jiggle about unpleasantly—the soldier pulled open the doors, and out the turkeys marched.

'They are the monsters' scouts,' came a gruff-sounding voice from outside the cage beside Bennie and Boris. 'They have orders to infiltrate farmland near military bases and spy on the country's defences.'

'WHO'S that *TALKING?*' Santa whispered. He turned sideways to find out but couldn't see past Alice's squished face.

Bennie couldn't see much better, either. Wedged inside the shelter, his vision was restricted by a framework of wooden slats—and Boris' enormous head. Whoever was lingering outside obviously didn't want to be spotted. 'What are you talking about?' Bennie whispered back. 'Turkeys don't take *ORDERS!*' And they *definitely* didn't spy on military bases.

'These ones do,' the stranger replied ominously.

'WHO *ARE YOU?*' Boris demanded. He eyed the column of turkeys filing from the barn with a troubled frown. It was like watching a bizarre episode of Countryfile—or a very low-budget horror movie.

'Maggie,' the stranger replied.

Bennie frowned. Maggie had a very deep voice for a girl. 'What are you doing here, Maggie?'

'I live here,' she said, and then she growled. 'The MONSTERS have taken my owner.'

Bennie gaped. *Blimey, I didn't think slave labour was a thing these days.* Maggie's revelation was almost as shocking as a barn bursting with mutant turkeys. *If Alice finds out, she'll have a hundred activists here by morning chaining themselves to farm machinery.*

'I think our new friend might just be able to help us,' Santa announced, stroking his white beard as if it were a big fluffy tomcat. 'There are two ways we can find out what's going on. One, we wrestle the giant turkeys to the ground and sit on them until they give us answers. Or two, and my personal favourite, we sneak behind their backs while they're not looking and jump through the portal.'

'Number two, please,' Boris whispered. Despite being the biggest and strongest boy at school, he couldn't abide violence. Nor did he like the idea of sitting on mutated farmyard animals with very sharp beaks. It sounded terribly uncomfortable.

'Two,' Alice grunted, barely able to breathe.

'EXCELLENT! Bennie, my boy, ask our new friend to create a diversion if you please.'

'We're going to JUMP through the portal?' Bennie was all for adventure, but leaping into the unknown was a risky business, wasn't it? 'How do we know where it leads? And what about JUMP SICKNESS? If we tumble out the other end in the same state you and Keith were in earlier, I can't see it ending well.'

Freeing a hand from where it was trapped beneath his substantial right buttock, Santa yanked a small handful of celery sticks from inside his trousers.

'I didn't only borrow sugar cubes from Sunset Rest,' he explained proudly, waving the limp green vegetables in front of the children's faces.

'I thought BORROWING without asking wasn't very nice,' Alice murmured feebly, gasping for air like a fish out of water. Santa's revised position inside the shelter hadn't awarded her any extra room. If anything, she now had less and started turning purple.

It was Santa's turn to look hedgehogish. 'Well, the thing is, in certain scenarios, the rules can be bent, just a little, for the greater good.'

Alice snorted. 'You should be a politician.'

Santa was horrified. 'NOT ON YOUR NELLY!! I can't think of anything worse.'

Boris put his hand up—at least as well as he could manage within the restricted confines of the cage. He looked like a baboon trying to scratch its ear with a dislocated shoulder. 'In what way are CELERY STICKS important?' he asked, believing that perhaps he had missed a previous conversation discussing their relevance.

Santa flapped the question away impatiently. He was far more interested in implementing his rather excellent plan than explaining elementary space travel procedures to eleven-year-olds. 'RIGHT, let's make our move!' Santa said. 'Tell the new girl to distract the guards.'

Bennie nodded and pressed his face against the side of the shelter. 'Did you hear, Maggie? Will you help us?'

There was a pause before Maggie's gruff voice whispered close: 'Be ready.'

'How will the others know about our plan?' Boris asked Santa. Huddled inside the shelter opposite, he could just make them out over the heads of the marching turkeys, their faces tinged blue by the portal's light.

'Keith and I have an understanding,' Santa answered smugly. 'It's like telepathy but with hand gestures. She'll know EXACTLY what we're about to do.'

While the old man inside the cage began manoeuvring his hands and arms into all sorts of peculiar positions, Maggie made her move. Creeping between the shelters, she stalked Farmer Grindle's lost birds as they strutted through the barn doors like a lioness hunting a herd of antelope.

Suddenly, she exploded from the shadows like a bat out of hell. Bolting past the floundering guard, she leapt at the turkeys, disappearing amongst the birds in a cloud of feathers, and in an instant, the calmness of the star-lit night was shattered by yelping animals.

'Oh, Maggie has a sheepdog. BRILLIANT!' Bennie said, watching the chaos unfold through the slats in the cage.

A black and white border collie was scattering the birds across the farmyard and, in doing so, had successfully drawn the giant turkeys from their posts, leaving the portal unprotected.

Santa sprung from the shelter like a jack-in-the-box. 'And AWAY we go!' he chirped merrily.

Bennie, Boris, and Alice stumbled from the cage like OAPs from a street fight—bruised, battered, and not entirely sure which day of the week it was.

Santa waited beside the pulsing blue portal, tapping his feet impatiently. 'We haven't got all day! Now poke these in your ears,' he said, thrusting celery sticks into the children's hands as they joined him.

'Hang on a minute,' he said. 'Where are the others?'

13

Into the Blue

Two minutes earlier…

Keith, Ravi, and Mabel gawped in bewilderment.

'What's he DOING?' Mabel whispered, frowning so hard she risked giving herself a migraine. She was familiar with military hand signals; her dad had taught her before she could walk, but she hadn't a clue what these were.

'Having a FIT?' Ravi replied, shaking his head. 'He'll get caught if he carries on much longer.'

'Just nod,' Keith advised. 'It easier to let him think you know what he means.'

That's precisely the same philosophy I use at school, Ravi thought, nodding like a loon.

Outside the barn, a cacophony of barking and yelping suddenly erupted, the night sky swirling with turkey feathers.

Mabel watched the turkey soldiers storm toward the commotion. When she finally looked back the other way, Santa was standing in front of the portal while her friends were hobbling across the barn toward him like zombies.

'Do we follow?' Ravi asked, glancing anxiously at the entrance for signs of trouble.

'Yes, follow,' Keith replied, prodding the children from the shelter. 'Quickly, before big turkeys return.'

Out of nowhere, a black and white dog launched itself at the cage. 'WAIT! They'll catch YOU!' the border collie barked, knocking all three of them back into the shelter.

'Did that dog just *TALK*, or am I HEARING THINGS?' Ravi stared at the hairy animal like it was an unexploded bomb.

'We haven't got time for this,' the border collie growled impatiently. 'My name is Maggie, and yes, I'm a talking dog. NOW GET OVER IT!'

'GET OVER IT?' Ravi blurted, his face beginning to twitch uncontrollably. 'How can we GET OVER IT! YOU'RE A TALKING–'

Mabel clamped a gloved hand over Ravi's mouth. 'Maggie's right,' she whispered, setting aside the mind-boggling revelation that she was in the presence of a linguistic canine to focus on the disaster currently unfolding before their eyes. The turkey soldiers had spotted their friends.

'WE'VE GOT TO WARN THEM!' Mabel hissed, trying to squeeze past the dog.

'It's too late,' Maggie warned, nosing the girl back inside the shelter before jumping on her lap. 'They'll see you, too.'

The monsters burst back into the barn, yelling and shrieking in their horrible alien language. Santa shoved Bennie and the others toward the VJP.

'OH, NO! LOOK!' Mabel groaned.

Another pair of soldiers materialised from the shimmering blue tunnel.

'IDIOTS. They've gone and got themselves caught!' Ravi moaned. 'What do we do now?'

Mabel covered her eyes. 'I can't bear to WATCH!'

Raising their guns, the turkey soldiers prodded their captives away from the portal and into the clutches of their captain, the turkey wielding the sceptre.

The creatures exchanged a few brief words—not words exactly, more a series of strange clucks and yelps—before one started pawing at Santa and the children. It probed each of them with long fingers, searching their clothes and pockets. 'Stop wriggling like a worm!' it shrieked at Boris. 'Or else, I'll gut you like a fish!'

'I can't help it,' Boris giggled. 'IT TICKLES!'

Finding nothing more than a bag of sugar cubes, a limp bunch of celery, and a snotty handkerchief between them, the soldier stepped away, looking rather disappointed.

'So you have discovered our operations here,' the Turkey Captain said. The creature spoke English, but his words were hard for Santa and the children to understand. The giant turkey twitched its hideous wart-ridden head as he scrutinised each of them in turn. 'You are very clever human beings, aren't you? But what to do with you?'

The Captain conferred with his soldiers, engaging them in a harsh, incomprehensible conversation that made Bennie's brain hurt.

One of the guards, its plumage quivering excitedly, brandished a selection of metallic bracelets.

'My associate insists that we cuff your hands. Alternatively, he is quite keen to remove them altogether. Which is it to be?'

As fast as lightning, Santa and the children thrust their hands out in front of them.

'Very clever human beings,' the Turkey Captain sniggered, his comrades yelping like hyenas.

The soldier secured the bracelets around the prisoners' wrists, the strange metal cold against their skin. Bennie wondered why the cuffs didn't have a chain linking them, but then the Captain pressed a button on his sceptre, and suddenly the metallic bracelets snapped together like magic.

Meanwhile, Keith, Ravi, Mabel, and a talking dog called Maggie watched from the safety of their turkey shelter.

'MAGNETIC HANDCUFFS!' Ravi mouthed gleefully. 'AWESOME!'

Mabel eyed Ravi with disapproval. The boy really needed to sort out his priorities.

'The wand has great power,' Maggie whispered. 'Watch, and you will see.'

The Turkey Captain's sceptre began radiating a mysterious orange light, which he directed at the captured children one by one.

'A scanner?' Ravi deduced. He had watched enough science fiction to know a scanner when he saw one. 'BRILLIANT!'

Keith dipped her head gravely. 'Now Elf Father will be discovered.'

'What will they do to him?' Mabel asked, fearing the worst.

Keith shook her head. 'I not know.'

'Maggie, can you cause another diversion?' Ravi suggested, trying to be helpful.

Maggie's ears drooped. 'I doubt they will fall for the same trick twice.'

It was too late. The Turkey Captain shone the orange light at Santa. Immediately, the bird's plumage shot to attention, and the longer the scan continued, the prouder the turkey's feathers stood.

'Oh... You are not like the others. Yes, you're him, aren't you? You're the one our glorious Emperor has been searching for.'

Yelping joyfully, the turkey monsters bobbed their heads furiously. The horrid things almost looked like they were rocking out to Megadeth at a thrash metal gig.

'Oh my! Emperor Gobble-Gobble will be pleased. Come, my friends, let us deliver our prize and bask in glory!'

Mabel gripped Ravi by the shoulders and spun him around until her face was pressed uncomfortably close to his. 'We have to stop them—NOW!!!'

Ravi dithered. He was only four foot six and equipped with a mobile phone and a pair of miniature tweezers he had won in a Christmas cracker at the school party; the monsters were seven-plus and armed with pointy beaks, razor-sharp talons, and enough hardware to obliterate the population of Larkbridge in less time than it takes to stuff a lemon up a turkey's bottom.

'You're outgunned, pretty girl,' Maggie said. 'There's nothing we can do.'

'Talking dog is correct. We cannot help,' Keith conceded. 'But do not lose hope. There is another way.'

They watched in miserable silence, dazed and helpless, as Santa, Bennie, Boris, and Alice were frogmarched through the glimmering azure portal, perhaps never to be seen again. The VJP closed behind them, plunging Farmer Grindle's turkey barn into darkness.

'I appreciate this probably isn't the most APPROPRIATE time,' Ravi whispered, 'but if somebody doesn't explain how there's a talking dog sitting next to me, I'M GOING TO FREAK OUT!!'

Maggie's ears twitched. 'I suppose now is a good enough time as any other,' she muttered. 'The turkey's wand also fires a green light.'

'A green light?' Mabel was intrigued.

'Yes, but this light doesn't scan you like the orange one; it evolves you—mentally, at any rate.'

'WHAT?' Ravi was close to bursting a blood vessel.

'They call it the AWARENESS RAY—capable of delivering a million years of evolution in under a minute. Hence, a talking dog who would quite like to learn CHESS and read SHAKESPEARE.'

'How will you move the pieces and turn the pages?' Mabel said. After such a monumental statement, it wasn't the most thoughtful observation. In her defence, she was *very* tired.

'I hadn't thought of that,' Maggie replied dejectedly. 'I could use my mouth, I suppose. I've only been clever for a week.'

Ravi was finding it difficult to breathe. It wasn't because he was scared; it was because he was excited. In fact, he was so excited that he had given himself a nosebleed. How many more ground-breaking technological revelations would he discover today? This Awareness Ray thingy was equally as astonishing as vortex manipulation.

'Hang on a minute, why do the mutants use it? What do they gain from evolving the odd *DOG?*' Ravi questioned.

'I'm not sure. I wasn't their intended target. After my owner's birds were taken, a few strays remained.' Maggie promptly looked rather guilty. 'I just *HAPPENED* to be amongst them when the green light shone.'

The elf growled nearly as deeply as the border collie. 'Dog's behaviour SICKENS Keith. Gorging on animals is ABHORRENT.'

'Don't listen to her. There's nothing wrong with a dog wanting to chase a few birds, Maggie,' Mabel said reassuringly. 'That's what dogs do.'

Maggie began whining miserably. 'Perhaps that was true before, but now I'm filled with remorse for the things I've done.'

'You didn't know any better,' Mabel said, patting her on the head.

Maggie just whined even more.

'Look at it this way,' Ravi said. 'If you WEREN'T snacking on turkey, you WOULDN'T be sitting here in the dark holding a conversation with us.'

Mabel frowned again. 'WHY are we sitting in the dark?' she asked quietly. The turkeys were gone, and the portal with them. There was no longer any reason to hide.

Ravi shrugged. 'We're probably in shock.'

He was right. Conversing with a canine and an elf inside a turkey shelter in a dark barn was distracting them from contemplating their friends' fate and what, if anything, they could do to resolve the situation.

'What will I tell Alice's MUM?' Mabel whimpered, her tough exterior blown wide open. She wiped tears from her eyes before sobbing into Maggie's fur.

'Sssshhh... There, there. Don't be sad.' Now it was the dog's turn to offer a shoulder to cry on. She nuzzled the unhappy girl affectionately.

Keith nodded while making a reassuring noise that sounded like a cat yawning. 'To save friends, we must not talk to ANYONE—including children's elders. UNDERSTAND? If they find us, they stop us helping.'

'Fine by me,' Ravi declared. He could happily go a few days without socialising with his boring parents.

'I understand,' Mabel said, sniffing. 'But how can we save them? THE PORTAL'S CLOSED!'

Suddenly, there was light again. It shone from Keith's VTM. 'We make new portal.'

At once, Mabel's face brightened—and so did Ravi's. He couldn't wait to have his entire body disassembled on a cellular level, sucked through time and space in the blink of an eye before being reconstructed atom by atom on the surface of an unknown alien planet.

Professor Brian Cox, eat your heart out, Ravi mused gleefully. *I'll be the first kid in the world to experience interstellar teleportation.* Then he remembered that Bennie, Boris, and Alice had already jumped. *Okay, fourth in the world isn't too bad, I suppose.* Ravi just needed to make sure he went in ahead of Mabel. He didn't care about Keith or Maggie. He was pretty sure animals and elves didn't count in the pecking order, even if they could talk and play chess.

'VTM locked onto turkey VJP…' Keith announced with all the enthusiasm of a tiger presented with a bowl of greens for supper.

'*BUT…?*' Ravi could spot that face a mile off, elf or not. His parents wore it as often as they wore socks. It was, 'I've bought doughnuts, *but* you need a brain transplant and five fillings before you can eat them' face. It promised Heaven but put you through Hell first.

'But… VTM needs power.'

'Well, that's not so bad.' Ravi had expected something a little trickier than plugging the thing into the mains. Why was the stupid elf making such a fuss?

'MUCH more power.'

Ravi sighed. 'How MUCH more?'

'One million volts.'

Ravi's jaw hit the deck.

'Is that a lot?' Mabel asked. She wasn't great with numbers and measurements unless it involved the diameter of a gun barrel or the weight of a battle tank.

Ravi despaired. 'Where are we going to find that sort of POWER?' Frustrated, he tugged the beanie from his head and began whacking it against the turkey shelter like he had his phone.

'Pylons cross the fields next to my owner's land,' Maggie said, wagging her tail. She opened her mouth, ready for a treat, but then remembered getting rewards for obedience and good behaviour was a thing of the past. She had evolved, but old habits die hard.

Ravi shook his head. 'YES, the pylons have the power, but we would need direct contact with the high-voltage cables, and that's a DEATH SENTENCE to whoever's INSANE enough to pull a stunt like that.'

'Keith will do it,' the elf chirped nonchalantly as if she was agreeing to something far less trivial like emptying the bins or doing the laundry.

'THAT'S FANTASTIC, KEITH! THANK YOU!'

Mabel wasn't usually so upbeat, but the sheer relief washing through her body couldn't be contained. They would charge the VTM, jump through the new portal, rescue Santa and her friends, and be back for breakfast!

Ravi didn't share Mabel's deluded optimism, but at least he wouldn't be the one climbing to the top of a 164-foot electricity pylon in the dark.

'Can we get out of the turkey shelter now, PLEASE?' Mabel whispered. 'I really need a wee.'

14

The Hall of Nine Windows

Bennie was propelled forward at unfathomable speed. It felt like hurtling down the world's highest, steepest, twistiest underwater flume in the dark.

A deafening roaring filled his ears, and a dazzling kaleidoscope of colours flashed before his eyes. *It's like being strapped to the front of a space rocket!* Then, after what seemed like an age but in actuality was only a millisecond, he was somewhere else.

'I think I'm going to be SICK,' he heard Boris mumble beside him.

'My body feels INSIDE OUT,' Alice whimpered, frantically checking herself for misplaced organs and misaligned limbs. 'I don't care where we are or how far we've travelled, but I'm walking home. There's no way I'm stepping into one of those things EVER AGAIN!'

Bennie's senses gradually rebooted. It was a phased return to normality, starting with his sense of smell and ending with a dramatically heightened sense of dread.

We're underground. Bennie wasn't sure how he knew. Perhaps it was the chill, dank air or the lack of windows. 'It's like Wooky Hole in Somerset,' he whispered. Bennie had visited the cave system with his grandad during a family holiday a few years ago.

Even though this place felt like a cave, it wasn't. The walls were built from yellow blocks, and the floor from thousands of tiny, coloured stones.

A mosaic, Bennie mused, marvelling at the detail and workmanship involved. He had learned about them at school. Mrs Spleen-Weasel had described them as 'Ornamental art for floors.' If Bennie remembered correctly, the Ancient Romans were partial to a mosaic or two. *The Romans and mutant turkeys.* He hadn't anticipated the monsters' love for decorative flooring.

The colourful scene beneath his Wellington boots depicted a ginormous turkey man wearing a crown of golden feathers perched on top of a weird, shiny throne. Presumably, this oversized *birdman* was the

Emperor. In front of him, columns of turkey soldiers were lined up in battle formation facing the portal.

On impulse, Bennie spun around to see the portal for himself. This wasn't how it appeared from the other side. This was a permanent fixture, a vast gateway spanning the chamber's width. 'WOW,' he uttered, impressed by the sheer scale of the VJP.

A whole army could march through, shoulder to shoulder, just like the mosaic. It was a grim thought that led him to question exactly what these strange creatures wanted and where they had been lurking all this time? Was a hidden underground city really feasible? It seemed impossible for such a place to exist secretly, yet here it was.

The turkey soldiers herded their prisoners into the centre of the chamber.

'I am Captain Claw,' the Turkey Captain announced, strutting back and forth, looking extremely pleased with himself.

Santa scoffed. 'Well, of course you are,' he replied sarcastically. 'And who are your henchmen? Razor-Beak and Peck-Me-To-Death?'

Captain Claw stopped his march and loomed menacingly over Santa. 'Would you like to know what the glorious Meleagris Empire calls you, old man?' he said, peering down with beady eyes.

Santa shrugged. 'Not particularly. I can't remember the names I've already got.'

Captain Claw's plumage quivered. 'Your humorous tongue won't save you. In fact, I think the Emperor will pluck it from your mouth.'

A barrage of high-pitched squawking burst from the giant turkeys. Bennie winced. It was excruciating. It sounded like a pack of screeching velociraptors chasing a horde of screaming preschoolers at a unicorn convention.

'Your treacherous deeds fill our history books. Never again will you be free to aid the evil causes of your despicable human allies. Today is a great day. At last, the Meleagris will have justice. At last, Rufus Diaboli—the red devil—is our prisoner!'

The birdmen hissed at Santa like angry swans. Their horrible hairless heads jutted back and forth, their sharp beaks snapping like hungry pterodactyl chicks.

To say Bennie, Boris, and Alice were in the dark was an enormous understatement. They were locked inside a dark box in a dark room on a dark night, blindfolded.

'It deeply saddens me that human chicks know nothing of our eternal suffering,' Captain Claw said, noticing the children's lack of understanding. 'Your elders have failed you, and because of them, you will pay. Now take them away!'

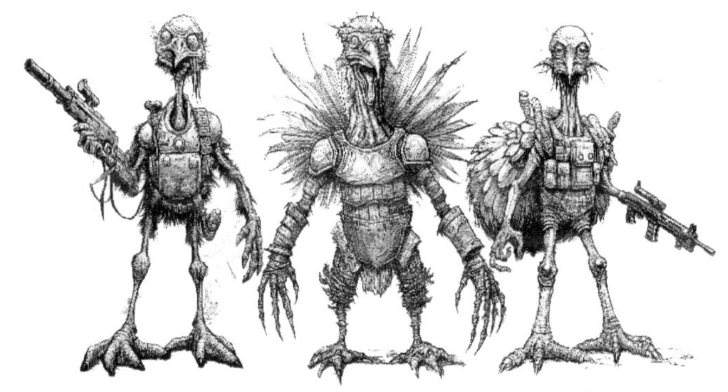

The prisoners were ushered from the chamber into an arched torchlit corridor. The route weaved past so many intersections Bennie lost count. It was more like a rabbit warren than a turkey coop. He didn't spot a single window along the way, confirming his suspicions that they were indeed underground. But then they started going up, blowing Bennie's theory to smithereens.

'You might have thought such a technologically advanced race like the MELEAGRIS would have installed a lift,' Boris moaned breathlessly.

'You're beginning to sound like Ravi,' Alice whispered, trying not to incur the wrath of their turkey guards. She hoped Mabel and Keith were okay back at the farm. And Ravi, too, she supposed, even though he wasn't very nice sometimes.

Bennie shook his head. 'We've only been climbing for FIVE MINUTES, and you're already puffing.'

Actually, Bennie wasn't concerned about Boris. Despite his complaining, he was as fit as any of them—except for Alice, who didn't know the meaning of the word *tired.* It was Santa gasping like a giant halibut that worried him. 'Are you okay, Santa?' he said over his shoulder.

'I... WISH... CAPTAIN... CACTUS... FACE... HADN'T... SNATCHED... MY... SUGAR... CUBES!'

Bennie sympathised. His own legs were beginning to burn. A few ounces of glucose wouldn't half help to power him to the top.

They plodded upwards, twisting around and around as if climbing an enormous corkscrew. Each time one of the gang stopped to rest, the soldiers prodded them with the barrels of their ray guns. 'Keep moving,' they hissed. 'Many more steps to go.'

'*SERIOUSLY?*' Boris grumbled.

As they gained height, they finally began passing windows.

'It's definitely not an underground city,' Bennie mumbled under his breath. *Where are we?*

The fiery pain in his legs was instantly forgotten. He wanted to stop and stare because what he saw through the windows was impossible. The landscape was barren and tinged a yellowy-orange. It was as if they were in the middle of a desert.

The city didn't only exist beneath the surface; it erupted into the sky. 'It's like a GIGANTIC termite's nest,' Bennie mouthed silently. Everywhere he stared, towers of sandstone protruded from the parched soil. *These turkeys have taken roosting in trees to another level.*

'They look like BLOOMING GREAT TURNIPS!' Santa said, wheezing like a set of deflating bagpipes.

'Don't you mean *TULIPS*, Santa?' Alice corrected. And she was right. The towers were all finished with a tulip-like dome on top.

'No, TURNIPS!'

Whatever they looked like, Bennie had never seen anything like them. They made the pyramids in Egypt look positively mundane, not to mention pitifully stunted. Yet this couldn't be right, could it? There was nowhere on Earth like it, not anywhere he had seen, at any rate. Admittedly, he didn't watch enough documentaries to be an expert, but surely, he would have learned about this at school. *Especially as the place is teeming with giant turkeys.* He couldn't work it out. It didn't seem like they were even trying to keep the city a secret. To be honest, the giant tulip towers were probably visible from space. So why hadn't he heard about them before now?

And that wasn't all. The sky wasn't right either. It was dark and brooding and tinged a yellowy-orange like everything else here.

'It wants to rain, but it can't,' Bennie murmured while twisting past another window. Was constipated weather a thing? *I need water... and a nap,* he decided, suddenly feeling incredibly weary. Staying up all night was a first for him. Not that it was night here. *But it is at home.*

At last, the torturous climb ended, bringing the party before a set of grand doors decorated with beautiful feather patterns and guarded by a pair of turkey soldiers adorned in ceremonial dress.

Alice sniggered. She had never seen so many feathers. *They look like giant birds.* And then she remembered they *were* giant birds.

'When you are presented to his Excellency, you will kneel,' Captain Claw instructed in his comedic

Germanic lilt. 'Failure to do so will result in your immediate demise.'

'Blooming charming,' Santa muttered into his beard. 'Hospitality at its finest.'

The ceremonial turkeys—the ones that Alice thought wore ostrich costumes—lurched from their posts to push open the doors. Captain Claw inflated his chest, stiffened his plumage, and strutted into the chamber. Santa and the children tramped after him, with Razor-Beak and Peck-Me-To-Death bringing up the rear, ensuring the prisoners didn't try anything stupid like leap out of a window.

The Emperor was perched on a gilded nest atop a grand wooden dais. It was skillfully crafted to resemble the branches of a tree—that, or it *was* a tree. He was draped in an enormous cloak of peacock feathers, and upon his elongated head, he wore what looked like a crown of golden beaks.

Bennie shuddered. The beaks looked hungry.

Except for the throne, the circular hall was empty of furnishings, allowing for uninterrupted views of the surrounding landscape through nine enormous arched windows.

'You are in the exalted presence of His Excellency, Emperor Gobble-Gobble,' declared a giant turkey standing beside the throne. The creature was clad in yet another assemblage of outlandish garments, the oddest of which was a silly-looking feathered bonnet.

Bennie struggled to contain a snicker. *Gobble-Gobble? They've got to be kidding, right?*

'Welcome to the Hall of Nine Windows,' the Turkey Emperor announced. The hall was located inside the dome—or tulip or turnip or whatever you wanted to call it—at the very top of the tower. 'Please, sit.'

Captain Claw and his soldiers shoved the captives onto their knees.

'Hall of Nine Windows? THAT'S NOT VERY ORIGINAL,' Alice blurted before she could stop herself.

Captain Claw rushed forward to prod Alice in the back with his sceptre. 'Silence, human scum!'

Emperor Gobble-Gobble held up a horrible leathery hand. 'Please, Captain, show restraint.'

'My apologies, Excellency,' Captain Claw said, dipping his head and moving away.

'Our guests require educating, that is all,' the Emperor continued. 'Please, speak, girl. Ask your questions.'

Alice gulped, suddenly becoming incredibly nervous. 'Why have NINE windows? I wouldn't want a single one with a view like THAT!' she said, appalled by what she saw outside.

'The honesty of youth,' Emperor Gobble-Gobble chuckled. 'The view is poignant to us. It reminds the Meleagris of humankind's impact on our world.'

'What do you mean?' Bennie asked. He knew enough about climate change to realise things needed to improve, but as far as he was led to believe, it wasn't too late, not yet.

'And another thing,' Boris said. 'WHERE ARE WE?' It certainly wasn't anywhere he had been before. It looked very different to Ipswich. 'Are we in SCOTLAND?'

'No, not Scotland, lad,' Santa said. 'I fear we've travelled beyond the British Isles—and not in the way you think.'

Boris felt like he had just been asked an incredibly complicated algebra question. 'Where then?'

Abruptly, the Turkey Emperor stood and flung his arms wide. 'The skies are a churning mass of rainless clouds and swirling pockets of poisonous fumes. The sun is rarely visible, which is a blessing because the world below screams in woe when she shines. Earth is a barren wasteland: nothing grows, at least nothing edible. We eat what can be created in our laboratories or caught in the wild. The oceans boil, and the rivers run dry. The only water fit for drinking must be mined like a precious metal from deep beneath the cursed soil.'

'OH, I KNOW!' Boris blurted. 'SKEGNESS!'

Santa grimaced. 'Shut your cakehole, lad, before you get us in trouble. If we aren't in enough trouble already,' he whispered through clenched teeth.

The Emperor descended the dais, and with his peacock cloak trailing behind him, he moved to a window and gazed into the far distance. 'Welcome to the city of Arvian,' he said sadly. 'Welcome to the future.'

15

Recharge

Keith hopped from the turkey shelter and scampered to the barn door as quietly as a mouse. Poking her head outside, she gave the farmyard a quick once over before waving the others forward to join her.

The children didn't share the elf's poise. Ravi stubbed his big toe, and Mabel succumbed to a sneezing fit. 'Feathers,' she spluttered. Maggie, at least, showed *some* elf-like stealth, padding to Keith's side without incident.

Keith programmed the VTM to locate the nearest power source capable of recharging its jump capabilities. Simply plugging the device into the mains wasn't an option, not if they wanted to open a portal this side of Christmas. It wasn't a toaster.

'Closest high-voltage pylon one kilometre northeast,' Keith announced, studying the VTM's glowing display.

'ONE KILOMETRE across the fields in the SNOW AT NIGHT?' Ravi questioned despairingly.

'The alternative is staying here and waiting for the magic gate to reopen,' Maggie offered, scratching an ear with a white paw.

Ravi immediately liked the idea; anything was better than a midnight hike in freezing conditions.

'And WHEN will that be?' Mabel asked.

'Maybe hour, day, week. Who knows? Maybe never,' Keith said with a shrug, tempering Ravi's enthusiasm for staying behind.

'A midnight hike it is then,' Ravi declared miserably. He wasn't happy about trudging halfway across the Suffolk countryside, but he also realised his friends were in danger and tomorrow might be too late.

'I'm coming with you,' Maggie stated doggedly. 'The monsters have my owner.'

Mabel rested her hand gently on the border collie's head. 'The farmer isn't your owner anymore, Maggie. You can think and act for yourself now.'

The dog twitched her head sideways in thought. 'You're right,' she said with a toothy grin. 'The monsters don't have my owner; they have my FRIEND!'

Mabel smiled. It was reassuring to learn that Farmer Grindle cared for his animals well enough to deserve their loyalty. Although she very much doubted his turkeys felt the same, not after working out what happened to them at Christmas.

'Keep close, and do not make noise,' Keith warned, her violet eyes glowing in the dark. Humans didn't know the first thing about keeping quiet and needed reminding of their inadequacies at every opportunity.

Leaving the barn, they crept through the icy farmyard, taking extra care passing beneath the cottage's overlooking windows.

Ravi glimpsed a blur of something feathery in Mrs Grindle's front garden. 'What was that?' he whispered, peering into the darkness. He gulped. The temptation to finger his earlobes was overpowering.

It was impossible to distinguish bushes from… well, other bushes. In fact, everything looked like a bush. It all blurred together, shadows hiding shadows.

'THERE! Behind Mrs Grindle's *BUSH!*' At least, he hoped it was a bush. It might just have easily been an enormous eagle's nest crawling with giant bird-eating tarantulas. The imagination could run riot on dark nights like this, even Ravi's.

Behind them, Mabel heard the patter of fast-moving feet through the snow. 'There goes another one,' she said, spinning around.

'TURKEY SPIES!' Maggie warned with a low growl.

Suddenly, a light flashed on above the cottage's front porch.

Mabel grimaced. 'Oh no, now we're in trouble.'

'CATCH THEM! Turkey masters cannot know we are coming.' Grabbing hold of Mabel, the elf shoved Ravi at Maggie. 'GIRL with Keith, and BOY with DOG.'

Ravi glanced anxiously at the floodlit farmhouse. 'What about Mrs Grindle and her shotgun?'

'No time to worry. Catch turkeys before they run.'

The gang separated. Keith and Mabel legged it into Mrs Grindle's front garden while Ravi and Maggie retraced their steps toward the barns.

Keith spotted a turkey loitering behind a holly bush. The elf crept around the shrub's prickly leaves one way and Mabel the other, cornering their prey between them on the other side.

With arms stretched out, Keith and Mabel closed in.

'Come to Keith, LITTLE BIRDIE!'

Startled, the turkey launched itself at the only viable avenue of escape: the dog flap set in Farmer Grindle's front door. After several quick steps and a head-first dive, the bird disappeared into the cottage.

'QUICK,' Keith said, 'find something to seal hole.'

Mabel began shoving against a big potted plant situated beside the porch, but it refused to budge. 'A little help, PLEASE!' she hissed, red-faced from her efforts. The elf added her strength, and soon, the pot began scraping noisily over the icy path. Once positioned in front of the door, preventing the flap from opening, Mabel and Keith swiftly retreated, seeking safety in the shadows.

Mabel couldn't help thinking they had just condemned the poor thing to certain death. *It looks like turkey is back on the menu for Mrs Grindle this Christmas.*

Meanwhile, Maggie had sniffed out the second bird. She herded the animal straight into Ravi's path, who waited beside the smaller of Farmer Grindle's barns, brandishing a broomstick.

'Here it comes,' Ravi whispered nervously, watching the turkey hurtle toward him. In the dark, it looked nearly as scary as its mutated cousins.

Flinging his arms wide, Ravi swished the broom through the air, hoping to frighten the bird directly into the open barn. But the thing didn't stop.

'Oh, no,' Ravi muttered just before the turkey bulldozed him into the snow.

Maggie shot after it, chasing the animal across the farmyard, around the barns, and back again, her legs scrabbling on the ice.

BANG!! BANG!!

Two thumping gunshots rang into the night, stopping everyone in their tracks, including the turkey.

'Mrs Grindle's SHOTGUN!' Mabel mouthed, hardly daring to breathe. 'NOBODY MOVE!'

After spending at least a minute resembling ice sculptures, the gang—and the turkey—simultaneously concluded that the shots had originated from inside the cottage and not outside, allowing the mayhem to resume in earnest.

Mabel winced. *Turkey number one is down*, she thought guiltily. Mrs Grindle certainly didn't mess about. As for turkey number two, it was running for its life, hoping to reach the open fields on the far side of the farmyard.

Keith and Mabel leapt from behind another bush, blocking its path. The bird slid to a halt, spraying snow into the air before back peddling like crazy… but Maggie and Ravi were waiting.

'Unless you want to end up like your FRIEND, I suggest you co-operate,' Mabel said with a cold stare.

The turkey searched for a way out, twisting around and around until its scrawny neck looked like a corkscrew, but there wasn't one.

'You promise not to feed me to the farmer's wife?' the hen said, her voice so high-pitched it sounded like she had been sucking helium from birthday balloons for the best part of the afternoon.

Mabel nodded. 'I promise.'

Ravi glanced at Maggie. 'She's negotiating with a turkey,' he whispered.

'And you're chatting to a sheepdog.'

Ravi chuckled. 'Fair point.'

Keith shooed the animal into the smaller of Farmer Grindle's barns. The others tailed behind, happy to be out of range of Mrs Grindle's shotgun. Once inside, Keith frog-marched their feathery captive onto an empty crate.

'What's this? An interrogation?' the turkey screeched.

Ravi shone his torch into the hen's face. 'Just a few questions.'

'And what if I don't want to answer?'

Ravi grinned devilishly. 'She'll *EAT* you,' he said, directing the light into Maggie's face.

Maggie bared her teeth and emitted a low, menacing growl.

Scared stiff, the turkey accidentally did its business on top of the wooden crate. 'Okay. I'll tell you anything you want. Just please keep that horrid dog away!'

Mabel snatched Ravi's phone from his hand and shined it straight into the turkey's beady eyes:

'WHAT'S YOUR MISSION? WHEN WILL THE PORTAL REOPEN? WHAT WILL HAPPEN TO OUR FRIENDS? WHAT DO THE GIANT TURKEYS WANT? ARE THEY ALIENS? HOW BIG IS THEIR ARMY? WHAT ARE THEIR MILITARY CAPABILITIES? DO THEY HAVE AIR POWER OR ARMOURED DIVISIONS? WHAT ARE THEIR KEY TARGETS? KEY OBJECTIVES? WELL?'

The turkey trembled with fear. 'To spy. Monday night at 9pm. Imprisonment, interrogation, execution.

Your planet. No. Not as big as yours. Advanced missile systems, forcefields, and ray guns. I don't think so. Turkey farms, military bases, London, capturing strategic sites, nullifying your armies, instigating a full-scale uprising, conquering the world, and enslaving the human race.'

The gang stared at Mabel open-mouthed.

'Blimey, you don't take any prisoners,' Ravi said. 'Have you ever considered a career in teaching?'

Mabel grimaced. 'No thanks. I would rather have my EYES POKED OUT!' She couldn't stand pen-pushers. She just wanted to play Risk until she was old enough to join her dad in the army.

Tentatively, the turkey raised a wing into the air. 'Erm... can I go now?'

'NO. BIRD STAY,' Keith stated firmly, ushering the others to the door.

'You can't just leave me here!'

'We haven't got a choice. We can't risk you spilling your beans,' Ravi explained with an apologetic shrug.

'I don't even like beans!' the turkey yelped miserably.

'We're sorry, but this is war… AND YOU STARTED IT!' Mabel said, following Maggie and Ravi from the barn.

'Come back, or I'll peck your toes off, you chicken-livered bird eaters!'

Keith put a finger to her lips. 'SSSSHHH... It best if farmer's wife does not hear noisy hen,' she whispered before slipping through the door.

Outside, Keith secured the barn and set off at a furious pace. According to the turkey's information, the portal wouldn't reopen for another two days, and with talk of imprisonments, interrogations, and, dare they think it, *executions*, time was perilously short. Who knew how long their friends had left before the giant turkeys strung them up? Recharging the Vortex Time Manipulator was their only hope.

The farm vanished behind them, and soon, they were wading through glistening white fields under the moonlit sky. They trudged deep into the night, their warm breath billowing in the freezing air. Mabel and Ravi had long since lost the feeling in their fingers and toes, but they didn't complain. Saving Santa and their friends was worth a little discomfort.

At last, the pylons loomed ahead, a frozen army of snow-crusted metal giants emerging from the darkness. The gang marched to the closest of them, gathering beneath the structure.

Ravi peered skyward. 'Wow… That's a long way to climb.' Before he knew it, Keith was shimmying up the pylon like a rat up a drainpipe.

'How are you going to connect the VTM to the cable without BLOWING YOURSELF UP?' Ravi yelled from below, watching the elf vanish from sight. He stamped his feet while he waited, desperately trying to restart the flow of blood to his extremities.

Keith's muffled voice answered from above. 'VTM does not require direct contact. It only needs to be close to absorb power. STAND BY.'

'How long is this GOING TO TAKE?' Ravi called back. 'Only, I think I'm slowly turning into a SNOWMAN FROM THE FEET UP!'

'Snow-boy, more like,' Mabel muttered.

Suddenly, there was an almighty bang, and Keith was lit up like a Christmas tree being struck by lightning.

Mabel cupped her hands together and yelled, 'Are you OKAY?' She feared the elf was getting fried alive.

The pylon cables crackled with dancing flashes of electricity. Then, unexpectedly, a blinding white glow pulsed into the sky.

Above the field, night turned into day.

'KEITH!' Mabel cried.

There was no reply.

Maggie raced around the pylon's enormous feet, barking frantically with worry the whole time.

The cables above their heads continued crackling and spluttering, showering glowing yellow sparks into the air like a giant firework.

'Oh, no. Keith is gone!' Mabel murmured despairingly.

Ravi winced. 'Barbecued elf. HARSH!'

And then they heard a small voice above them, 'Keith alive, STUPID HUMANS. VTM now charging.'

'Thank goodness,' Mabel sighed.

Ravi nudged Mabel in the back. 'Look,' he said, pointing into the distance.

Mabel gasped. One by one, Larkbridge's lights began blinking out until the whole town was plunged into darkness.

'WOW! That thing just sucked Larkbridge DRY!' Ravi exclaimed excitedly.

Keith reappeared beside them. 'Now we jump,' she said, pulling a handful of celery sticks from her pockets.

16

Future Earth

The blue portal spewed Mabel, Ravi, Keith, and Maggie onto a rocky outcrop high on the slopes of a jagged mountain.

'Where are we?' Mabel said, scrambling to her feet after finding herself sprawled on top of the others in the dust. She shaded her eyes with her hands. It was daytime here. Wherever *here* was.

Jumping from a gloomy barn in the middle of the night straight into morning light was disorientating, to say the least—especially for the eyeballs.

Keith glared at the VTM as if it were lying to her. 'Future Earth,' she finally muttered, her violet eyes widening. 'If device to be trusted, we in 8989.'

Ravi leapt up so fast he nearly fell off the ledge. Which, considering how high they were, would have been seriously bad for his health. 'Did you say, 8989! THAT'S MENTAL!'

However, Ravi's enthusiasm swiftly died a death. 'Well, by the look of things, I'd say global warming has caught up with us,' he said, joining the others by staring into the distance.

For as far as they could see, the land was sun-blasted and barren. A city of red towers dominated the horizon, its many spires reaching into an orange sky where turbulent storm clouds writhed like living shadows. Beneath the strange orange sky and churning clouds, rolling banks of choking smog crept over the landscape. It looked like a vast predatory spirit searching for victims to engulf and consume.

Mabel screwed up her face. 'The air smells like ROTTEN EGGS.'

'And tastes like CHARRED SAUSAGES,' Maggie added, wriggling her nose.

'Is that where we're headed?' Mabel said, nodding toward the distant city.

'Yes,' Keith confirmed sharply after blowing a thick coating of red dust off the VTM.

Ravi frowned. 'Why are we so far away?'

'It prudent to arrive safe distance from Santa. Keith did not want to materialise INSIDE turkey barracks.'

'Fair enough, I suppose,' Ravi said, sighing. 'How far to the city?' It seemed a long way. He hoped it was an optical illusion caused by the peculiar atmosphere. Sometimes, distances seemed further away when the air was distorted with fumes and heat shimmers.

'Five kilometres or so.'

Ravi's heart sank. 'FIVE KILOMETRES! Haven't we walked enough tonight?' Not that it was night in this terrible *future Earth*. Ravi wondered if dark ever fell here, or was this twisted half-light perpetual? Had day and night become one?

A shrill cry echoed through the mountains, followed moments later by an answering call which was much closer. Then another and another.

'What was THAT?' Mabel whispered. Having spent much of her youth exploring the outdoors, she was accustomed to calls of the wild, but never had she heard an animal make such a noise.

Ravi shrugged. 'Some sort of ape?'

Whatever it was, it was getting nearer.

Tilting her head, Maggie sniffed the bitter air. 'Humans.'

'HUMANS?' Mabel said. 'But they don't sound like humans.'

'Unless whatever's chasing the humans is making the noise?' Ravi surmised, utilising his brain to devise a logical answer. Dissecting and analysing a situation helped stop being overrun by anxiety and panic. It was a useful discipline Ravi often used to his advantage. However, after careful consideration, he decided that neither of his two conclusions were reassuring. *We're either being hunted by unknown savage creatures or humans who sound like unknown savage creatures.* Feeling suddenly anxious, Ravi began to panic.

Keith pointed the VTM toward the mountains from where the unnerving calls were coming. 'Twelve life forms approaching FAST.'

'Can't you tell what they ARE?' Ravi asked.

'Not until Keith scans them,' the elf replied.

Ravi desperately searched the terrain beneath the ledge for the quickest way down. He grimaced and then started feeling sick. A near vertical slope strewn with boulders and stones disappeared below. It looked impossible to traverse. 'Unless you're a GOAT,' he mumbled glumly.

'Let's hide, and you can scan them when they run past,' Mabel suggested eagerly.

Much like Ravi's *analysing* helped combat his fears, Mabel's inane love of adventure distracted her from the perilous reality of her situation. The consequences of being caught hadn't crossed her mind.

Maggie's long snout began twitching again. 'Caution,' she growled in warning. 'These humans smell hungry.'

'HUNGRY? How can someone smell *HUNGRY?*' Ravi questioned. 'Anyway, we haven't got anything to give them, have we.'

'Only ourselves,' Keith replied ominously.

Ravi gulped. 'Shouldn't we be rescuing our friends instead of skulking about up here?' He really didn't want to meet *hungry* savage future humans who didn't seem the least bit bothered by eating their long-lost cousins.

'Aren't you curious? They might be our descendants.'

'No, not in the slightest, thank you very much, Mabel,' Ravi stated firmly. 'And in any case, we shouldn't allow ourselves to be side-tracked however interesting the locals are.'

The elf nodded. 'We must go.'

'Finally, some common sense,' Ravi said. 'Now, how do we get off this thing?'

'TOO LATE!' Mabel gasped, pointing a gloved hand toward a spikey-looking ridge.

Ravi was horrified. 'What are THEY?' His rational thought process was having terrible trouble computing.

The creatures scurried across the serrated ridge on all fours, leaping skillfully from rock to rock. From where the gang stood, they appeared very much like apes, just as Ravi had said—but they weren't.

'Humans,' Keith announced, having completed her scan. 'DNA ninety-nine percent match.'

Ravi fingered his earlobes aggressively. 'Ninety-nine percent? BUT THERE'S NOTHING REMOTELY HUMAN ABOUT THEM! And Maggie's right. They look hungry.'

Suddenly, the future humans screeched excitedly. They had spotted the strangers ahead and began bounding over the remainder of the jagged crags with renewed vigour. They were hairy, filth-ridden, and desperate. Humanity on Earth had seemingly de-evolved. In fact, the once-dominant all-conquering species had recessed so far that they appeared very much like Neanderthals once more.

'RUN!!!' Ravi squawked. And this time, the others didn't argue.

'THIS WAY!' Keith slid down a short sandy gully, scrambled over a knobbly spur, and then tip-toed across a scarily exposed rock bridge with nothing on either side except thin air. 'Do not look down,' she shouted over her shoulder.

Abruptly, the elf skidded to a halt, teetering precariously on a ledge jutting over a steep scree slope strewn with boulders all the way down to the valley floor. An acrid smog wreathed the lowlands beneath her, hanging over the scorched plains like a mysterious mist.

Pumping their arms and legs at a furious rate, Ravi, Mabel, and Maggie negotiated the knobbly spur, traversed the death-defying rock bridge, rounded a jagged crag that looked remarkably like a giant duck, and then barged straight into Keith like a freight train.

All four of them toppled over the edge.

Rolling head over heels, they tumbled down the mountainside, banging elbows and knees on rocks and stones. After a chorus of torturous cries, they finally slowed themselves enough to control the rest of the descent—and thankfully, in a much less painful manner.

Soon, they were negotiating the scree slope like pro surfers riding Cornish waves. Great big dust clouds trailed behind them, spewing into the sky. Near the bottom, the gang regrouped to catch their breath. But not for long. Shrieking like Marjory from Sunset Rest—i.e., like howler monkeys—the future humans flew down the mountain with frightening speed.

Keith pressed on, leading Maggie and the children into a boulder field. Eager to lose their pursuers, they weaved between the enormous stones, zigzagging like they were competing in a downhill slalom race.

Mabel pointed to a huge rock ahead. It had cracked in two, and between the halves was a significant gouge in the red soil, deep enough to perfectly conceal a boy, girl, elf, and dog inside.

Keith gave an affirmative nod and swerved from the path. The others followed, diving headfirst into the hole one after the other.

'HERE THEY COME!' Ravi gasped, panting nearly as hard as Maggie. Sports and outdoor pursuits were a time-consuming distraction for academics. But now Ravi wished he had joined Larkbridge Lightning Bolts, the school's football team, and Mrs Spleen-Weasel's cross-country club, Little Weasels, at the start of term. It would have put him in good stead for encounters like this. *Whoever said keeping fit was good for you should take a bow.* He only wished he had listened.

Mabel scowled and shoved a finger against Ravi's lips. Didn't the stupid boy know not to make the slightest sound when attempting to evade an enemy?

The future humans loped past without noticing them. They looked like wild dogs, snarling and sniffing the acrid air, their leathery feet pounding through the red soil.

'I think we might actually get away without being seen,' Ravi whispered. And he was right. At least, he would have been if he hadn't sneezed—really, really loudly.

'AAAAAACHHHHHHOOOOO!!!!'

The others glared at him, holding their breath, waiting for the inevitable bark of alarm.

'SORRY!' Ravi mouthed, wiping a gloved hand across his nose. 'It's the dust.'

One of the creatures split from the pack and moved closer, shuffling toward the gang's hiding place. And then it grinned, revealing horrible, pointed black teeth.

'SHE'S SPOTTED US! AND IT'S ALL YOUR FAULT!' Mabel hissed, subjecting Ravi to her crossest scowl—the one with disconcerting snake eyes and lips so puckered they made her look like an angry trout. 'What do we do?'

Suddenly, a glaring light flashed before their eyes, and the creature was blasted into the dirt. Before the future humans knew what had hit them, they were caught in a crossfire of pulsing yellow laser beams. In seconds, they were all face down in the arid red soil beside their fallen comrade.

'Are they DEAD?' Mabel murmured in a low, frightened voice. She had momentarily forgotten to maintain complete silence in combat zones.

Keith shook her head. 'Stunned.'

The gang quickly ducked their heads as black-armoured turkey soldiers stepped into view. To make certain their victims were unconscious, the turkeys poked them with their ray guns or prodded them with their horrible, clawed feet.

Next, rumbling over the ground like distant thunder, an open-sided wagon halted beside the bodies. Yoked and chained like oxen, the wagon was hauled by more humans. They looked desperate, miserable creatures.

Once the turkey soldiers had slung their prey onto the wagon, they swiftly withdrew, melting into the smog swirling between the boulder field like wraiths.

Maggie sniffed the air. 'I'll scout ahead to make sure it's safe,' she whispered, slinking from the hole. Before long, she reappeared above them. 'They have gone. You can come out now.'

Keith helped Mabel and Ravi squeeze from the hole and then between the huge split boulder. 'We follow turkeys into city,' she stated as the children brushed red dust from their clothes. 'Come, nasty fog help conceal us.'

The journey felt much further than five kilometres, and the whole way was spent coughing and spluttering in the noxious mist. They passed dried-up riverbeds and lakes of yellowy water bubbling like gigantic vats of foul-smelling parsnip soup. The parched soil beneath their boots scalded like hot ash. Everywhere they looked, the terrain was barren and devoid of life.

The children hadn't experienced anything like it. Not even last year's summer drought that turned the countryside into a tinderbox and everyone's gardens into a wasteland populated with fried flowers and crispy grass came close. At least it had been temporary. Here, it was permanent.

A trail of discarded clothing littered the gang's approach to the city. Clad in winter coats and woolly hats, the searing temperatures had become too much to handle. Keith advised against disrobing. Even though it was hot, the garments protected them against the smog's toxic fumes and the sun's harmful rays, but the children wouldn't listen. 'If I don't take my clothes off, I'll pass out,' Ravi whined glumly.

Without warning, the fog dispersed—one minute it was there, and the next, it wasn't—leaving the would-be rescuers dreadfully exposed to the turkey guards atop their sentry towers.

'WHERE did they come from?' Mabel gasped, berating herself for failing to identify the enemy's outposts.

'That's rather inconvenient,' Ravi muttered. 'You just can't rely on the weather, can you?' The boy's sanity was beginning to unravel.

The giant structures reared into the sky right in front of them. Their appearance did at least confirm the gang's arrival at the city's outskirts, which would be a small comfort if they were captured.

'How are we going to get past that lot without being spotted?' Ravi wasn't optimistic about making it into turkey town unseen.

Keith shared the boy's concerns. 'We find cover or go back.' The elf's violet eyes scanned the desolate terrain for another hiding place. It wouldn't take long before the turkeys perched high in their watchtowers noticed them.

Beyond the lookout posts, several enclosures caught the gang's attention. 'WHAT are THEY? And what's inside them?' Mabel saw what looked like animal pens fenced with a crisscross of glowing wires.

'There are humans inside,' Maggie said, peering into the distance.

'HUMANS? But that's AWFUL! They're kept no better than CATTLE! They can't hold prisoners like this. It's in violation of the Geneva Convention!' From what Mabel could see, there were no facilities to speak of. *What happens if they need to go to the toilet?* It was barbaric. And what's more, these humans weren't future humans but men, women, and children from their own timeline. It was easy to identify them; most still wore the winter clothes they were abducted in.

It's a good job Alice isn't with us, Ravi thought. *She would have marched straight to the nearest turkey tower quoting human rights at the top of her voice.*

Maggie sniffed the air and whined dolefully. 'I hope my *FRIEND*, Farmer Grindle, isn't in such a place.'

One of the enclosures, which without a roof was at the mercy of the sun's damaging rays, contained future humans. Left to rot, they huddled together, moaning like starved animals.

'What do they want with them?' Ravi questioned, for once appearing equally as dismayed as Mabel.

Keith shook her head. 'Nothing good.'

Ravi glanced up at the sentry towers. 'We can't stand here all day. WE'RE SITTING DUCKS!' Quite frankly, he was amazed they hadn't been spotted yet.

Mabel agreed. 'We need to find a new hiding place and infiltrate the city under the cover of darkness. AND THEN THEY'LL WISH THEY'D NEVER BEEN BORN!!'

Ravi had different ideas. He wanted to continue. 'As much as I would like to hide until it's dark, can we afford to wait? The others might not have much time left. And what happens if it doesn't get dark here?'

There was no guarantee that this *future* Earth was anything like their own. It was entirely feasible that days could last weeks and nights only minutes.

'There is ANOTHER WAY!' the elf announced triumphantly. 'Keith find tunnel system beneath soil. Entrance near.' She turned one way and then another, following the VTM with its flashing display. 'THERE!' she suddenly blurted. 'QUICKLY, HEAD FOR RIVERBED!'

17

The Turkey Princess

'Blooming heck, this isn't going *AT ALL* well, is it? I'm beginning to think you should have left me in Sunset Rest with all the other relics,' Santa mumbled miserably.

Alice squeezed Santa's hands. 'Don't be silly. You couldn't have known investigating Mr Grindle's farm would lead us here.'

'That's true enough,' Bennie said. 'No one on *EARTH* could have predicted that.'

Boris rummaged about in his pockets before pulling out a bulging handful of sugar cubes. 'Here, these will perk you up.'

'I'd rather not if you DON'T MIND!' Santa growled, turning his head away from Boris' outstretched hand like a petulant toddler refusing his greens. 'I'm sorry for putting you all in this situation. I'm supposed to make children happy, not inadvertently instigate their imprisonment.'

Bennie shrugged. 'It's not all that bad.'

'Yeah, it's just a bit dark and dank, that's all,' Boris said. Then he wrinkled his nose. 'Oh, and a bit smelly.'

'Just like a boy's bedroom,' Alice stated haughtily.

Finding themselves detained in what could only be described as a medieval dungeon wasn't where they had expected to end up this morning. They could hardly see a thing, and what's more, everything they carried had been confiscated, including their mobile phones. Not that the things would be of any use here. Even if there was a signal, it was doubtful that calling 999 would bring help, and goodness only knew what the call would cost.

'I'm TOO OLD for all this nonsense,' Santa moaned, sounding like a wailing spirit from the Otherworld. 'I've served my purpose. Can't you just let me sleep?'

'Oh, no,' Boris whispered to Bennie. 'Not this again.'

It appeared Santa was struggling with another bout of overwhelming bleakness. *He's like Jekyll and Hyde. He's all smiles one minute, and the next, he looks like he's just been force-fed Mrs Scrange's toad-in-the-hole.* Boris hated Mrs Scrange's toad-in-the-hole. He often wondered what was in her recipe because it certainly wasn't sausage. *Probably toad*, he thought with a shudder.

Boris supposed Santa felt just as terrible as he did on Sunday evenings before school the next day. *And being locked in an apocalyptic dungeon in the dark probably isn't helping his mood either.*

Bennie had an idea. 'I think we should administer him a sugar hit,' he whispered.

'You mean stuff them all into his mouth when he's not looking?'

'Yep. It will be for his own good. What do you say?'

By the look on Boris' face, he wasn't comfortable with Bennie's plan. In fact, he felt guilty just thinking about it. But he also realised it was their best chance to dispel Santa's dark thoughts and kickstart his flagging spirits.

After a few minutes chewing over Bennie's proposal, during which time he contorted his face into a wide variety of ridiculous poses, Boris reluctantly agreed. 'It's best if we don't tell Alice. She won't approve.'

Bennie nodded and moved into position. *Alice will forgive us... eventually.* After all, it *was* for the greater good.

Santa continued his descent into despair: 'I've squeezed down my last chimney, delivered my last present, eaten my last mince pie… I'm done for. Dump me on the scrap heap like a broken toy.'

Alice gripped Santa's hands again and squeezed harder than ever. 'You're not done for. What a silly thing to say,' she stated firmly. 'Come on, ONE LAST CHRISTMAS! Do it for us. I know you can.'

Santa shook his head sadly. 'You'll be okay. You don't need me. I'll just slow you down or get you all hurt… or worse. Leave me here; it's the only way.'

'NOW!' Bennie yelled.

In the blink of an eye, the two boys leapt at Santa. Bennie pinched the old man's bulbous nose with one hand and yanked on his white beard with the other. Gasping for air, Santa's mouth popped open. Boris wasted no time shoving the sugar cubes inside.

'WHAT ARE YOU DOING?' Alice shrieked, shocked by her friends' dastardly assault on an elderly pensioner. 'HAVE YOU GONE MAD?'

Having accomplished the deed, the boys slumped to the straw-covered floor beside Alice.

'Job done,' Bennie declared happily.

Alice glared at him. 'I can't believe you just did that. Violating a defenceless old man just because he doesn't want to help us is SHAMEFUL.'

Boris couldn't look at her. He stared at his hands as if he blamed them for his part in the heinous act. 'It was only some sugar, Alice.'

'Speak up; I can't hear you, HORRIBLE BOY!'

'He said it was only some sugar,' Bennie said. 'We weren't giving him RAT POISON for not wanting to help. We're just trying to get him going again, that's all.'

Alice's face softened. 'Oh, why didn't you say so?'

Bennie snorted. 'You didn't give us much of a chance.'

Alice narrowed her eyes. 'It still wasn't a very nice thing to do.'

Santa began mumbling again, and this time, his words were hardly audible. 'I AM... THE LAST... IMMORTAL,' he whispered. It was like he was in some sort of weird trance.

'Are you hearing this?' Alice said to the others. There was a good chance it was nothing but gibberish, but she was intrigued. She listened carefully as if Santa was sharing something profoundly important with them.

'PAAARRRP-PAA-PAA-PAA-PAA-PAA-PAA-PAA-PAARRP!'

The dungeon echoed with a mournful tune composed and conducted by Boris' musical backside.

'Oops,' Boris whispered, smirking bashfully once the final note rattled from his bottom like a trumpet. 'It's my nerves.'

'BORIS!' Alice scolded. 'YOU'RE DISGUSTING!'

Bennie was impressed and, if truth be told, a weeny bit jealous. *Beethoven? Perhaps Mozart?* He wished he could fart classical music.

'IN PAST TIMES, BELIEF SUSTAINED US... YET AS HUMANITY'S FAITH DIMINSHED... SO WE FADED FROM THE WORLD... ALL BUT ME... I AM THE LAST.'

'What is he going on about? I reckon Boris' bottom burp addled his brain,' Bennie said.

Santa's blathering sounded suspiciously similar to the beginnings of a church service. Reverend Dullard, the vicar at Larkbridge's Church of Saint Norbert, was the most boring man Bennie had ever had the misfortune to hear. He made watching paint dry an exhilarating pay-to-view event.

'SSSHHH! I'M LISTENING!' Alice didn't have a clue what Santa was trying to say, but she was hanging on his every word. 'Do you think it's something to do with what Keith told us? You know, about Santa being the last hero?'

Bennie shrugged. 'I hate to say it, but it sounds like the ramblings of an old man.' *Or an old vicar*, he thought wryly.

Huffing and puffing, Alice folded her arms and scowled. 'I thought you believed in Santa?'

Bennie sighed. 'I do. But not so much in this particular version. I shouldn't worry, though,' he added with a grin.

'WHY NOT?' Alice snapped impatiently.

'Because Santa's about to have an upgrade.'

'WHAT?'

'SUGAR RUSH! Get ready, here it comes… Five, four, three, two, ONE!'

Suddenly, Santa's eyes bulged, and he sat bolt upright like he had just been electrocuted with a cattle prod.

'I'll take forty-two, please, Mrs Cox. You can never have too many Christmas Puds! Rudolph, Prancer, Dasher… AWAY!'

Then things got weird. 'HELP! PIGLETS ARE NESTING IN MY BEARD!'

Then, even weirder. 'GOOD TIDINGS WE BRING TO YOU AND YOUR KIN! WE WISH YOU A MERRY CHRISTMAS AND A HAPPY–'

Abruptly, Santa paused mid-chorus, barked like an Alsatian and then slumped against the wall, falling unconscious.

'Blimey,' Bennie exclaimed. 'SUGAR OVERLOAD!'

Alice wasn't impressed. 'YOU IDIOTS! You've given him too much!' She fussed over Santa, pressing her ear to his chest—being extra careful to avoid a rather unpleasant custard stain on his shirt—to make sure his heart was still beating. 'Are you okay, Santa?'

The old man's eyelids gradually lifted. 'Blooming heck, my head is banging as if there's a miniature bull charging about inside. It feels like I've necked too much Christmas Eve sherry.'

'Oh, thank goodness,' Alice said, sighing with relief. 'You gave us quite a scare.'

Santa smiled, and it was one of his great big beaming smiles that lit up his whole face like he had just won a Christmas hamper in the church raffle. 'Don't worry, little lady. There's a bit of magic left in the old dog yet,' he said with a wink.

'We never doubted you for a second, Santa,' Bennie said. 'Right, Boris?'

Boris smiled ruefully. 'Not for a second.' He was just relieved he and Bennie hadn't been responsible for murdering an old man in cold blood.

Happy that Santa was himself once more and that a catastrophe had been averted, Alice focused on the next equally catastrophic problem—their incarceration.

'What will the turkeys do to us?' she asked quietly.

Santa blew out his cheeks and then scratched his beard. 'Well, they'll probably CHOP OFF our heads, STUFF our backsides with sage and onion, and ROAST us at two hundred degrees until our skin is NICE AND CRISPY and our JUICES RUN CLEAR.'

Boris was appalled. 'You think the turkeys will EAT US?'

'Why not? We're the fresh dish on the menu, and they haven't had anything new for centuries,' Santa said, and by the look of him, he wasn't joking.

Alice snorted. 'You've been scoffing down turkey burgers ever since I've known you, Boris. You shouldn't be surprised when your food returns the favour. On the other hand, *I* have never eaten turkey—OR ANY ANIMAL—which I shall explain to our captors,' she said rather smugly, holding her head high with pride.

'I don't think that's going to save you, Alice.'

'And WHY is that, Bennie?'

'Trust me, it just won't. They're not going to find you any less appetising just because you're a veg head.'

Alice suddenly looked terrified. 'Oh, no. I'm going to be SLICED and DICED and SPOONED INTO A PIE!'

Santa chuckled. 'Don't fret. I'll not let anything bad happen to you. Not while I'm still breathing, in any case.'

Alice was far from reassured. A few minutes ago, Santa very nearly wasn't breathing, and who knew how he would be feeling in a few minutes more? If he succumbed to another bout of bleakness, it was goodbye life, hello big chopper.

Boris frowned and began staring into nothingness, just like he did during one of Mrs Crispwhistle's science lessons. 'Do you suppose that's why the giant turkeys—THE MELEAGRIS—want to invade Earth? Is it so they can take revenge on us for EATING their ancestors?' He had obviously given the subject some serious consideration.

Santa stroked his beard as if it were a beautifully soft, long-haired rabbit, making Bennie and the others question whether he had, in fact, returned to full health or was still feeling the effects of excessive sugar consumption. 'I think Gobble-Gobble is invading our Earth because his Earth is DOOMED!'

The gang's sombre musings left them quietly subdued. Was their own timeline directly responsible for this travesty? Had the mistakes of the past led to Earth's downfall? The evidence was difficult to dismiss. It seemed humanity had created these monsters, and now they would all pay the price.

'You are both right,' spoke a voice from the darkness.

The gang nearly jumped out of their skins, except for Santa, who remained unmoving on the filthy floor, still grinning from ear to ear. It seemed that he was still processing the obscene quantities of glucose rushing through his system.

'Who's there?' Alice demanded, scrambling to her feet. Did she detect a comedic Germanic lilt?

'Humanity's treatment of our ancestors is reason enough to exact revenge, but their disregard for the planet is a far greater crime. When Earth became all but inhabitable, they abandoned it for a new life among the stars, condemning those left behind to survive in the most extreme conditions imaginable, as you have seen for yourselves. Over time, the Meleagris became the dominant species, but because of our bitterness, we grew crueller year by year. There is no rain. The sun burns. The very air we breathe is poison. Nothing grows. We hunt the remaining humans, feasting on their flesh to sustain our pitiful existence. The invasion of your Earth is our salvation.'

Bennie edged closer to the adjacent cell where the voice was coming from. 'Who are you?' he whispered, peering through the bars.

From the gloom appeared a giant turkey. 'I am Princess Cluckety of the Meleagris, Emperor Gobble-Gobble's eldest daughter.'

The children stared at one another, not knowing what to do or say. The Princess spoke in a less screechy tone than her male kin, which thankfully was less grating on the ears, but what she had said was a cruel truth to hear.

'I must apologise for my father's behaviour. I would never treat guests in such a manner—even *human* guests.'

Alice stepped nearer. The Turkey Princess was as filthy as the future humans who had chased them down from the mountains. And she hated herself for thinking it, but Cluckety was just as hideous as the rest of her kind. She didn't have a frilly comb protruding from the back of her neck like the males, but a colourful ruff of blues and greens that cupped her head and scrawny neck like the petals of a flower—admittedly not a pretty flower, but a flower nonetheless. Her beady black eyes weren't menacing like her father's either. They were sad.

'What are you doing here?' Alice asked, wondering why Emperor Gobble-Gobble's eldest daughter was locked up in a cell just like them.

'Not all the Meleagris favour my father's plans, and me least of all.'

'So he chucks you in the dungeons for disagreeing with him?'

The Princess sniggered, which sounded like a dolphin having a sneezing fit. 'I did more than disagree with him. I openly opposed him during a Meeting of the Elders in the Hall of Nine Windows.'

The Turkey Princess became sombre again. 'I accept my fate. Yet yours and your people's, I cannot. The sins of your fathers are not yours to bear. However, while I am locked in this dismal place, I can do little to remedy the situation.'

'Are you saying that if you escaped, there's a chance you could stop the invasion?' Bennie said, his veins suddenly flooding with optimism. Had fate dealt them a winning hand at last?

The Princess' eyes blazed with passion. 'I will start a rebellion! Although you must understand that if I do this, and the invasion is cancelled, I condemn my race to certain doom. There is no future here, only death. We will need to make a new home on your Earth. Can you promise us a future in the past?'

This was interdimensional politics on an unimaginable scale.

'Yeah, we can sort that for you, can't we, gang?' Bennie announced matter-of-factly.

Boris began nodding like crazy. 'Of course, not a problem. Interdimensional politics is our speciality.'

'I'll personally request an audience with the president of the United Nations to get the ball rolling,' Alice promised with a cheesy grin. It was her, *'You look absolutely lovely today, Mummy. Oh, by the way, can I have a pony for my birthday?'* grin.

Santa nearly choked on his beard. 'GOODNESS GRACIOUS ME! If I did have a naughty list, I'd blooming-well put this lot right at the top for this,' he mumbled, shaking his head.

Purring like a giant feline, Princess Cluckety's feathery ruff quivered excitedly, but her celebrations soon faded. 'Alas, caged as we are, I fear our glorious scheme for a bright new future will never come to fruition.'

'I wouldn't be so sure,' Santa said.

Alice frowned. 'What do you mean?'

'LISTEN!'

In the darkness beyond the dungeon, a kerfuffle was in full motion. There was a blue flash, followed by a yelp and then a thud. Suddenly, a light shone into the cells.

'KEITH FIND SANTA!' chirped a familiar voice.

18

Professor Wattle-Pluck

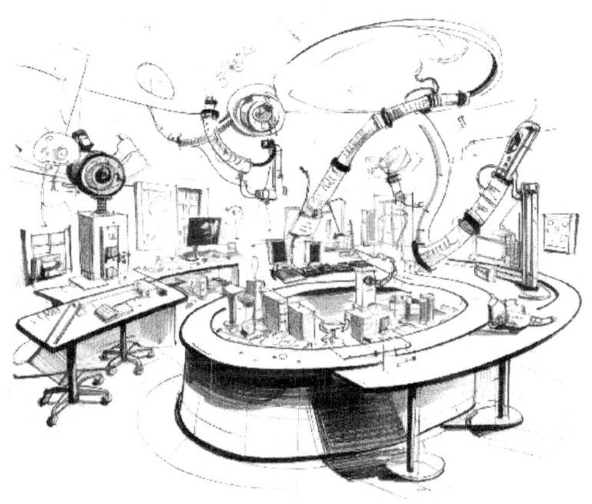

'Stand back,' Keith warned.

Crackling blue lightning shot from the VTM held in the elf's small hand. The metal lock turned orange, then white, and then, with a bang, it exploded into tiny shards of red-hot shrapnel that shot across the dungeon like mini fireworks.

Bennie shoved open the cell to greet his friends. 'Blimey, are we glad to see YOU LOT!'

'We had the horrible feeling we were going to be too late,' Mabel replied. She was relieved to find that

Bennie and the others still had their heads attached to their bodies.

'Yeah, from what we've seen since arriving in this awful place, you're lucky to be breathing,' Ravi added. He turned his nose up at an unsavoury aroma wafting from the dungeons. 'Is that CABBAGE again?'

Alice bolted from the cell and hugged each of her saviours in turn, even Ravi. 'THANK YOU! THANK YOU! THANK YOU!'

'Okay. Calm down. We're not safe yet,' Ravi mumbled, desperately trying to prise the girl from his body. She reminded him of an alien face hugger from a science fiction movie. *That would explain the smell*, he thought. The reasoning behind Ravi's assumption that aliens smelt of cabbage was uncertain.

'Oh, you've brought Maggie's sheepdog with you,' Bennie said, giving the border collie a good stroking.

'I *am* Maggie,' replied the dog gruffly.

After an animated ten-minute discussion regarding talking animals and Awareness Rays—and the need for Santa to update his repertoire of baffling hand signals—the gang were finally ready to escape the dungeons. Well, almost.

Boris eyed the unconscious turkey guard sprawled in the dust with concern. Was the thing really sleeping, or was it waiting to leap up and strangle him with its disgusting warty fingers if he ventured too close?

Suddenly, the creature's arm twitched. Biting his lip, Boris bravely suppressed the urge to scream like a four-year-old. 'Shouldn't we get moving before that *THING* wakes up?'

'All in good time, my boy,' Santa said, yawning his head off. He emerged from the cell like a big bear roused from hibernation. 'I'm assuming you jumped here using your VTM?' he asked Keith, stretching his arms above his head. 'And now the blasted thing needs recharging before we can jump home?'

Keith nodded.

'As I suspected,' Santa declared, finding himself momentarily distracted by the whiffy scent of cabbage. He sniffed his armpits and very nearly passed out. 'Keith, before we go any further,' he continued, hastily repositioning his arms by his sides, 'I want you to unlock the next cell.'

Keith narrowed her violet eyes. 'Is Elf Father sure?'

Santa shook his head impatiently. 'Of course, I'm sure. I wouldn't have asked you if I wasn't, would I?'

'But prisoner in next cell is turkey?'

'GOD'S TEETH, KEITH! I KNOW THAT!'

'You want to release one of them?' Ravi questioned incredulously.

'YES!' Santa boomed, looking to the heavens. 'Goodness gracious me! What's wrong with you all?'

Keith shrugged her slender shoulders and zapped the lock, skipping backwards as it clattered to the dungeon floor in a shower of sparks.

Ever so slowly, the door squealed open, but there was no sign of the occupant.

Alice crept forward. 'You can come out now,' she encouraged, speaking softly into the darkness. 'We won't harm you; I promise.'

Maggie growled warily.

'Sssshhh, Maggie,' Boris said, patting the dog's head. 'The Princess is a friend.'

Ravi scowled suspiciously. 'The Princess? Princess WHO?'

A tall, menacing shape appeared from the shadows. 'I am Princess Cluckety. And soon, I will be living with you all on your Earth.'

Mabel and Ravi traded a bemused look.

'I'll explain later,' Bennie whispered. 'We may have accidentally agreed to a peace treaty we weren't entirely authorised to promise.'

'You've done WHAT?' Mabel exclaimed.

'SSSHHH! LATER!'

Craning her long, slender neck, the Princess ducked through the cell door toward them. 'But first, I will help you escape.'

That sounds like a much better idea, Ravi thought, beginning to worry that his friends had taken leave of their senses and had been bewitched by Big Bird's turkey magic.

The Princess stepped over the slumbering guard with an elegant, willowy stride, leading the escapees from the dungeon. 'I will introduce you to Professor Wattle-Pluck. He is the Emperor's chief scientist and a very dear friend who will aid us.'

United once more, the gang were taken through a series of deep, dark tunnels, the existence of which, according to Princess Cluckety, was a secret even to the Emperor.

'The tunnels allow the rebellion to stay one step ahead of my father. At least, they did until I took a step too far and got caught.'

Eventually, after stumbling through the gloom for what felt like hours, the Princess guided them into the light once more. 'Wait here. I will make sure the way is clear,' she said before scrambling up through a metal grate above their heads.

Ravi wasn't convinced they were doing the right thing. 'How do we know we can trust her?' he whispered once she had vanished through the grate in the tunnel's roof. 'She claims she's a friend, but that's what all the baddies say, isn't it?'

Alice couldn't believe what she was hearing. 'Of course she's not a baddie!' she stated firmly.

'But how do you know?'

'I just do.'

Mabel cleared her throat. 'I hate to side with big ears, but he's got a point. Conspiring with the enemy is a dangerous game.'

'She's not the enemy. She's AGAINST her father!'

'So she says,' Mabel replied stubbornly. 'At the end of the day, she's one of them.'

Santa had heard enough. 'HUSH IT! If you don't, we'll get caught again, and none of us want that,' he barked. 'And take it from me, the Princess is a friend.'

'Where's your proof?' Mabel pressed. For all they knew, Princess Cluckety had run off to fetch the guards.

Santa huffed and puffed with indignation. 'For your information, little lady, I happen to be the finest judge of character in ALL HISTORY! I DON'T NEED PROOF!'

'OF COURSE!' Bennie blurted. 'It's how you tell who's naughty and nice, right?'

'Something like that,' Santa said, scratching at his beard like he had a flea infestation.

Princess Cluckety's monstrous face reappeared above them. 'Come, it's safe. The professor's laboratory is close.'

Trusting Santa's judgment, the gang hauled themselves through the gap and joined the Princess in a broad corridor.

Soon, they came upon a closed door. The door was solid metal and secured with more locks and bolts than any of them could count.

'How are we supposed to open that?' Bennie whispered. He had picked a padlock or two—only for fun and definitely NOT to borrow things from Larkbridge Primary School's stationery cupboard—but the security protecting this door was on another level. It made Fort Knox look like… Well, like Larkbridge Primary School's stationery cupboard.

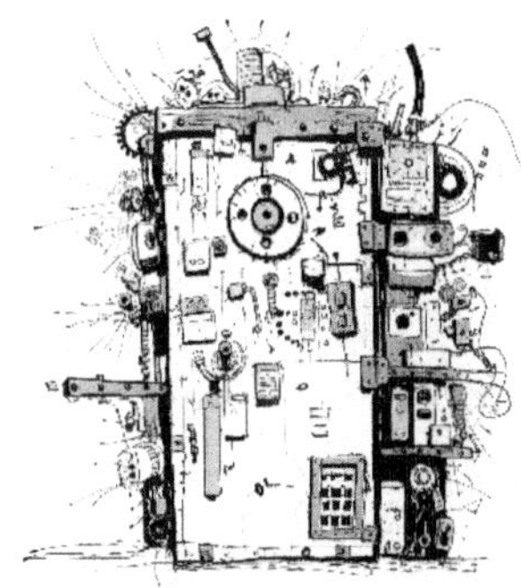

Ignoring Bennie's despairing expression, the Princess began rapping her bony knuckles against the door, creating a mournful chime like a misfiring grandfather clock striking midnight.

Bennie quickly detected a pattern. 'OH, A SECRET KNOCK!'

'If your brain worked any slower, you'd start talking backwards,' Ravi mocked, having identified the *secret knock* instantly.

In quick succession, the locks and bolts slid open, and with a loud groan, the door swung inward. On the other side, they were greeted by a turkey man wearing a long white coat.

'MY PRINCESS!' The professor surged to his feet from where he was perched on an absurdly tall stall, its nest-like seat cushioned with feathers.

As giant turkeys go, Professor Wattle-Pluck was a little on the short side. Neither was his plumage as colourful and vibrant as those creatures Bennie had so far encountered nor did it stand so erect. And it came as no surprise to see a pair of round-rimmed spectacles perched on the turkey's bony beak. Geekiness, it seems, transcends race, space, and time.

The professor's beady eyes bulged when he noticed the gang loitering with intent behind the Princess. Searching his coat with trembling hands, he produced what looked like a futuristic screwdriver from the top pocket.

'RELEASE HER AT ONCE!' Professor Wattle-Pluck demanded, waving the thing at them in a threatening manner. In truth, it wasn't an especially intimidating screwdriver.

'Lower your tool, Professor. You have nothing to fear,' the Princess said, indicating the gang sheltering behind her in the doorway with a clawed hand. 'These are my friends.'

The professor slowly lowered his screwdriver. '*Friends?*' he said. It was almost as if the word was alien to him. 'But... but... they're savages! Look at them. They're nothing like us. They are hideous creatures with smooth skin and squishy faces.'

The Princess shook her head. 'They are from an Earth before the cataclysm. They are our hope.'

The professor didn't look convinced, but he clearly trusted the Princess. 'Quickly, enter and secure the door. If anyone sees us together, we'll be sent to the Liquifying Chamber and turned into cattle feed.'

Cattle feed? Bennie hadn't seen any livestock, and the Liquifying Chamber didn't sound like the sort of place he wanted to visit anytime soon.

Santa wasted no time investigating Professor Wattle-Pluck's lab. He was like a child in an expensive gift shop. He picked things up, inspected them with grubby, chubby sausage fingers and then plonked them down without care or consideration.

'AH, HA! This is a *TIME BOMB*, if I'm not *MISTAKEN?*' he said, hooking a space-age-looking piece of equipment from a shelf.

The professor snatched the object from Santa's hands. 'You are mistaken,' he snapped irritably. 'That's my lunch!'

'What do you do in here, Professor?' Boris asked.

'I design Arvian's defences and weapon systems.'

'Like the ray guns?' Mabel said eagerly.

'Indeed. As you can see, it is mainly theory here. The working labs are on the next level. But I can control many of the city's systems from here.'

Professor Wattle-Pluck tapped a computer screen inlaid in the centre of a workstation. At once, a three-dimensional image materialised from nowhere, leaping into the air right in front of their eyes.

'WOW! AN INTERACTIVE HOLOGRAPHIC DISPLAY SYSTEM!' Ravi screeched gleefully, his eyes on stalks. If only he could get his hands on this technology. What a Christmas present that would be!

The professor began hitting the control screen with his claws, revealing missile launches, ray guns, laser cannons, forcefields, and jump portals. It was almost like he was playing a video game.

'And I presume you can control the vortex portals from here?' Santa said, trying very hard to sound like he knew what he was talking about—and failing.

The turkey professor pushed his spectacles back along his beak. *'Obviously,'* he answered haughtily. 'The jump details can be set and the portal primed.'

Keith promptly shoved her VTM under the turkey's beak. 'Big turkey recharge?'

The professor's feathers quivered whenever he looked at the elf. 'Let me see,' he said, taking the device from Keith. 'Erm… A primitive vortex time manipulator.'

Keith hissed like a disgruntled cat while Santa grumbled something inaudible that included the word 'rude'.

The professor scanned the VTM with a purple ray. Afterwards, he withdrew another screwdriver-like tool from another pocket—of which there were dozens—and set about dismantling the thing. 'Although many of its features still function to an acceptable degree of operational readiness, the device's internal power cells have been rendered unrepairable,' he explained, giving the VTM's innards a final prod with the screwdriver.

Alice yanked her pigtails impatiently. 'In English, please.'

'Its circuits are fried,' Ravi said with a shrug.

'Indeed.'

'Why does everyone wearing a long white coat sound like a nerd no matter who or where they're from—even if they're giant turkeys from the future,' Alice mumbled under her breath, echoing Bennie's thoughts moments earlier.

'So we're stuck here,' Mabel said dejectedly. She didn't much like the idea of spending Christmas somewhere that didn't serve turkey for lunch. *Do they even have Christmas lunch? Do they even have Christmas?*

Santa chuckled. 'Of course we're not stuck. We'll just use one of *THEIR* VTMs, that's all.'

Boris looked anxious. 'How are we going to sneak into that portal chamber place without being spotted?' Under no circumstances did he want to be sent back to the dungeon, especially knowing what happened to prisoners after their stay. Getting pulped into turkey feed wasn't how he envisaged his future.

'I'm sure Professor Wattle-Pluck will come up with something. He's very clever, you know,' the Princess said, bobbing her head toward the professor with obvious affection.

The professor's wattle turned an embarrassing shade of purple. He pondered the dilemma, pacing about the lab, muttering to himself. Then, all of a sudden, he stopped, his feathers shooting to attention like miniature guardsmen on parade. 'We will utilise holographic projection resonators embedded within magnetic beam capsules!'

'WHAT?' Bennie said. He made a face at Ravi. 'Translation, please.'

Ravi rolled his eyes. 'The professor is going to disguise us with TURKEY MAGIC.'

'Oh,' Bennie said. 'WHAT AS?'

'One of them, I'm guessing.'

Alice gagged. 'I really don't think I can.' The thought of being transformed into a revolting, warty-looking monster was enough to make her heave.

The professor started rummaging through various draws and cabinets, knocking equipment—and his lunch—to the laboratory floor in his haste. In a matter of seconds, he had assembled what looked to most of them as nothing more than a collection of useless junk, but Ravi knew otherwise. He squawked with delight as each new component was piled on the workstation.

'While Wattle works, I must inform you of my Father's plans regarding your world,' Princess Cluckety began solemnly. 'He intends to invade—this you know—but despite our superior technologies, he does not have the numbers to achieve this goal.'

Boris looked confused. 'How will he do it then?'

'The Awareness Ray,' the Princess replied ominously.

Ravi sniggered. 'I hardly think a few evolved animals will give the Emperor the upper hand. No offence, Maggie.'

'None taken,' she answered with a gruff bark.

'You do not understand,' the Princess continued. 'There is a bigger device.'

Bennie experienced a sinking sensation. 'How much bigger?'

'Big enough to instantly evolve every living thing on the planet.'

'THAT'S RIDICULOUS!' Ravi spluttered. 'You'd need to convert the ray into a sonic pulse and discharge it from at least five hundred feet above sea level. And even then, you'd need to simultaneously bounce the signal from dozens of satellites.'

'Forty-seven satellites, to be precise, at an altitude of six hundred and twenty-seven feet. Which, coincidently, is the exact height of London's British Telecom Tower.'

'The BT Tower?' Ravi muttered thoughtfully. 'Yeah, that would do it.'

'Blooming heck,' Santa rumbled. 'And when pray tell, is this travesty scheduled to take place?'

'Tomorrow night.'

Alice almost fainted. 'BUT THAT'S CHRISTMAS EVE!'

Santa chuckled. 'Well, it would be, wouldn't it. If I haven't already got enough on my blooming plate.'

Boris put his hand up. 'Erm… What's so bad about all the animals being able to talk and stuff? Maggie loves it, don't you, girl?'

Maggie tilted her head thoughtfully. Becoming *evolved* had amplified her feelings; they whirled about inside her head like an uncontrollable snowstorm. It was easier before. She did as she pleased, relying on her instincts and senses. But now, her conscience questioned her every move, every thought. It felt like being continually interrogated by herself. Being evolved was hard work. 'There's nothing better,' Maggie lied.

The chamber fell silent. 'Who wants to explain the situation to Boris?' Ravi said as if he really didn't want to be the one to do it.

Santa sighed. 'Take a seat, boy,' he said softly. 'Yes, that's it. Good lad. Now, I'll make this simple. What do you think might happen if, come Christmas morn, the farm animals in the fields suddenly understood what they were doing there?'

Boris scrunched up his face. 'I'm not sure.'

'Why do farmers keep animals in fields?'

'So they can milk them?'

'Yes, go on.'

'And… shear their wool?'

'Yes, very good. And…'

'Oh.' Boris' stomach lurched. 'And eat them.'

'BINGO!' Santa bellowed. 'And what do you think they might do, having learnt the awful truth?'

'They'll get a bit angry?'

Santa despaired. 'BLOOMING HECK, BOY, YOU'RE MAKING HARD WORK OF THIS! Yes, they'll get a bit angry. So angry, in fact, they'll want revenge. Wouldn't you if you'd been caged against your will and all your family and friends had been turned into beef burgers? You couldn't blame them for it, lad.'

Alice gasped. 'There'll be a full-scale uprising!'

Mabel's eyes gleamed excitedly. 'IT WILL BE WAR!'

19

Back to the Past

'We have a problem. I only have enough capsules to disguise four of you,' Professor Wattle-Pluck announced, poking his round-rimmed spectacles back along the length of his beak for the umpteenth time. 'Princess, you must have one,' he said, bowing respectfully, 'and the dog another.'

No living turkey had ever seen a dog, and Maggie would undoubtedly attract unwanted attention. And as for the strange little creature with the violet eyes. Well, they wouldn't make it to the end of the first corridor without being stopped. 'The... elf the third.'

'And Santa the fourth?' Bennie said.

'Indeed. It would be wise to disguise the plump, bearded specimen. Many Meleagris will want to eat him.'

The professor stared at Santa with hungry eyes as if picturing him roasting over a roaring fire with a big rosy-red apple stuffed in his mouth.

Santa suddenly felt very uncomfortable. 'Blooming heck, you best give me one of those capsule thingies sharpish before one of your lot puts me on the menu for CHRISTMAS LUNCH!'

'How do they work?' Mabel asked while the professor distributed the devices.

'They simply need to be within the user's immediate proximity.'

Mabel was eager to see them in action. What she wouldn't give to have one. *I'd take espionage to another level.* She would be a spy like James Bond, Ethan Hunt, or Alex Rider. *Only I'd be loads better because I'm a girl.*

Boris glanced at the dog. 'How will you hold yours, Maggie?'

Maggie opened her mouth, and the professor duly popped a capsule on her lolling tongue.

Boris raised an eyebrow. 'Is that a good idea? You might accidentally swallow it.'

Maggie emitted an angry, low growl. 'What do you take me for? I may still be a dog, but now I'm a clever dog, remember?'

'You shouldn't talk with your mouth full,' Boris warned.

'I'm perfectly capable of holding a conversation without—'

Maggie swallowed the capsule.

'WHOOPS…'

'You were saying?'

'Only activate the capsules when you must,' the professor continued. 'They only hold enough power for a few minutes.'

'What about the rest of us?' Alice asked.

'You will be our prisoners,' the Princess said.

The professor scratched his beak with a clawed hand. 'Even so, you will be fortunate to escape detection, especially in the Portal Chamber. We will require something more to increase your chances.'

'Any ideas, Professor?' Bennie questioned.

'I will create a diversion, and I know just how to do it!'

The gang ventured underground again, using the tunnel system to get as close as possible to the Portal Chamber. Once more, the Princess was their guide. 'Come, not much further,' she said, hastening along the dark shaft.

After ten minutes of bumping their heads and stubbing their toes, the Princess stopped them.

'We are beneath the Fattening Chamber. The Portal Chamber is near. We wait here until Professor Wattle-Pluck's diversion begins.'

'Do you know what he's got planned, Princess?' Bennie asked quietly. He was hoping for something dramatic, like an earthquake or a giant explosion.

'I have my suspicions. But let us wait and see.'

Unlike the previous tunnel, this one terminated with a grate set into the chamber's eastern wall and, as such, commanded a clear view of what was beyond.

'What happens here?' Bennie questioned, staring through the grate's metal bars. It reminded him of a makeshift hospital ward in an old bomb shelter. It was almost like they had been evacuated here because of a national disaster. Rows and rows of patients filled the chamber. There was hardly enough room to squeeze between them. *They're not patients; they're prisoners,* he reminded himself.

'In the Fattening Chamber, the livestock are–'

'*LIVESTOCK?*' Alice interrupted, not liking where this was headed, especially as the place was full of humans.

'Yes, Alice. The *livestock* are administered an engineered feed to increase their body mass. However, I have never seen so many humans. When our hunters return to the city with their prey, they bring them here. We eat what we can catch, but our hunters return with less each day, and more often than not, they return with nothing at all.

I know it is abhorrent to you, but it is how we live. We eat meat, and when we cannot, we eat the same feed as the livestock. The feed is made from a mixture of fungi grown in the catacombs, liquified remains, and genetically modified matter created by our scientists.'

Ravi narrowed his eyes. 'Remains of *WHAT?*'

'Nothing is wasted in Arvian. The dead are put to good use.'

Alice was shocked.

'But… but that's BARBARIC… AND DISGUSTING!' The very thought of it made her want to be sick, which, in the tight confines of the tunnel, wouldn't have been appreciated by her friends.

'It is how we survive, barbaric or not. Sadly, we do not have the luxury of choice.'

It got Bennie thinking. *It's no different to humans eating meat. Not dead people, though.*

What was happening on Future Earth put everything in perspective for Bennie. Well, almost. He knew what the Princess was trying to say. Her people had no other option but to eat *people* meat. Without it, they would die. The fungi and engineered produce weren't enough to sustain them. But back home in the past, there *was* a choice. In fact, there was an inexcusable number of choices. If truth be told, what right did he or anybody have to enslave and exploit another species, especially another species unsuspecting of their fate?

Perhaps Emperor Gobble-Gobble's Awareness Ray wasn't such a bad idea after all? *If food started talking back, we might feel less inclined to eat it,* Bennie thought. One thing was for sure: there was no way he would eat another bacon sandwich ever again.

'Excuse me, YOUR MAJESTY, but how much longer do we have to wait here?' Boris asked in his poshest voice. He was reluctant to moan, but he was so cramped up that he was beginning to lose the feeling in his legs. It was like the turkey shelter in Farmer Grindle's barn all over again. He could only imagine the discomfort Princess Cluckety was experiencing. Her long neck was bent double.

'We must wait for the professor's diversion.'

'How will we know when it starts?' Alice whispered.

'Oh, I think we will know.'

Mabel nodded in agreement. Any diversionary tactic worth its salt wouldn't need an introduction. If implemented correctly, it would be more than obvious when it began. Her dad had taught her that. It was basic military know-how.

Meanwhile, Maggie, who had disappeared down the tunnel to relieve herself in private, had picked up a familiar scent in the air, and now she came bounding back into view like a charging wildebeest. She barged past the others and promptly stuck her snout between the metal bars.

'What are you *DOING*, Maggie?' Alice hissed, trying to sound authoritative as quietly as possible.

Maggie didn't reply; she was too busy sniffing the air.

'Is dog sick?' Keith asked, eyeing the animal with disapproval. 'Or possessed by EVIL SPIRIT?'

'Whatever's wrong with her, she'll give us away if she sticks her nose out any further,' Ravi said.

'Can't she see those two guards with ray guns in there?' Boris added anxiously.

Suddenly, Maggie pulled her head away from the grate. 'Mr Grindle is here. I can't see him, but I can smell him.'

Bennie was horrified. 'Farmer Grindle is in *THERE?*'

Maggie's ears drooped, and she began whimpering. 'I can't leave this place without him. Promise me you will help?'

Bennie nodded. With a face like that, how could they refuse? 'We promise, don't we, gang?'

In the dark tunnel, Santa beamed. 'That's the spirit, my boy.'

'A delay might jeopardise your escape. It would be best if we stuck to the plan,' the Princess warned.

'Only boring people stick to plans,' Santa whispered excitedly.

Mabel suddenly grinned. 'I've got a new plan,' she said, caught up in the moment. 'Let's rescue them all and then BURN THIS PIGSTY TO THE GROUND!'

'YES!' Alice agreed passionately. 'But maybe without the burning.'

The Princess' plumage quivered uncontrollably. 'But that's impossible! How will we smuggle so many into the Portal Chamber?'

'It may be IMPOSSIBLE, but we're going to do it anyway,' Bennie declared boldly.

Santa chuckled. 'Now you're talking my kind of language. DOING THE IMPOSSIBLE IS RIGHT UP MY ALLEY!'

Princess Cluckety was taken aback. She hadn't expected them to care so much. The Meleagris had been led to believe humans were a selfish, compassionless race. 'If you are an example of your people, I cannot understand how Earth fell into ruin.'

'I'll fill in the blanks, shall I. Firstly—'

Fortunately, Ravi wasn't given the opportunity to bore them all senseless with an endless list of reasons for the planet's downfall because, precisely at that moment, an ear-splitting siren started screaming.

Bennie's eyes widened. 'Professor Wattle-Pluck's diversion!'

'Look, the turkeys are leaving!' Boris exclaimed, pointing through the grate as the Fattening Chamber's guards raced for the exit.

'Now's our chance!' the Princess squawked.

'AWAY WE GO!' Santa kicked the grate open and launched himself headfirst through the tunnel. Unfortunately, he didn't get far.

'What a ruddy EMBARRASSMENT!' Santa mumbled into his beard, wedged halfway between the tunnel and the Fattening Chamber. 'A little help, please, boys and girls!'

The children took turns shoving Santa's substantial rump until, with a 'POP', the tunnel gave birth to a bearded old man.

Finally dislodged, Santa was unceremoniously dumped into the chamber on his head. 'Cor, blimey. That's not good for the OLD NOGGIN!'

Even though Professor Wattle-Pluck had successfully deactivated the laser cuffs and security systems, the humans—or livestock as the Meleagris called them—couldn't escape. Pipes and tubes protruded from their bodies, binding them to their chairs.

They look like they're at the dentist, Bennie thought with a shudder. Nothing was more terrifying than a dentist's chair—especially one with weird alien probing equipment.

'Quickly, pull feeding tubes from prisoners!' Keith instructed.

The gang rushed into the chamber, dispersing amongst the feeding stations. Thankfully, the feed had stopped pumping. Even so, yanking the pipes from people's throats and nostrils wasn't pretty.

'YUCK! THIS IS REPULSIVE!' Alice complained, her face pebble-dashed with a repugnant, foul-smelling gruel.

'This way,' Maggie barked, weaving between the captives, snout twitching.

Boris was right behind her.

'There! The human wearing a flat cap!'

Farmer Grindle had a grotesque tube sticking from his mouth. It was attached to a machine behind his chair that looked and sounded like a washing machine, but instead of dirty clothes stuffed inside, it was filled with a repugnant, luminous green slime.

Boris began untying Farmer Grindle's bindings while Maggie pulled the pipe from his throat with her teeth.

'Maggie, is that you, lass?' Farmer Grindle croaked.

Maggie rested her front paws on the farmer's lap. 'Yes, Mr Grindle, it is Maggie, your friend.'

Farmer Grindle nearly fainted in shock. 'CAWD A HELL, when did you LEARN TO TALK, LASS?'

'It's a long story,' Boris said, unfastening the last of the straps and helping the farmer onto his feet. 'There. You're good to go.'

'I don't think much of the hospitality around here. Mind you, the food's not half bad.' Farmer Grindle poked his balloon-like belly. 'I've put on at least a stone—IF NOT MORE!'

Boris cringed. It was probably best if Farmer Grindle didn't know what the turkey feed was made from.

The gang raced from one captive to another, releasing them from their terrible chairs. But then…

ZAP! ZAP!

The guards had returned, firing their ray guns above the prisoner's heads. The creatures lowered their weapons, yelling and screeching in their strange language.

Bennie and his friends raised their hands—and paws—into the air.

'What do we do now?' Alice whispered, anxiously tugging her hair.

'I don't know,' Bennie admitted.

Boris groaned miserably. 'Please, not the dungeon!'

They were all feeling incredibly frustrated. To have come so close to achieving the impossible was soul-destroying.

Mabel was so angry she felt like nuking Arvian sky-high then and there. Ravi, on the other hand, was trying to look on the bright side. At least he was guaranteed a personal demonstration of the Turkey Emperor's futuristic torture equipment.

And then Bennie spotted Santa, and he knew the great escape was very much back on. *Good old Father Christmas!*

Unbeknown to the turkeys, *good old Father Christmas* had tiptoed behind them as quietly as a mouse wearing two pairs of exceptionally comfy slippers. Putting a sausage-like finger to his hairy lips, Santa crept closer. Then, when he was right behind the unsuspecting birds, his hands shot forward as fast as striking cobras. Grabbing their long, scrawny necks, he twisted them together as if he were making balloon animals at a children's birthday party.

After successfully turning the guards into something loosely resembling a two-headed giraffe, Santa disarmed them as easily as taking smartphones from babies.

'If you lot want to get out of here in one piece,' Santa said, addressing the liberated prisoners, 'I suggest you follow me and my friends.'

The prisoners started clapping and cheering like Americans do while watching movies or the English when observing random people inadvertently hurting themselves.

'Bleeding heck, we escape in SILENCE!' Santa boomed, vibrating the walls and shaking dust from the ceiling. 'Haven't any of you been rescued before?'

The Princess ushered everyone across the corridor toward the Portal Chamber. Outside, she halted. 'It's time to activate our capsules.'

'Right, here goes!' Fumbling inside a pocket, Santa activated his holographic projection resonator. Immediately, he began shimmering, warping in and out of focus. And then, in a flash, he was a seven-foot turkey.

'WEIRD,' Bennie mouthed, watching Keith change next. One second, she was a fiery little elf, and the next, a long-limbed, scrawny-necked giant bird creature.

'Ready, Maggie?' Alice asked the dog. 'It's your turn.'

'I have a confession to make. I may have ACCIDENTALLY eaten my projection capsule.'

'WHAT!'

'I didn't mean to. It just slipped down before I could stop it.'

Alice began to panic. 'Okay. I'll stuff you up my jumper. No, that won't work; you're too big. THINK, ALICE! There must be something we can do.'

They wouldn't be going home if they couldn't hide the border collie. Worse, they would be sent to the Fattening Chamber, force-fed gloop until they burst and then roasted and served to Emperor Gobble-Gobble on a silver platter.

Maggie howled miserably. 'I don't feel so good. Oh, I feel funny, and not in an amusing way. SOMETHING IS HAPPENING!'

The dog's belly began making all sorts of peculiar sounds until, quite suddenly, an enormous explosion of gas ripped from her hairy hindquarters.

Alice gasped. 'Oh, Maggie! You're a TURKEY!'

Somehow, the projection capsule had triggered inside the dog's digestive system. The downside was now everyone was gagging half to death shrouded in a thick, reeking gas that hung in the air like a poisonous fog.

'Remember,' the Princess began, coughing and spluttering, her eyes weeping, 'even though you look like us and will be able to understand us, you won't sound like us. So leave the talking to me.'

Santa and the Princess led the long line of liberated prisoners while Keith and Maggie brought up the rear. They marched into the Portal Chamber and were immediately confronted by turkey troops armed to the teeth stomping the other way.

The turkey officer in charge of the column saluted Santa and the Princess. It wasn't a salute Bennie had seen before. It was a firm nod, like a short, sharp peck.

The turkey officer scrutinised the prisoners. 'Where are you taking the livestock?'

The Princess saluted sharply. 'Processing, sir.'

'All at the same time?'

'Emperor's orders, sir.'

The officer hesitated, casting his gaze over the humans again. 'Very good. Carry on.'

The turkey stomped away until he approached the back of the line, where he noticed an irregularity. 'Where's your weapon, soldier?' he demanded of Maggie, the creature's beady black eyes narrowing.

Maggie didn't know what to do, so she started barking.

The turkey officer leapt backwards. 'Bird Flu?' he questioned fearfully.

Maggie nodded like crazy.

'Nasty. Best get yourself to the infirmary and sharpish. We don't want it spreading.' The turkey officer saluted—nearly pecking Keith's holographic beak off in the process—and marched his troops into the corridor.

'That was close,' Maggie whispered, her heart pounding like she was centre-stage at Crufts and really needed a poo.

Inside the chamber, the gang were presented with six gigantic archways. Each was inlaid with strange symbols and intricate carvings, mostly depicting angelic flying turkeys adorned with halos.

Beneath the archways were shimmering portals as blue as the ocean. The chamber was even bigger than the one with the mosaic floor Bennie and the others had passed through when they first arrived in Arvian.

'Which one?' Ravi whispered, awed by the enormity of the gateways. The Meleagris were barbaric, but boy, were they clever.

'Portal number two,' the Princess announced. 'Professor Wattle-Pluck has primed the gateway for your departure. Quickly, while the chamber is deserted.'

Tentatively, the humans approached the gate, uncertain what might be waiting for them on the other side. Was this really freedom? Or was this a shortcut to the slaughterhouse?

Santa deactivated his capsule. 'Trust me, home is through that blue swirly thing. I've used them gazillions of times, and they hardly ever go wrong.'

While the chamber echoed with the discontented chattering of humans debating whether or not to put their trust in a *blue swirly thing that hardly ever goes wrong*, Santa suddenly remembered something important. He jerked his gaze toward Princess Cluckety. 'We haven't got any CELERY STICKS to put in our EARS!'

The Princess appeared decidedly confused.

'CELERY STICKS!' Santa repeated impatiently. 'IN YOUR EARS!'

'Why would you do such a thing?'

'Jump sickness, of course!'

Princess Cluckety giggled at the notion, which just happened to sound like a distressed marsh warbler trying to negotiate a particularly rowdy storm. 'I can assure you, there are no side effects when using Arvian jump portals.'

Santa snorted. 'Blimey, that's progress, I suppose.' It seemed future turkeys weren't all bad.

'Right, then,' Santa boomed, making sure everyone in the chamber could hear him—and half of Arvian besides. 'Let's get this show on the road. Come on, we haven't got all day! JUMP INTO THE BLUE!'

Farmer Grindle was the first to step into the light. The others followed him, slowly at first but soon with ever-increasing enthusiasm. Eventually, they all disappeared into the past, leaving only the gang behind.

'I cannot go with you,' Princess Cluckety explained. 'I have a rebellion to instigate! Do your best to stop my father's plans. When next we meet, let us hope it is in better circumstances.'

Before their departure, the Princess presented Santa with a gift. 'Something to help you in the coming days. It is one of our devices. You need not worry about jump sickness anymore.'

'Oh, thank you kindly, Your Majesty,' Santa gushed, tossing the VTM over his shoulder. 'Here, Keith, a new toy for you to play with.'

As the gang marched toward the portal, they each saluted the Turkey Princess in the Meleagris way. Ravi's salute was so vigorous he nearly gave himself a black eye. 'Good luck!' they called as the swirling blue swallowed them whole.

'And to you!'

20

Hasseldorf

Santa filled his lungs with clean, cold mountain air. 'I'm home,' he whispered.

Hasseldorf was a winter wonderland, a fairytale hamlet cocooned deep within the snowcapped Alps.

Christmas Hall stood at the centre of the settlement, a colossal timber building adorned with ornate carvings and sturdy timber beams, a blend of elf craft and ancient Viking workmanship. It was a sanctuary, a place out of time, the symbolic heart of Christmas itself… At least it would have been if giant mutant turkeys from the future hadn't blasted it all to bits.

Keith was crestfallen. 'Turkeys have much to answer for.'

Wherever the gang looked, there were signs of destruction: trees felled, elf cabins flattened, toy factories burned to the ground, and worst of all, Christmas Hall reduced to a blackened shell.

Bennie saw how upset Santa and Keith were. 'You can rebuild, right? Start again.'

'The hall was centuries old, boy. It was Hasseldorf's soul. You can't rebuild a memory.' Staring at the scorched and broken beams half buried in the snow, Santa sighed. 'PAH! It was nothing more than a museum, anyhow. It hadn't been used for years besides the occasional rave or elf wedding. What is done is done.'

Taking another deep breath, Santa pulled himself together. 'Right, let's get to work. There's no point crying over spilt milk. Keith, gather the elves. Boris and Maggie see to the rescued prisoners. Mabel, prepare the defences against another attack. The rest of you, with me. WE HAVE REINDEER TO FIND!'

Santa set off through the deserted village and down a wooded slope with Bennie, Alice, and Ravi on his heels. Snow began to dance from the grey skies. After experiencing the acrid heat of Future Earth, it was a welcome sight. At least, it was until the children began to resemble small human icicles. In hindsight, jettisoning their hats and coats in Arvian was a regrettable decision.

'Why do we need the reindeer?' Ravi asked Santa as they trudged their way through the snow.

Santa glared at Ravi like he was one prawn short of a cocktail. 'So we can fly to London and save Christmas, of course!'

'Fly?'

'YES, FLY! For goodness sake, boy, you really need to keep up.'

'Reindeer can't fly.'

'Well, these ones can.'

Ravi shook his head. *The daft old codger has finally lost his marbles.*

At the bottom of the slope, nestled amongst the trees on the shoreline of a frozen lake, stood another timber cabin. It wasn't as big as Christmas Hall but was certainly large enough to accommodate a small elf wedding or, if push came to shove, a modest rave.

'It's beautiful,' Alice whispered.

Blanketed in snow, the scene looked like it belonged on a Christmas card, which, as a matter of fact, it did.

The landscape glistened white, the lake and surrounding pine trees sparkling as if coated with icing and dusted with sugar.

'Come on, before you catch your deaths,' Santa said, guiding his guests in through the front door. The children obliged, kicking the snow from their feet before stepping inside.

'Welcome to my home,' Santa announced, spreading his arms wide. 'And thank heaven, it's still in one piece.'

It wasn't what Bennie and his friends were expecting. Having supposedly lived in the same house for hundreds of years, Santa hadn't exactly stamped his mark on the place. In fact, it hardly looked lived in at all. It felt more like a holiday home, cold and lifeless, devoid of warmth and creature comforts. There were no pictures on the walls, books on the shelves or collectable knick-knacks lining the mantlepiece. Santa's home felt like it didn't have a heart.

'Was there ever a Mrs Claus?' Alice asked, grimacing at a thick layer of dust coating the hall mirror. In her opinion, the place lacked a woman's touch.

Santa caressed his beard, his blue eyes distant for the briefest of moments. 'Once, a very long time ago.'

By the look on the old man's face, it wasn't something he wanted to discuss. Alice wondered why he didn't at least have any pets. 'You need a cat or dog,' she said. 'And more chairs, perhaps a rug or two, and, if I'm perfectly honest, A COMPLETE MAKEOVER!'

'I don't need more chairs, and I certainly don't need a MAKEOVER—whatever that is? And no, I don't have a cat or a dog… bothersome so-and-sos. But I do have reindeer. Want to meet them? OF COURSE YOU DO!'

Without waiting for an answer, Santa cupped his hands around his mouth and started bellowing like a demented yak.

Yep, he's gone totally doolally, Ravi concluded. He wondered how they were going to stop Gobble-Gobble with a misfiring Santa in charge. *We'd be better off with Keith running things.* Yes, she was annoying and nearly as scary as Mrs Crispwhistle, but at least she wasn't deluded.

Suddenly, the big double doors at the end of the hall banged open and in stomped not one but a whole herd of reindeer.

'You've got to be joking,' Bennie mouthed in disbelief.

'AH, HA! THERE YOU ARE, MY LOVELIES!' Santa greeted the animals with open arms, rubbing their noses and patting their necks affectionately.

'Hang on one blooming minute,' Ravi blurted incredulously. 'THEY'VE ACTUALLY GOT WINGS!'

'Well, of course, they have. How else do you expect them to fly? MAGIC?'

Their wings weren't feathered like a bird's or leathery like a bat's, but something in between. *Feathery leather?* Perhaps not. It was difficult to describe.

'What are their names?' Bennie asked, stroking one of the magnificent beasts.

Alice couldn't believe her eyes and quickly descended into hysteria: 'YOU KEEP REINDEER IN YOUR *HOUSE?* YOU DO KNOW THAT IT'S INCREDIBLY UNHYGIENIC, DON'T YOU? BUT AT THE SAME TIME, IT'S PROBABLY THE BEST THING I'VE EVER SEEN. OH, *PLEASE* TELL ME THEY'RE DIRECT DESCENDANTS OF RUDOLPH! ARE THEY?'

Santa chuckled. 'They are,' he confirmed with pride. 'See that big one? That's SHADOXHURST.' Then Santa pointed at the reindeer one after the other. 'Grafty Green, Mockbeggar, Guston, Sissinghurst—'

'WAIT!' Alice interrupted, suddenly scowling as well as Mrs Crispwhistle. 'Why haven't they got nice names like Dasher, Prancer, and Vixen?'

Santa shrugged. 'If you must know, I got bored. After exhausting all the common reindeer names, I started labelling them after flowers and shrubs like Rose, Juniper, Sneezewort, Skunk Cabbage, Mother-in-law's Tongue… That sort of thing. Then it was kings and queens, then movie stars, household appliances, Welsh mountains—which even the elves couldn't pronounce—and now I name them after English villages in Kent.'

Ravi shook his head again. *Insane.*

'Oh,' Alice said with a feeble smile. 'That's nice.'

Sucking in his belly, Santa squeezed past his reindeer and stomped off through the house. 'Come on, lots to do and not much time to do it in!'

Exiting the cabin via the back door, the gang again found themselves outside in the bitter cold. In front of them, the lake stretched into the distance until it became lost in a swirling white and grey sky. The falling snow had thickened, and now the mountains circling Hasseldorf were hidden.

Alongside a small fishing shack on the lakeshore, Santa entered the stables. 'BLIMEY! This place is long overdue a good MUCKING OUT!' Pinching his nose, he tiptoed past the pens through a minefield of steaming reindeer dung and pulled open a large wooden door. On the other side was a dusty old storeroom, which mercifully was less smelly. In the centre, wrapped in red cloth like an enormous Christmas present, was something big.

'Is that a car?' Alice said.

Santa rolled his eyes. 'Blooming heck, girl, use your noggin. Why would I keep a car in the ruddy reindeer stable?'

Muttering something into his beard that sounded decidedly rude, Santa yanked the cover free.

'OH, IT'S YOUR SLEIGH!' Alice squealed, clapping her hands excitedly.

'Predictably red,' Ravi said, seemingly unimpressed. 'Is it airworthy? It doesn't look like it. In fact, it looks like it belongs in a museum just like…'

'Just like ME?' Santa said. 'That's what you were going to say, wasn't it? Well, I've got news for you, big ears—there's life in the old dog yet, and that goes for ME AND BERTHA!'

'Who's Bertha?' Alice whispered to Bennie.

Bennie shrugged. 'The sleigh, I think.'

Santa placed a hand on the sleigh's bodywork and began stroking the paintwork like he did his beard. 'Bertha is airworthy, alright. You'll see. At least, she will be after a little fine-tuning.'

'I think she's MAGICAL,' Bennie whispered. He couldn't stop grinning. *Santa's sleigh. I can't believe it!*

It was Ravi's turn to roll his eyes. 'It's just a bit of old wood. There's nothing remotely magical about it.'

'PAH! You won't be saying that when you're up in the sky.'

'WE'RE GOING TO *FLY* IN HER?' Alice exclaimed, very nearly exploding with joy.

'How else do you think we're going to get to London and stop Gobble-Gobble?'

'A jump portal?'

Ignoring Ravi, Santa strode across to a small area cordoned off from the rest of the sleigh barn. 'I call this my snug.'

Tugging a gold-tasselled rope, a red velvet curtain opened to unveil a comfy-looking armchair, an ancient wood burner, and a rickety wardrobe. In truth, it looked significantly more homely than his actual home. There was even a collage of black and white photos of Santa posing by famous landmarks: Stonehenge, the Statue of Liberty, the Taj Mahal, the Great Pyramid of Giza, the McDonald's in Luton... Bennie's favourite was a photo of Santa's sleigh parked atop the Great Wall of China.

'A fire to defrost my toes and a bottle of the strong stuff to warm my cockles,' Santa said with a grin. 'There's nothing better on a cold Winter's night.'

'What are COCKLES?' Alice whispered to Bennie.

Bennie frowned. 'I haven't got a clue. And to be honest, I'm not sure I want to find out.'

Santa opened the wardrobe, its hinges creaking as the doors slowly swung toward him. Hung from a wooden rail was a big red coat.

'Please don't tell me you're going to put that on?' Ravi said, screwing up his face like he had just bitten into a mouldy lemon after cleaning his teeth.

'Why wouldn't I?'

'Because it's so clichéd—and it's got moth and smells like my nana.'

'POPPYCOCK!' Santa barked, his beard quivering. 'Your nana smells of Mint Imperials and lavender.'

Alice clasped her hands together in prayer. 'PLEASE WEAR THE COAT, SANTA!'

Bennie grinned. He had the feeling Alice was going to get her wish.

Reaching into the wardrobe, Santa grasped a red sleeve, the fabric soft beneath his rough fingers. His touch lingered and lingered and lingered…

Awkward, Bennie thought, deciding to stare at his feet.

It was as if touching the coat awoke a lifetime of memories, and Santa had lived a hundred lifetimes. His worn features softened, and for a second, the children saw tears glistening in his blue eyes. Then he snorted like a walrus, blew his bulbous nose into his beard, and pulled the coat from the wardrobe. 'It's Christmas. I wear the suit and ride the sleigh.'

Alice punched the air in triumph. 'YES!'

'Right, out you go. Give an old man some privacy while he gets changed.'

On the other side of the snug, Bennie, Alice, and Ravi stared at one another as all sorts of strange noises began emanating from behind the curtain, including a colourful assortment of expletives that, until now, had never before been heard by children. *Getting changed* was seemingly proving to be a challenge for Santa.

Screeching on their rusted rail like a tortured banshee, the faded velvet drapes parted at last, revealing not an old man who turned the air blue with foul language, smelt of boiled cabbage, and appeared less likely to fit down a chimney than a pregnant hippopotamus, but the *real* Saint Nicolas. Well, almost.

Santa genuinely looked twenty years younger. His sapphire eyes gleamed, his white beard glistened, and his big nose shone as red as his suit. 'So, how do I look?'

'Alright, I suppose,' Ravi admitted.

Bennie nodded approvingly. 'You look awesome.'

'No,' Alice said, bursting with pride. '**YOU LOOK PERFECT!**'

Santa's big smile returned, knocking at least another ten years off his age. 'I have to admit. I feel **BLOOMING FANTASTIC!** Right, now it's your turn. In you come.'

Bennie frowned. 'What do you mean, ***OUR TURN?***'

Santa chuckled. 'You can't ride the sleigh without looking the part, now, can you, hey? What if somebody sees you?'

Ravi experienced a moment of grim foreboding. 'I've got a bad feeling about this.'

Santa pressed a bundle of clothes into each of their hands. 'Honorary elves for a day! Well, a night, at least.'

Ravi held up a red and green shirt and shuddered. 'You can't be serious?'

Santa shrugged. 'If you want to fly, you put on the costumes.'

'But these are nothing like what Keith wears?' Ravi moaned miserably. He had a point. If they walked into a fancy dress shop requesting elf costumes, these were precisely the sort of things they would be sold. Keith's attire, with its rustic greens and bark-armour accessories, wasn't remotely similar.

Santa grinned boyishly. 'No, but you're not elves, are you. You're elf HELPERS. We dress all the boys and girls in the things when they come to visit. Or at least we did. They like to look the part. Do you think I wear the red suit out of choice? I don't. It's what the little scamps expect to see.'

'Children used to VISIT?' Alice couldn't imagine Santa entertaining quests. He was always so grouchy.

'Only the most well-behaved. We don't let any old RIFF-RAFF in off the street.' Santa glowered at the gang, his gaze lingering on Ravi. 'Until now.'

Alice wasted no time donning her garish new clothes. Bennie eagerly joined her, pulling on the green shirt, the red and white bobble hat, and the red woollen tights that really didn't look right worn over jeans.

Turning around, Ravi eyed the sleigh with longing. 'The things I do in the name of science.'

21

Attack of the Giant Mutant Turkeys!

'I LOOK RIDICULOUS!' Ravi whined unhappily.

'No more ridiculous than the rest of us,' Bennie replied.

'SPEAK FOR YOURSELF!' Santa said, blowing an enormous raspberry that sounded like a small aeroplane taking off.

Alice giggled. 'Where's your Christmas spirit, Rav? Just go with it. It's Christmas Eve, and we're in Santa's village, for heaven's sake! If you can't dress as an elf here, you can't anywhere.'

'Suits me.'

All of a sudden, the whole building shook. The children grabbed hold of one another as Santa's home trembled all around them. The velvet curtains swung side to side, and the wardrobe rocked back and forth as if there was a monster trapped inside, trying to smash its way out.

'AN EARTHQUAKE?' Bennie said breathlessly.

But the rumbling didn't stop. Bucketfuls of dust and debris fell from the rafters, and the beams above their heads groaned like the undead.

'A THUNDERSTORM?' Alice said.

'NO!' Santa said, shaking his head. 'WE'RE UNDER ATTACK!' He rushed from the stables, leading Bennie, Alice, and Ravi back into the snow beside the lake. 'GOBBLE-GOBBLE'S SOLDIERS HAVE FOUND US!'

Through the trees, Bennie saw flashes of red and green at the top of the slope. It looked and sounded like Hasseldorf was hosting a giant fireworks display, but instead of claps and cheers, the loud bangs and exploding lights were accompanied by screams and shouts.

Bennie hadn't expected a terrifying full-scale invasion to look so pretty. The pulsing reds and greens reminded him of the coloured bulbs on a Christmas tree. *Very festive*, he mused absently.

Head down, Santa bulldozed through the deepening snow like a human plough, aiming straight for the thick of the action.

'Shouldn't we be running in the opposite direction?' Ravi muttered, trying to keep up.

'Mabel and Boris are somewhere up there,' Alice snapped. 'Or had you forgotten?'

'Good point,' Ravi conceded.

Emerging from the snow-clad trees at the top of the slope, Santa and the gang were presented with chaos.

Bennie's mouth dropped open. 'It's definitely not a fireworks display,' he whispered. 'IT'S A SPACE WAR!'

Laser beams streaked through the falling snow, illuminating the dark skies red and green. Everywhere the children looked was on fire.

Alice's breath caught in her throat. 'IT'S AWFUL,' she said, her eyes wide with fear.

'Yeah,' Ravi agreed. 'It's worse than the school Christmas disco.'

Alice tugged her pigtails and scowled.

Pulsing blue portals spewed legions of giant turkey soldiers into the heart of the village. Elves and the rescued prisoners met them in battle. Bennie and his friends couldn't watch. Sticks and stones were no match for ray guns.

'Keep your heads down,' Santa warned, ducking a crackling red laser beam that incinerated the tree directly behind him. After a groan and a snap, the spruce crashed to the ground.

'LOOK!' Bennie shouted, pointing into the mayhem.

Several figures were stumbling toward them, perfectly silhouetted by the roaring orange flames behind. It didn't take long to see who they were. 'Oh, thank goodness, it's Mabel and Boris,' Alice said, sighing in relief.

It wasn't only Mabel and Boris but Keith and Maggie too.

Beneath the trees, Santa stooped low to examine them once they were reunited. 'Is everyone okay?'

'Yeah,' Boris replied. 'Just about.'

'And you, Mabel?'

Mabel grinned. 'Never better.'

Santa's bushy white eyebrows lowered. 'You look like you're enjoying yourself a bit too much, little lady.'

Mabel quickly wiped the smile from her face, replacing it with a look of sincerity. 'Honestly, I'm not. I THINK WAR IS ABSOLUTELY DREADFUL.'

Despite an intergalactic battle raging behind him, Boris couldn't help wondering why his friends were dressed in fancy dress costumes. 'Why do you look like ELVES?'

Santa glowered. 'Because it's CHRISTMAS, and I TOLD them too! Now, more importantly, what's the situation?' he said, addressing Keith.

'Dorothy leading defence and Morag the evacuation.'

Bennie wondered if Dorothy and Morag were girl or boy elves? There really was no telling.

'Good. Now hurry. We need to hitch the reindeer to the sleigh before the turkeys find us.'

A tall, menacing shadow loomed above Santa.

'TOO LATE!' Alice screamed. And then something grabbed her from behind, and she was hoisted into the air.

More turkeys materialised from the trees, yelling gobbledygook and pointing their ray guns.

'FOR CHRISTMAS!' Spinning on his heels like a Strictly Come Dancing contestant, Santa butted a turkey into the snow before launching himself at another. Santa shoulder-charged the monster holding Alice like a Welshman rugby tackling a sheep on the slopes of Yr Wyddfa.

Mabel helped her friend to her feet. 'Come on, we need to find cover.'

Alice shook her head. 'No, we have to get to the stables.'

Mabel glanced down the hill. 'We'll never get through.' The turkeys had them surrounded.

'We'll see about that, little lady! CHARGE!'

Santa pounded headfirst toward the turkeys blocking their path, swerving searing bolts of red energy as the creatures blasted him with their ray guns.

Bennie couldn't believe his eyes. *Did Santa just cartwheel over a laser beam?* And then, even more amazingly, the old man drop-kicked a turkey soldier halfway up a tree. Was the red suit giving him superpowers? Bennie was beginning to believe that Santa was a *real* hero after all.

Inspired by the Elf Father's daredevil antics, the gang chased after him, screaming their own war cries through the woods.

Keith hissed like a cat. She leapt from turkey to turkey like a frenzied whirlwind of pain, scratching and biting.

Boris hauled a fallen tree branch from the snow before using the gnarled log like a lance, toppling turkeys from their clawed feet one after the other.

Maggie darted between the creatures' legs, snapping at their heels while snarling like a wolf.

Alice and Mabel hurled snowballs.

Bennie threw sugar cubes.

And Ravi tried his best not to get in the way.

The gang weaved through a gauntlet of grasping claws, dodging red and green laser beams that exploded beside them in the snow.

'WE'RE NOT GOING TO MAKE IT!' Bennie cried, darting between the pine trees. Then, from the bottom of the slope, he saw something coming.

'Oh, no. Now what?' He couldn't make out what exactly. It was as if the trees had come alive and were marching up the hill toward them. Thunder preceded them, making Bennie's ribcage shake and the ground beneath his feet tremble.

'TAKE COVER!' Santa cried. 'Shelter behind a tree trunk!'

Hunkering at the bases of pine trees, Bennie and his friends waited for the dreadful thunder to swallow them. They held their breath and covered their ears with shaking hands. The ground shuddered and the trees swayed. Suddenly the thunder crashed past them like an avalanche, showering them with crushed snow and sods of freezing soil.

'YOU BLOOMING BEAUTIES!!' Santa hollered proudly.

With their antlers lowered for attack, dozens of reindeer stampeded straight up the hill, heading for the enemy.

'LOOK, KNOCKHOLT'S LEADING THEM! GIVE 'EM HELL, MY BEAUTIES!'

Whooping with glee, Santa set off down the slope again. At the stables, the gang kept watch while Santa and Keith hitched the remaining reindeer to the sleigh. It wasn't long before laser beams started blasting the lakeshore.

Bennie shouted a warning: 'THE TURKEYS ARE COMING BACK!' Soon, the stables were on fire, and seconds later, Santa's house burst into flame. 'HURRY!'

The gang spotted turkey soldiers creeping through the trees like twisted shadows. There were hundreds of them, and they were all aiming their terrible weapons their way.

'DONE!' Santa hollered from inside the stables. 'TIME TO FLY!!!'

Mabel pushed her friends into the burning building. 'GO, GO, GO!!'

Ducking through the door, they ran past crackling orange flames, the air thick with black smoke.

Grinning like a loon, Santa sat ready and waiting in the sleigh with reins gripped and reindeer primed. 'ALL ABOARD!'

Coughing and spluttering, the boys and girls leapt inside.

'AWAY, SHADOXHURST! AWAY!'

The huge reindeer jolted forward, and the six behind him responded to their leader. In seconds, the majestic animals were dashing toward the sleigh barn's doors—doors that were still shut.

Santa flicked the reins for more speed. 'Open the doors, KEITH!'

Alice screamed—and so did Boris. 'We're not going to make it!'

'KEITHHHH!!!'

The elf repeatedly hammered the VTM. 'Doors not responding. SIGNAL JAMMED!'

'Hit the sensor,' Ravi shouted, pointing to a flashing red light positioned high on a crossbeam between themselves and the doors.

'What with?' Boris shrieked, frantically checking his pockets for something they could use.

'WITH THIS!' Bennie fished out a hairy sugar cube from deep inside his jeans. 'LAST ONE!' He tossed it to Mabel. 'You've got the best aim.'

Mabel swallowed hard. This was a pressure shot. Steadying herself, she gauged the distance to the target, accounting for the sleigh's speed and her shaking hands. Satisfied, Mabel let fly. The cube sailed through the cold air, heading straight at the sensor.

It was a direct hit!

At least it would have been if the sugar cube hadn't disintegrated an instant before reaching its target.

'OH, NO!' Bennie cried.

'ABORT MISSION! ABORT MISSION!' Santa yelled, preparing to yank on the reins.

'NO, WAIT!'

Maggie scampered past Santa and hurled herself onto Grafty Green's broad back. Then, leaping from reindeer to reindeer until reaching Shadoxhurst at the front, she climbed his massive antlers and, with a final herculean leap, hit the sensor with an outstretched paw before tumbling into a bale of straw.

The doors began trundling apart.

'Blooming heck! This is going to be TIGHT!' Santa yelled. Shadoxhurst and his team squeezed through the widening gap. 'BRACE YOURSELVES!'

With a great big bang, the sleigh bulldozed into the doors, smashing them off their runners.

'AH, HA! YES! GOOD OLD BERTHA! AWAY WE GO!'

Bennie mouthed a silent thank you to Maggie as she watched them race past her and out of the barn.

'AWAY SHADOXHURST! AWAY GUSTON, MOCKBEGGAR, FROGHAM! AWAY HOGBEAN, GRAFTY GREEN, DUDDLESWELL!'

The reindeer cantered onto an angled jetty with nothing ahead of them except a vast expanse of icy water. Bennie held on for dear life. He had never been so scared. In the back of the sleigh, behind Santa and Keith, the gang subconsciously linked their arms and clasped their hands together.

'HERE WE GO!'

At the end of the jetty, the reindeer leapt into the air, and as the sleigh rumbled over the edge, it followed them up into the sky.

Bennie leaned over the side. Beneath them, through the tumbling snow, Hasseldorf was a blur of colours: oranges, reds, blues, and greens. *I hope Maggie will be alright. I'm sure Farmer Grindle will look after her.* He wondered if they would ever see her again. *Once Gobble-Gobble realises Santa has escaped, he'll call off the attack,* Bennie told himself. And then his heart sank. *But then the Turkey Emperor will be after us, and he'll be ready and waiting in London.* It wasn't a nice thought. In truth, it filled Bennie with dread.

Santa twisted around in the driver's seat. 'Now that we're in the clear, you two can put these on.' He threw Mabel and Boris a bundle of elf clothes. 'If you don't, you'll likely FREEZE TO DEATH.'

Bennie suddenly realised he didn't feel cold, not even a little bit. In fact, he hadn't felt cold since pulling on the elf clothes. He smiled. *Elf tech is fantastic.*

'Right, Keith. Begin programming the VTM. We'll use a jump portal. Bring us out as close to the BT Tower as you dare—but stay clear of those awful city high-rises. I don't want to pop out the other end to find one RIGHT IN MY FACE!'

22

Saving Christmas

Above the clouds, Santa's sleigh zoomed through the darkening skies like a red spaceship. For a time, Santa guided the reindeer into the setting sun, the horizon a beautiful candyfloss-pink.

'It's wonderful,' Alice whispered.

'Yeah, I suppose,' Ravi said, 'but you do realise we're flying in the WRONG direction. If I'm not mistaken, the sun sets in the east. We should be travelling northwest.'

Santa grunted noisily from the driver's seat.

'RUDDY HECK, BIG EARS. You haven't got a romantic bone in your body, have you?'

Ravi looked confused.

'I'm guessing we're going this way because Santa thought we'd appreciate the view,' Bennie said. 'It's not every day you get to watch the sunset in a SEVEN-REINDEER open sleigh at FIVE THOUSAND FEET. And besides, it doesn't matter which way we're heading if we're using a jump portal. Am I right?'

'PRECISELY! At least some of you have a soul as well as a brain.'

Ravi still looked confused. The pretty sunset didn't particularly excite him, at least not like it did his friends. However, the fact that he was riding in a sleigh drawn by winged reindeer certainly did—especially while feeling warm and toasty when he should have been frozen half to death. Ravi examined the sleeve of his elf shirt. He couldn't wait to get the material under a microscope.

'Coordinates locked,' Keith chirped, finally glancing up from the VTM.

Santa nodded. 'Be a good elf and take the reins for a bit, Keith.'

Handing control of the sleigh to his deputy, Santa swivelled his bulging frame until he faced the children. 'Room for a little one?'

Not waiting for an invitation, he clambered clumsily into the back, parking his substantial posterior between Alice and Mabel. 'HA, HA! There we are—as snug as bugs, hey?'

'More like CRUSHED bugs,' Boris winced. Like Bennie opposite him, he had become uncomfortably squished against the side of the carriage. 'I think my circulation is about to be cut off again. I can't feel my arms.'

Santa cleared his throat awkwardly. 'I want to take this opportunity to thank you. You know, for bringing me back from the dead, so to speak.'

'Don't be silly,' Mabel said.

'No, it's true. I was ready for the final curtain, but you kids have made me realise the show isn't over. Not yet. I can still make a difference.'

Alice gave Santa a hug. 'Aah, you're so lovely… like a big cuddly bear.'

Santa sighed. 'If you can believe it, I wasn't always so nice.'

Ravi snorted. He dreaded to think what Santa must have been like if he thought he was nice now.

'Have you got something to say, BOY?'

Ravi flinched. 'No, sorry, Santa. I just had something stuck in my throat, that's all.'

'Probably a fly. Luckily, you don't see many in the Northern Hemisphere this time of year, but Australia is a COMPLETE AND UTTER NIGHTMARE! We have to wear visors, don't we, Keith—including the reindeer. And take it from me, they're not keen on the things, not one bit! Are you, my beauties?'

Santa's mind had wandered... again.

'Where was I? Oh, yes. Back when I was a young man. In truth, I was a thief before I was a saint. I stole from the rich to give to the poor.'

Ravi sniggered. 'You mean a bit like an obese Robin Hood?'

It was Santa's turn to snort. 'I wasn't always so round of girth, I'll have you know. Unfortunately, centuries of scoffing mince pies and swigging eggnog expands the waistline. It's an occupational hazard.'

Santa opened his mouth to continue his story, but nothing came out. 'Now look what you've done, I've lost my train of thought… DAMN AND BLAST!'

'Robin Hood,' Mabel prompted patiently.

'AH, YES! In those days, the poor had very little. Come Christmas, children went without presents while the boys and girls living in the big houses didn't. I couldn't abide that. So, one Christmas Eve, I decided enough was enough. I hid inside a great big coat and started a crime spree.'

Alice gasped. 'Saint Nicholas, YOU'RE A CROOK!'

Santa smiled ruefully. 'I'm afraid so. It was the locals who began calling me Saint Nicholas. The police and the posh folk called me Claws.'

'Why Claws?' Mabel asked.

'On account of my surname being CLAUS, YOU BANANA... and because of my crowbars, of course. Blooming useful things if you need to break into doors and windows. They protruded from the sleeves of my big coat, making it look like I had metal hands. So CLAUS became CLAWS.'

Bennie grinned. 'Cool.'

'And then, one fateful Christmas Eve when I was smashing my way into Mr Detrick's mansion, the town's mill owner, I WAS SHOT!'

Alice almost jumped out of her seat in shock. In fact, she would have done if she hadn't been so tightly wedged between Santa and Boris. 'OH, NO! THAT'S TERRIBLE!'

'Was it Mr Detrick who shot you?' Boris asked, now unable to feel his legs as well as his arms. Why did sitting next to Father Christmas always result in paralysis?

Santa shook his head. 'No, ironically, it was his little boy. The young scamp had got wind of my antics and didn't take kindly to me half-inching his presents.

Understandable really. He was only defending his property.'

'But that's awful,' Alice said.

'Yeah, blooming well hurt, too, I can tell you. Well, that should have been my lot, but I was in luck, or so I thought.'

Santa pointed a finger toward the emerging stars twinkling above the clouds like millions of fairy lights.

'It seemed the powers that be—I MEAN *HIM UPSTAIRS*—had need of a silly old thief. I was offered a deal. Go to HELL—which, let's be honest, isn't the most attractive of options—or repent for my sins by carrying on with what I was doing. I chose to live. Who wouldn't? It didn't take long to realise I'd been tricked... but in a good way. Well, sort of. If that makes sense?'

Santa looked at Alice. 'You asked me back in Hasseldorf if there used to be a Mrs Claus, didn't you? Well, there was once upon a time... my darling ANTHEA. A wonderful woman, strong-natured and sweet-minded. Or was she SWEET-NATURED AND STRONG-MINDED? Either way, she was my soulmate. Alas, she grew old and died while I didn't age a day. Watching those you love fade in front of your eyes is a curse. After Anthea, it was easier to live alone.'

Keith spun one hundred and eighty degrees and glared at Santa.

'NOT that I was ever truly alone. I had KEITH and my beloved elves, my MAGNIFICENT animals—and my WONDERFUL job! Being immortal is a hardship few can imagine, but it is also a blessing.'

Santa sniffed loudly before wiping his nose with the back of his hand. 'I'm not sure why I'm telling you all this, but hey-ho, there you go. Actually, I do feel a whole lot better.'

Santa might have been feeling a whole lot better, but the children definitely weren't. Bennie and Mabel were sniffing, Alice was blotting her tears with Santa's beard, and Boris was positively blubbing like a baby who had lost his dummy to a family of aggressive ferrets. Even Ravi looked sad, and that hadn't happened since a power cut curtailed his plans for resurrecting his pet hamster from the dead using a second-hand heart defibrillator.

'Thanks for listening. You've cheered me right up,' Santa said after a gigantic sigh. 'And now that you've done your jobs let me do mine.'

Bennie frowned. 'What do you mean, Santa?'

'I mean, the VTM is programmed to jump us to Larkbridge before London. I'm taking you home.'

The gang began protesting all at once:

'NO, YOU CAN'T!'

'WE CAN HELP!'

'WE'RE NOT GOING!'

'PLEASE, DON'T SEND US HOME!'

Santa held his hands up. 'You all saw what happened in Hasseldorf. Gobble-Gobble will be waiting in London. It will be too dangerous. What would I tell your parents if something happened to you? AND ON CHRISTMAS EVE! Goodness gracious me, it doesn't bear thinking about.'

'If we don't help, there might not be a Christmas,' Alice argued solemnly.

Mabel was having none of it. 'Well, I don't care what you think or what you'd say to our parents if we didn't come back because we're coming with you whether you LIKE IT OR NOT!'

'Well said, Mabel!' Boris declared with an affirmative nod of his bobble hat.

'You owe us, Santa. Without our help, you'd still be sucking sugar cubes and playing "Guess that Movie" with Shirley at Sunset Rest,' Bennie stated firmly.

'Oh, blooming heck! Alright, alright. But if you get yourselves KILLED, don't come RUNNING TO ME!'

'We won't,' Bennie said.

'Not even the geeky one?'

'Not even me,' Ravi said.

Santa slapped his thighs. 'WELL, ROAST MY PARSNIPS AND CALL ME BRIAN! It looks like we're all going to London after all. Open the portal, Keith. IT'S TIME TO SAVE CHRISTMAS!'

A glowing blue gateway materialised in the sky. Santa manoeuvred Shadoxhurst on an intercept course. Beneath them, the grey clouds swirled and writhed with the promise of more snow. Ahead, the blue VJP pulsed closer and closer.

'HERE WE GO!'

Shadoxhurst disappeared inside. An instant later, Santa's red sleigh exploded from the gateway into London.

'BLOOMING HECK!' Santa bellowed.

A tower block reared into the black sky directly in front of them. Santa hauled on the reins. Shadoxhurst banked hard right. For a dozen strides, the reindeer's hooves clattered against the side of the building before launching into the air again. In turn, the sleigh rolled ninety degrees, its rails sliding along the walls with a dreadful scraping noise.

'Blimey, Keith. That was *TOO CLOSE FOR COMFORT!* What are you playing at?'

Keith looked sheepish. 'Sorry, Santa.'

In the clear again, Santa saw the BT Tower in the distance. At over six hundred feet high and lit up like a Christmas tree, it was easily spotted. The telecom building was a beacon of light—blue, red, and then purple.

'At least we know where we're headed,' Mabel said. Most targets didn't have flashing neon lights guiding you toward them.

'Let's hope it doesn't turn green any time soon,' Bennie said. They all knew what that would mean. Green was the colour of Gobble-Gobble's Awareness Ray. If the BT Tower pulsed green, it was game over.

Suddenly, it wasn't only their target illuminating the night sky but a barrage of blazing red laser beams fired from the high risers on either side of Santa's sleigh.

'HOLD ON!' Santa cried. 'We'll have to make a low-level approach!'

With turkey snipers blasting at them, Shadoxhurst led his reindeer into a vertical nosedive. The icy black road and snow-white pavements raced toward Bennie and his friends as they plunged from the sky. Then, just when they thought they were going to be turned into red goo and splattered all over London, Shadoxhurst pulled level.

'YES, SHADOXHURST!' Bennie shouted with a celebratory fist pump.

With their wings hammering up and down like hyperactive pistons, the reindeer powered the sleigh onward.

Despite the terrifying nature of their mission, the children couldn't help grinning from ear to ear. 'Santa, don't we get a HO, HO, HO!!' Bennie asked as they streaked like lightning fifty feet above the busy city street. Beneath them, traffic stopped, and people pointed into the sky.

'IT'S A MYTH!' Santa yelled back, swerving past a laser beam that sheared off Grafty Green's left antler. 'I caught whooping cough back in 1776, and ever since, all I bleeding-well get is *HO, HO, HO* wherever I go!'

The enemy firepower intensified. The sleigh was caught between a barrage of red and orange lasers.

Santa couldn't dodge them all. 'TAKE COVER!'

They were hit again and again. A crackling blast of energy even set fire to Boris' elf hat.

'WE CAN'T TAKE MUCH MORE, SANTA!' Keith warned, her violet eyes glowing in the dark almost as brightly as the laser beams flying all around her.

'This is a DEATH STAR TRENCH RUN!' Ravi cried in despair, watching sizzling bolts of colour streak past him, one after another. 'WE'RE DOOMED!'

Santa stared ahead, focusing on the lights pulsing from the target. 'Not much further,' he muttered as the sleigh was buffeted by wave after wave of enemy fire. 'Stay on target, Shadox, my lovely!'

And then, out of the corner of his eye, Santa saw them… sleigh-seeking missiles. 'BLAST!'

Yanking on the reins, Santa launched Bertha straight up into the sky like a space rocket. He glanced over his shoulder. The missiles were still on their tail.

'QUICKLY, KEITH. EMERGENCY PORTAL JUMP! GET THE KIDS OUT OF HERE!'

'What about you, Elf Father?' Keith cried.

'You do your job, and I'll do mine! Ready?'

Ducking and diving through the night sky, Santa kept their unwelcome shadows at bay. 'HURRY!'

Taking a deep breath, Keith leapt into the back with the children. 'HOLD ON TO KEITH!' the elf yelled.

Bennie and his friends each grabbed a limb. They didn't know what was about to happen, but they trusted Keith. By the look in her eyes, she wasn't messing about.

'GOOD LUCK, ELF FATHER!' Keith shouted into the wind. Then she hit the VTM, and she and the children vanished in a flash of blue.

Keith and the gang reappeared on the snowy banks of the Thames. Gathering together, they stood shoulder to shoulder, staring above the tower blocks and high risers.

Santa's sleigh was on fire. Bertha looked like a flame-wreathed comet streaking across the night sky. Against all the odds, Santa had outrun the missiles, and even though the sleigh resembled a firework about to explode, he was nearly within reach of the BT Tower.

'He's going to make it,' Bennie whispered, crossing his fingers and toes.

'Stay on target,' Keith repeated over and over. 'Stay on target.'

'OH, NO,' Mabel cried. 'LOOK!'

Another missile screamed from a skyscraper straight at Santa. And that wasn't the only bad news. At exactly the same time, a blinding beam of light shot into the air from atop the tower—and it was emerald-green in colour.

Bennie stared up into the night sky with dread. 'THE AWARNESS RAY!'

'I can't watch,' Alice whimpered, tearing her eyes away from the dreadful scene.

There was a flash and a bang, and when Alice dared look again, she saw Santa's red sleigh engulfed in flame.

Bertha plummeted from the sky toward the busy London streets like a fireball… and then Santa was gone.

23

A Very Merry End of the World

Bennie's eyes pinged open. His heart was hammering inside his chest like a herd of stampeding reindeer. 'It's okay. It was just a nightmare,' he whispered in the predawn dark. Wasn't it?

Yawning, Bennie sat up in bed. *Since when did I own a set of elf pyjamas?* he mused, noticing what he was wearing. 'OH, DEAR.'

It wasn't a nightmare at all. However impossible as it seemed, everything that had transpired over the last few days was real.

Bennie groaned despairingly before retreating beneath his covers. *This can't be happening.*

After Bennie had returned late last night, his mum said it was going to be the happiest Christmas ever. His safety was the best present she or his dad could have wished for. Bennie wasn't so sure. He had the nagging feeling Christmas was going to be a disaster. His parents didn't even want to know where he had been. 'Don't worry about it now,' they had said. 'You can tell us in the morning. All that matters is that you're okay.'

Bennie didn't feel okay. In fact, he felt downright gloomy. Not even the bulging sack of presents dumped at the end of his bed lightened his mood. Something terrible was going to happen. He just knew it. Despite their best efforts, they hadn't stopped Gobble-Gobble's Awareness Ray. And if that wasn't bad enough, poor old Santa was gone, too.

'Shot down over London,' Bennie whispered disbelievingly. He couldn't comprehend what had happened. Now there was no one to stop the turkey invasion. *No one except the gang*. But what could they do?

Bennie relived Santa's terrible demise over and over inside his head. He couldn't stop seeing the sleigh hurtling out of control toward the ground in flames. It was horrible.

By the time Bennie managed to think of something that wasn't Father Christmas plummeting to his doom, daylight had brightened his bedroom. Downstairs, he could hear Christmas music on the radio and his parents banging about in the kitchen. *They're probably getting the Christmas lunch ready.*

It amazed Bennie how one meal required so much preparation. To be honest, he would be happy with a takeaway. He shrugged. So long as he didn't have to help, he would force it down with a smile on his face—except for the sprouts. Sprouts were pure evil.

Bennie yawned again. Then, halfway through a big stretch, he heard his mum scream. His blood ran cold.

'MUM?'

Bennie had never moved so fast. He sprung from his covers, banged through his bedroom door, and launched himself down the stairs like a lightning bolt.

Hedgehog and Miss Fluff-Face greeted him in the hallway.

'Morning, Bennie,' Hedgehog said.

'Morning, Hedgehog,' Bennie replied. 'What's going on? Where's mum?'

'She's hiding in the kitchen cupboard,' Miss Fluff-Face answered. She was nonchalantly licking a grey paw before repeatedly dragging it across her face.

'She's WHAT?'

'She's locked herself inside like a big scaredy-cat.'

'Why would she do that?'

'You tell me,' Hedgehog said, wagging his tail. He stared up at Bennie with what could only be described as a smirk.

Dogs don't smirk, Bennie thought.

'Oh, and your dad's passed out on the living room floor,' Hedgehog added as an afterthought.

Bennie's eyes narrowed. There was something different about Hedgehog and Miss Fluff-Face. What was it? Bennie's face dropped. *Dogs don't smirk... and cats don't talk.*

'You're speaking to me, aren't you?'

Hedgehog laughed. Well, not a laugh, exactly. It was more of a gruff-sounding cough at the back of the dog's throat. 'It took you long enough, YOU DOUGHNUT.'

Bennie just stood there gawping. *Nope, I must still be asleep. This has to be a dream. Please, let it be a dream.*

'Don't worry,' Miss Fluff-Face said. 'We're not remotely interested in anarchy, are we, Hedgehog. Although, paying extra attention to our needs might be in your best interests, if you know what I mean? Shall we say an additional four strokes a day and a live meal on Sundays? Perhaps a mouse or baby rabbit? It's so much more stimulating when my food runs about. I doubt the other animals will be so easily appeased, though.'

'Other animals?' Bennie mumbled in confusion. 'WHAT ANIMALS?'

Hedgehog tilted his shaggy head toward the front door. 'Best you take a look. Just a peek, mind. You don't want them seeing you. It would be bad for your health.'

In a daze, Bennie stumbled to the end of the hallway before gently pushing open the front door.

'They started marching into town at first light, and by the look of 'em, they mean business,' Hedgehog explained, scratching an ear with a paw. 'Now, enough about them. When are you going to feed us?'

Peering through a crack in the door, Bennie watched wide-eyed as legions of farm animals stomped through the snow. It was by far the most peculiar thing he had ever witnessed. Cows, pigs, sheep, goats, chickens… You name it, it was marching past his house.

They're coming straight from the fields and farms surrounding the town, Bennie mused.

He had seen enough. *This is bad. Really bad.* Apparently, the Turkey Emperor's Awareness Ray was a resounding success.

Pulling the front door closed, Bennie ran past Hedgehog and Miss Fluff-Face—who were both waiting patiently for their breakfast—and into the kitchen.

'MUM,' Bennie called through the cupboard door, 'if you can hear me, I'm popping out for a bit. I'll be with my friends, so no need to worry.'

He sped away, skidded to a halt, and then scampered back again. 'MERRY CHRISTMAS, BY THE WAY!'

Before slipping out the back door and into the garden, Bennie checked on his dad. *He's fine.* He looked like he was having a nice little nap. He was forever complaining about how he didn't get enough sleep. *Well, now's his chance.*

Outside, Bennie took a deep breath. *Right, first things first, I assemble the gang.*

The snow had drifted across the garden, and once more, Bennie was forced to dig the gate free before squeezing through.

'GOING *SOMEWHERE?*' squawked a crow perched on a branch above the fence. 'You can't hide, little boy.'

'LEAVE ME ALONE!'

Bennie bolted along the path behind the houses. He was sure he could hear the bird laughing at him. 'This is like a bad dream,' he mumbled, ducking for cover beneath the wiry branches of a hawthorn tree.

A formation of pigeons swooped overhead, searching the landscape for stray humans with their beady eyes.

Snowflakes began tumbling from the sky again. Bennie hoped the weather would hide him. He waited anxiously until the birds had flown out of sight before edging cautiously from behind the tree trunk.

Bennie ran to Boris' house. Yanking open the garden gate, he almost bumped heads with his friends bundling the other way. 'BLOOMING HECK, am I glad to see YOU LOT!'

Mabel smiled sadly. 'You sound like Santa.'

The gang's faces crumpled, and for a moment, they looked ready to give up.

'Poor old Father Christmas,' Alice whispered.

'It's down to us now,' Bennie said, trying to rally his friends.

Boris sighed. 'I'm not sure we can help, Bennie.'

'Yeah,' Ravi said, 'I hate to say it, but we've lost.'

Bennie shook his head, the white bobble on his elf hat twitching like a hungry ferret. 'Not yet, we haven't. Not while we're FREE.'

'What can we do?' Alice asked quietly. 'This is worse than we ever imagined. Cows have taken over our house and kicked my family into the street. I snuck out the back before they could catch me. Mother's beside herself. We'd only just had new carpets fitted, AND

NOW THEY'RE ALL COVERED IN COWPATS!!'

Alice was becoming hysterical again.

'It's alright, Alice. We'll think of something,' Mabel said, wrapping her arms around her friend. 'Where's Keith when we need her?'

'I don't know. I think we're on our own, at least for now,' Bennie said. 'Let's hide in the woods until we think of a plan.'

Reluctantly, the others nodded. Bennie felt safe in the woods. It was where they had first encountered Keith. He hoped she was already there waiting for them.

'Christmas in the woods. It doesn't sound too bad,' Ravi said. 'It's got to be better than pretending to like sprouts and parsnips whilst having to wear a silly hat.'

Emerging from the path beside the road, the gang ducked beside an abandoned police car as a column of animals stomped past. The vehicle's windows were smashed, and its roof was squished as if a cow had parked its enormous bottom on top. Bennie shuddered. He really didn't want a cow parking its rear end on him anytime soon.

The animals talked amongst themselves while they marched, and the topic of conversation was their treatment at the hands of humanity: 'Well, they'll not get another drop of milk from me, I can tell you,' a plump black and white cow said. 'If they like the stuff so much, it's about time they started DRINKING THEIR OWN!'

'You're lucky they only want your milk,' answered a brown hen. 'They snatch my unborn chicks, *BOIL* them in water, *BREAK* open their shells, and *POKE* them with lengths of *TOASTED BREAD!*'

'That's nothing,' a dirty pink sow grunted. 'They turned all my brothers and sisters into SAUSAGES!!!'

'SAVAGES!' bellowed the cow.

'MURDERERS!' squealed the pig.

'They'll get their *JUST DESERTS!*' clucked the hen.

The gang listened, wincing with every alleged crime. If the exchange was anything to go by, the prospect of a peaceful solution to this uprising was unquestionably slim.

'Oh, no,' Alice blubbed once the coast was clear. 'They're going to eat my family.'

'And everyone else after,' Ravi added unhelpfully.

'Of course, they won't,' Mabel said. 'They'll be under strict instructions from Gobble-Gobble not to harm the prisoners. After all, we're his livestock, remember. He won't want us damaged before sending us to the LIQUEFYING CHAMBER.'

Alice sobbed harder.

'I don't think you're making Alice feel any better, Mabel,' Boris said.

'The animals are vegetarians, don't forget, Alice,' Mabel stated, desperately trying to come up with something to lift her friend's spirits. 'They won't want to eat us.'

Ravi snorted. 'Pigs aren't. They'll eat anything, humans included. And as for the turkeys? Well, I doubt they'll waste a MORSEL!'

Bennie rolled his eyes.

Suddenly, the police car's onboard radio crackled to life: 'Chief? Are you there?' came a voice over the airwaves. 'More bad news. The zoo animals have caged their keepers and are demanding immediate transport to their homes of origin, except for the baboons. They're happy to stay but want fifty percent of the profits and their own daytime TV show. CHIEF? ARE YOU READING ME?'

'The farmyard animals may have evolved mentally, but until they sprout fingers and thumbs, they're not really a threat,' Ravi explained as the gang ran across the road and into the safety of the woods. 'It's those baboons we need to worry about. They'll take charge. It'll be like *PLANET OF THE APES* before you know it. You wait and see.'

'You tell my family that,' Alice snapped, ducking under a snow-laden branch. 'A lack of fingers and thumbs didn't stop cows from kicking them into the STREET!'

Finally, after trudging through the ever-deepening snow, they reached the clearing where they had first met the elf. It felt like a lifetime ago.

Brushing the snow from a fallen oak tree, they hopped onto the horizontal trunk, dangling their booted feet over the edge before proceeding to stare into nothingness. Now they were here, they didn't know what to do. None of them had any ideas, never mind a plan.

'I suppose we wait for Keith,' Bennie said. 'Or until one of us comes up with something.'

The others murmured in agreement before gazing into space again.

'What are we going to do about food?' Boris finally said, his belly rumbling. 'I'M STARVING!'

'Nuts and berries are best,' squeaked a small voice beside Boris on the trunk. 'Although, I bet you're into MEAT, aren't you?'

Frowning, Boris glanced sideways.

A small grey squirrel stood on its hind legs, scrutinising him with a pair of tiny black eyes. 'Have you tried squirrel? I bet you have, haven't *YOU*? I can see it on your STUPID FACE!'

All of a sudden, the thing looked decidedly scary.

'You're a squirrel murderer, aren't you? ADMIT IT! YOU EAT SQUIRRELS!'

Screaming, Boris leapt from the tree trunk and armed himself with a broken branch. 'STAY AWAY!'

'LOOK EVERYONE!' the squirrel cried in its little voice. 'The *STUPID* human is going to strike me dead with a BIG STICK!'

The animal scurried back and forth along the trunk, which was now unoccupied because Boris' friends had all scarpered like cowards.

'And after he's BASHED ME TO DEATH, he's going to *EAT ME!!*'

Boris whacked at the creature with the branch. He couldn't help himself. 'BE QUIET, YOU HORRIBLE TREE RAT!'

'Did you hear? He called me a *TREE RAT!* Blatant derogatory abuse directed at another species!'

No matter how hard Boris tried, he couldn't dislodge the squirrel from the trunk. It danced side to side, scurrying from one end of the fallen tree to the other, its nose twitching constantly.

'Erm… Boris,' Ravi said. 'It's probably best if you put the stick down.'

Boris slashed again and again. 'I'll get the blighter in a second! Stay still, you NASTY LITTLE THING!'

'BORIS!'

'WHAT?'

'We have company.'

'OH.'

Boris dropped his stick into the snow.

'Didn't I say you couldn't hide?' cawed the crow sitting on a branch at the edge of the clearing. An assortment of woodland creatures crept from the trees to join her: badgers, foxes, rabbits, and deer. The children huddled back-to-back as the animals surrounded them.

Bennie scowled at the crow. 'I can't believe you grassed on us. My mum and dad have been feeding you in our garden for years. TRAITOR!'

The bird hopped irritably on the tree branch. 'Where your nest of bricks is built, there once stood a mighty horse chestnut tree.'

Bennie was confused. 'So what?'

'My father was born high in its branches... and his father before him, and every crow in my family for over a hundred years. I don't think a few nuts and seeds can make amends for your family's *TREACHERY.*'

Bennie didn't know what to say. 'I'm sorry,' he muttered feebly. 'I suppose we don't think enough about things like that.'

Chopping down a few trees to make room for a new house wasn't something most people worried about.

The crow shook her head. 'No, you don't. But perhaps we'll have a second chance when you've all gone.'

Ravi didn't like the sound of that. 'What do you mean WHEN WE'VE ALL GONE?'

'It's best if you come quietly,' growled a black and white striped badger, baring his teeth. 'Don't try anything SILLY!'

The gang put their hands up.

A trio of giant stags lowered their antlers and ushered the children from the clearing.

The squirrel began chanting from the fallen trunk as the gang and their captors disappeared amongst the trees:

'JUSTICE FOR ANIMALS!
HOMES FOR BIRDS AND BEASTS!
CULL THE HUMANS!'

After a solemn frogmarch through the woods and across the park, the animals escorted their prisoners into town. Bennie heard church bells.

DONG! DING! DONG!

However, they weren't ringing in celebration for Christmas Day but as a warning to the folk of

Larkbridge—trouble was afoot. The bells fell silent as the gang entered the town square.

Boris nudged Bennie. 'Isn't that our headteacher over there?'

'Oh, blimey. So it is.'

Herded by bullocks, Mr Markles was forced toward the town's Christmas tree at the centre of the square.

'And look, there's Mrs Spleen-Weasel.'

Screeching turkey soldiers prodded the poor teacher mercilessly along the snow-covered pavements.

Alice gasped. 'AND MRS CRISPWHISTLE!' A gaggle of geese pulled the teacher by her hair, dragging her through slush, cowpats, and pig slurry. Alice grunted. 'If anyone deserves to be eaten, it's her.'

'HARSH,' Ravi said. 'What happened to goodwill to all men?'

'She's not a man; she's a HORRIBLE WOMAN!' Alice's goodwill didn't extend to cruel, cold-hearted teachers, no matter what her mum or the Bible preached.

Bennie saw where the turkeys were taking them. 'We're all headed for the same place. The laser pen.'

The sight reminded Bennie of the human prisoners in Future Earth. Hundreds and hundreds of people crammed together like animals awaiting the abattoir. Was this humanity's fate? Had the tables turned? Was it time for the birds and beasts to rule?

Towering above the square, the enormous Christmas tree suddenly started shaking. It shivered so vigorously its decorations began shedding like needles.

A rain of colourful baubles plummeted from the tree's trembling branches like festive bombs. Then, immediately after, there was a crackling flash of blue followed by a thunderous boom.

At the foot of the tree opened a magic blue door.

Bennie's face lit up. 'VORTEX JUMP PORTAL!'

A huge, winged reindeer stepped through the shimmering azure gate, and on the animal's broad back rode an old man in a red suit.

24

Santa's Army

If seeing Santa emerge from the portal riding a gigantic, winged reindeer wasn't jaw-dropping enough, then what followed him was on a whole new mind-boggling level of ridiculousness. An army of Santas and elves sprung into the square, packing enough weaponry to start World War Three.

'Forward!'

The turkey soldiers sent their animal allies to attack, and the square swiftly became a battlefield. Yet highly evolved or not, farmyard animals versus gun-toting

Santas and angry ninja elves was only going to end one way, especially as the Santas fired de-evolving laser beams from their ray guns.

Flashes of bright yellow fizzed across the town square, transforming crossword solving, chess playing, Shakespeare reading, fully sentient beings back into moaning, meandering livestock.

The elves took care of the turkey soldiers. Morag led a posse of ninja elves against them. Clad all in black—except for some lovely Yuletide embroidery on the cuffs and hems, including silver stars and red baubles—they wielded samurai swords and weaponised candy canes. Somersaulting over laser beams, they hooked turkeys by their long necks before chopping their ray guns into match sticks.

'Cease this madness!' shouted one of the Santas.

To be seen, he had climbed onto the shoulders of another Santa, and now both Santas swayed like seasick piggyback contestants competing in the North Atlantic Piggyback Championships aboard a floundering ship firmly gripped in the clutches of a particularly troublesome storm named after one of the Bronte sisters. Then, in less time than it takes to shout the word 'PING!' *he* became a *she.* And what's more, she wasn't a Santa anymore; she was a giant future turkey.

'Forgive the disguise. We did not want to scare any of you,' explained the hideous-looking mutant turkey monster. 'I am Princess Cluckety, Emperor Gobble-Gobble's daughter.'

The fighting abruptly stopped, and everyone—and everything—turned to look and listen.

'The rebellion is a triumph! My father's rule is at an end. Yet, refusing to concede, he and his supporters have fled our world to yours. Before doing so, he stole a powerful new technology from Future Earth. And now we must all work together to prevent him from using it.'

A huge bull raised its horned head to speak: 'Your father has given us our freedom! He is a HERO! Why should we help those who oppose him?'

'My father intends to use this new technology to de-evolve the entire human race–'

The animals roared and squealed in delight.

'It's about time the humans got a taste of their own medicine. At last, animals will be the custodians of Planet Earth, and humans shall be our slaves. Let's see how they like it.'

The Princess waved her arms frantically, begging for calm. 'Used on such a scale, the technology cannot be controlled. Humanity will not be the only casualty. All life on Earth will be affected.'

The animals gasped before exploding with anger, bellowing their disgust for all to hear, their hot breath misting in the frosty winter air.

'Your new-found enlightenment will be snatched from your grasp. Do not let my father destroy your futures and shatter your dreams. Join us, and together, we can prevent this travesty from happening. We must learn to coexist—animals, humans and the Meleagris harmoniously.'

The town square erupted with noise once more.

'How can we trust the humans?' the crow cawed.

It was Santa's turn to take centre stage. The *real* Santa. Astride Shadoxhurst he pushed himself in amongst the animals.

'Now that you have a voice, humans can't ignore you. Not any blooming longer! And they can't ignore Earth's future, not now the Meleagris have revealed the grim truth. They'll listen, and they'll change. Give them another chance. Under your wisdom and guidance, the world can be saved. TOGETHER, THERE IS A WAY!'

The animals began bickering amongst themselves.

Santa leaned low and whispered into one of the reindeer's twitching ears. 'How did I do, Shadox? I wasn't TOO CHEESY, was I?'

'You did splendidly, sir,' Shadoxhurst replied proudly. 'It brought tears to my eyes.'

The big bull bellowed for quiet. 'We shall debate the issue,' he announced, stamping his hooves. 'And then we shall cast a vote.'

Santa nodded. 'Don't take too long deciding. Once Gobble-Gobble shoots that yellow beam into the London sky, IT'S GAME OVER FOR ALL OF US!'

Santa pointed to those animals that were de-evolved during the fighting. 'You can see the results of this technology. Fortunately, the Princess and her turkey friends can restore their minds, but if we are all turned by Gobble-Gobble's treachery, there'll be no one to save us.'

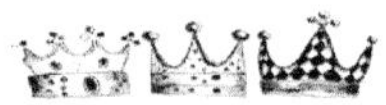

The laser pen was deactivated, and the prisoners were released. After the gang had checked on the wellbeing of their families and teachers—who were all dumbstruck and scared witless but otherwise perfectly fine, except for Mrs Crispwhistle, who was smeared head to toe in something even smellier than boiled

cabbage, old mushy sprouts, and Boris' musical farts combined—they squeezed their way through the crowds to Santa. He had dismounted and was feeding Shadoxhurst a nice big carrot.

Bennie grimaced. 'What happened to your EYE?'

A nasty gash was carved into the old man's face, running vertically from his bushy left eyebrow to his rosy cheek.

Santa winced. 'Ah, the eye. Yes, well, getting blown up had something to do with it. It's not all that bad. I can still see through the thing.'

'It makes you look like a pirate,' Boris said.

'Or a BOND VILLAIN,' Ravi added.

Mabel studied Santa with a scowl. Apart from the eye and numerous cuts and bruises, there was something else different about him. What was it? *Oh, I know!* 'Have you TRIMMED your beard, Santa?'

Santa winced again. 'BLAST! You noticed. The ruddy thing caught fire during the crash,' he explained, rubbing his chin. 'Very disappointing. I would have rather lost the blooming eye than the beard.'

Alice couldn't hold back any longer and hugged Santa as tightly as she could. 'We thought you were gone forever.'

'Careful, mind my grenades, little lady,' Santa said, chuckling. He patted the girl's head as if she were one of his reindeer. 'There, there… Father Christmas can never die, remember? It's a shame about Bertha, though. Nothing left but cinders.'

The gang's faces drooped. They all knew how much Santa's sleigh meant to him.

'Right, enough of all this sentimental nonsense,' Santa croaked, clearing his throat, which had suddenly developed rather a large lump. He popped a red candy cane between his lips and began sucking in earnest. 'I hope you kids are ready for ONE LAST ADVENTURE?'

'Let me guess,' Bennie said. 'It's not an enchanting return trip to London and the delightful BT Tower, by any chance?'

'SPOT ON! What better way to spend Christmas Day?'

'I can think of a few,' Ravi huffed. 'By the way, what's with the Santa impersonators?' he said, bemused at the sight of dozens of spritely, red-suited pensioners darting about the place.

'Turkey tech glitch, THAT'S WHAT! Wattle-Cluck's holographic capsule thingies threw a tantrum and decided to disguise the Meleagris as me.'

'It could have been worse,' Bennie said. 'It might have been Ravi's ugly mug.'

'OI!'

Alice eyed the animals with worry. 'Do you think the birds and beasts will help us?' It was so very strange watching them talk to one another. Whatever happened today, the world was going to be a very different place tomorrow.

Boris put a hand up. 'If we're going to London, how are we going to get there without Bertha, and how will we reach the tower without getting BLOWN UP AGAIN?'

Santa grinned. 'All good questions, my boy. And in answer to your first, here comes our transport.'

With a blinding flash, another portal yawned open. Santa's reindeer materialised from the swirling blue surface, swiftly followed by Keith, Maggie, and Farmer Grindle.

'CAWD A HELL! Them reindeer took some roundin' up,' Farmer Grindle explained. 'We spent the best part of the morn traipsin' through them ol' London streets. We found Grafty Green munchin' the Wembley pitch, Duddleswell doin' his business atop Nelson's Column, and Mockbeggar posing like a right ol' so-and-so on HIS MAJESTY's royal balcony up there at Buckingham Palace. I int never sin nuth'n like it, buh.'

Santa didn't care—not that he understood half of what the farmer had said. He was overjoyed to find his reindeer safe and sound after what had happened in London. 'It's wonderful to see you all fighting fit, MY BEAUTIES!'

'I suppose we can't portal jump straight into the tower, or we would've done it the first time?' Bennie asked, already thinking about the mission ahead.

'Correct,' Keith answered. 'Emperor will use anti-jump field—magnetic pulse that disrupts surrounding atmosphere. VJP not open within anti-jump field.'

'DUH, OBVIOUSLY! Everyone knows that!' Ravi commented in his customary charming manner.

Santa scratched at his singed beard. 'As for the part about not getting blown up for a second time, well, that's something we need to work on and fast!'

Bennie knew the perfect candidate for the job. 'You're up, Mabel.'

If anyone could conjure a plan from thin air, it was Mabel. Not only was she the undisputed queen of battlefield snowball warfare, but she was also Larkbridge's reigning Risk champion for the fourth year running.

The animals fell silent. At last, they had reached a decision. The big bull and the black crow came to give their answer.

'We have agreed to a truce,' the crow said, hitching a ride on one of the bull's horns.

'And we will help you stop Gobble-Gobble,' the bull added. 'But once the deed is done, there must be change.'

'If not,' cawed the crow. 'PREPARE FOR WAR!'

25

Thundersnow

After eating their Christmas lunch, Mr and Mrs Cheeseman settled on the sofa to watch the King's Christmas Day speech on television.

'What's that noise, DEREK?'

The Cheesemans could hear and feel a low rumbling. The Christmas tree lights flickered, and then the whole house began shuddering.

'I've never heard thunder like it. Go and have a look outside, Derek. Hurry, mind. You don't want to miss the speech.'

Mr Cheeseman sighed. 'Yes, dear,' he answered obediently, struggling up from the sofa.

'Take your tea with you,' Mrs Cheeseman instructed. 'Otherwise, it will get cold before you can drink it.'

'Yes, dear.'

Mr Cheeseman stooped to claim his cup, and when he thought his wife wasn't watching, he nabbed a mince pie from the table on his way into the hall.

'I SAW THAT!'

Ignoring his wife, Mr Cheeseman opened the front door and poked his head outside. It was already getting dark. The snow fell thicker than ever, and the strange rumbling grew louder.

Biting into his mince pie, he glanced toward the end of the street. The BT Tower was lost in the bad weather, but he could still see the building's lights twinkling through the snow.

'Can't they turn them off for once?' he moaned, huffing like a scrooge. 'IT'S CHRISTMAS DAY FOR HEAVEN'S SAKE!'

Admittedly, Christmas was one of the few occasions during the year when twinkling lights in the sky *were* appropriate, along with Guy Fawkes Night and Star Wars Day.

On the other side of the street, people stood in their doorways or peered through their icy windows, all intent on investigating the peculiar phenomenon from the comfort of their homes.

'Merry Christmas, Mrs Fowler!' Mr Cheeseman called to the lady opposite. She appeared a little worse for wear and had come to her door holding a wine glass and a candle, its flame dancing in the wind.

'Merry Christmas to you, too, MR CHEESY... WHEEZY!'

Mrs Fowler's gold-coloured paper crown sat lopsided on her head, and her speech was slurred like she had recently endured seven hours of dental surgery. 'Can you hear it?'

Mr Cheeseman smiled. *Mrs Fowler's been at the Christmas sherry.* 'Yes, Mrs Fowler, very odd, isn't it?'

'Thunder... SNOW, Mr Cheesy—wotsit—man. That's what they call it... DID YOU KNOW? Those weather boffins said we might get a bit.'

Then Mrs Fowler laughed hysterically for a whole minute. Mr Cheeseman thought it sounded like a demented peacock having a heart attack.

'I do declare,' she continued, despite having difficulty co-ordinating her sentences, 'that it's the first time they have got the forecast correct THIS YEAR!'

'Yes, Mrs Fowler. I think you might be right,' Mr Cheeseman replied, raising his cup of tea in salute.

The rumbling intensified, making the ground beneath their feet shake and the icicles dangling from the rooftops above their heads sheer off and plunge earthward like mini harpoons launched by Jack Frost's snow pixies.

Suddenly, a roaring thunder echoed through the street.

Mr Cheeseman and Mrs Fowler watched wide-eyed as an avalanche of charging animals pounded right past them before disappearing into the gloom toward the tower.

Mr Cheeseman spilt his tea.

'What ON EARTH was that, DEREK?' Mrs Cheeseman called from the living room.

'Oh, nothing, dear. Just a stampeding army of farmyard animals with Christmas Santas and elves riding on their backs.'

'WHAT?'

Mr Cheeseman was beginning to think he needed medical attention. Last night, he could have sworn he saw Santa's sleigh blown up by missiles. And now, he had just watched the London Farmyard Grand National hurtle past his front door.

'What has Maureen put in these BLASTED mince pies?' he muttered, examining the half-eaten snack. He subjected the filling to a quick sniff for good measure.

Across the street, Mrs Fowler gawped open-mouthed. She didn't notice her wine glass smashing to the ground. Nor did she bat an eyelid when her party hat went up in flames after accidentally setting fire to it with the candle.

Astride the mighty bull, Keith led the charge. Beside her rode Dorothy, Morag, Maggie, a host of snarling Hasseldorf elves, giant turkeys disguised as Santas, and Farmer Grindle atop an enormous sow—his childhood dream fulfilled. Well, almost. Unlike Gertrude, this pig couldn't fly. She also lacked machine guns, but courtesy of his new Meleagris friends, Farmer Grindle was armed with a massive ray gun.

Overhead flew squadrons of birds. Cawing furiously, the crow and her black-feathered dive-bombing legions spearheaded the airborne armada.

Angry red laser beams streaked through the snow. Positioned across the width of the street, Emperor Gobble-Gobble's soldiers guarded the tower, which disappeared into the stormy clouds like a giant alien monster. In answer, the turkey Santas fired back, blasting the defenders with sizzling blue lasers.

'BRACE FOR IMPACT!' Keith cried. Hopping onto her feet, she balanced on the bull's broad back like she was surfing a giant wave.

Cow-surfing in the snow was all the rage in London that Christmas. All the elves were having a go, even Farmer Grindle—although he was pig-surfing of course.

The two armies crashed together, causing a cacophony of noise that shattered the peaceful Christmas skies with a barrage of mooing, bleating, snorting, squealing, and squawking. As they clashed, the elves—and Farmer Grindle—were catapulted deep into the enemy's ranks.

Brandishing their weapons, they screamed into battle.

The ground assault was merely a distraction. High above the tower, the real attack was closing at speed.

'DIVE, DIVE, DIVE!' Santa boomed into the rushing wind.

'Roger that, Santa,' Shadoxhurst confirmed. 'Initiating final descent... *NOW!*'

As one, the reindeer plunged through the tumultuous snow clouds. Tight on Shadoxhurst's tail flew Princess Cluckety on Guston, Alice on Mockbegger, Mabel on Frogham, Ravi on Hogbeam, Boris on Duddleswell, and Bennie on Grafty Green minus her left antler—all clinging on for dear life.

Bennie was glad he hadn't eaten today. *Especially not an enormous Christmas dinner. If I had, I'd be scattering my innards all over London by now.* His stomach was threatening to escape up his throat and out of his mouth.

Bringing up the rear, Ravi and Hogbeam were forced into evasive manoeuvres.

'BRACE, BRACE, BRACE! Incoming friendly fire! Take cover!' Hogbeam hollered as a flurry of steaming reindeer dung exploded from Duddleswell's backside.

Ravi found himself momentarily upside down as Hogbeam skillfully evaded the offending discharge.

'Sorry about that,' Duddleswell apologised, shouting over his shoulder. **'I get *NERVOUS* flying in the snow!'**

Ravi rolled his eyes. *Now I've heard it all. A reindeer that gets twitchy in the snow. Next, he'll be telling us he's allergic to carrots.*

It was fair to say that Ravi was more than a little nervous himself. To be honest, who wouldn't be. Hurtling through thundersnow on flying reindeer toward a six-hundred-foot tower heavily guarded with evil mutant turkeys armed with space lasers was, quite frankly, totally insane. Most grown-ups wouldn't be capable of such daring bravado. In fact, most would have passed out somewhere over Hampstead Heath.

Bursting from the clouds, their destination was revealed. Wreathed in swirling snow, the British Telecom Tower reared into the sky like a giant lighthouse. It was an enormous spherical concrete tube encased in mirrored glass and adorned with hundreds of aerials and dishes—and enough LED lights to dazzle London's pedestrians, pilots, and pigeons for twenty miles in every direction.

Turkey soldiers blasted at the gang as they dropped from the storm.

'BLOOMING HECK!' Santa cried, ducking just in time to avoid a fizzing red laser beam from incinerating what was left of his beard. 'The roof's too dangerous to land on! We'll have to find another way in!'

Beneath the tower's summit, with its blinding lights and deadly lasers, was an observation level. Santa and the gang swooped to investigate, circling the perimeter for a weakness to exploit.

'It's all glass,' Bennie yelled. 'I can't spot a door anywhere. THERE'S NO WAY IN!'

After dodging turkey lasers for another three circuits, Santa lost his patience. 'Well, we'll see about that, WON'T WE!'

Seemingly appearing from thin air, the old man brandished two gigantic machine gun pistols. It looked like he was carrying a pair of bazookas. 'Who needs doors when we've got WINDOWS!' he bellowed, squeezing the triggers.

Orange and yellow flames flashed from the massive gun barrels, spewing a deluge of bullets into the air. With an almighty crash, the glass encasing the observation level shattered into a million pieces, exploding into the building like a shrieking hailstorm.

'IN WE GO!' Santa boomed merrily.

Shadoxhurst ducked into the now windowless thirty-fourth floor. One after the other, the gang swooped inside, landing beside Santa.

'Be careful of the broken glass,' Santa warned as they slid from their reindeer. 'Blimey, wasn't that fun!' he said, tossing the empty machine gun pistols to the floor. 'Those little beauties would have come in handy in the good old days. Blasting my way into children's homes would've been a blooming sight easier than squeezing my backside down chimneys.'

The gang stared at Santa as if he had lost his mind, even Princess Cluckety. They really didn't think blowing stuff up was a responsible means of gaining access to properties—especially when *not* waking the occupants was an absolute necessity.

'Is it just me, or are we moving?' Alice said. She was convinced the room was turning ever so slowly clockwise. It was an unnerving sensation.

'We're on the observation level. It rotates,' Ravi replied with a shrug.

In recent years, much of the tower had become obsolete, nothing more than a tourist attraction for those seeking uninterrupted views of the capital. The Observation Lounge was even once home to a novelty restaurant.

'What are you doing, Ravi?' For reasons Alice couldn't fathom, Ravi was more interested in searching through the broken glass scattered across the floor than saving Christmas.

'Come on, there's no time for sightseeing,' Mabel said, making for the lift. 'WE'VE GOT AN OVERGROWN PHYCHOTIC TURKEY TO STOP!'

'NOT SO HASTY!' Santa called. 'I think it best if we take the stairs. They'll see us coming if we use the lift.

And besides, I ruddy well hate the things. I got stuck in one back in the seventies. A monkey in the works, apparently. Actually, literally. There really was a monkey in the works. The little blighter caused havoc, I can tell you. It almost ruined Christmas that year.'

Ravi briefly paused his search to shake his head at Santa's ramblings.

'Anyway, you've given me an idea, little lady. Let's deliver the turkeys on the floors above a Christmas present, shall we?'

Unpinning a smoke grenade, Santa tossed it into the open lift and sent it upwards. 'That'll give them something to think about. AH, HA! BOOM!'

'RAVI! WE NEED TO GO!' Mabel yelled from the bottom of the stairs.

'NEARLY FINISHED!' Ravi wrapped the belt from his trousers around a large piece of glass salvaged from the debris. Once the strap was secured, Ravi pulled it nice and tight before hefting it into the air. 'SHIELD!'

Alice shook her head. 'A WINDOW SHIELD? It won't last five seconds. You better be careful not to cut your fingers on the thing.'

Ravi glared. 'Ye of little faith. You'll see.'

Leaving the reindeer behind, they tackled the stairs, quickly reaching the next level. Princess Cluckety craned her long neck through the doors to take a peek before making an odd yelping sound that might have been a giggle. 'Sleeping like chicks,' she whispered after winding her neck in.

Santa's smoke grenade had done the job.

'MARVELOUS!' Santa said, leading the gang onwards without delay.

Scrambling up another flight of stairs, they burst out onto the next level—the last before the roof where they knew Gobble-Gobble was lurking—and skidded to an abrupt halt. An old enemy barred their way.

Santa narrowed his old blue eyes. 'AH, CAPTAIN CLAW, WE MEET AGAIN!'

26

Bad Turkey

'You're too late,' Captain Claw hissed, flexing his horrible razor-sharp claws. 'My master's plans cannot be halted.'

'GO!' Santa cried, shoving the children toward the final flight of stairs. 'You can't help me! Find Gobble-Gobble. Hurry! I'll take care of our FRIEND.'

Two gleaming crowbars slid into Santa's hands from the sleeves of his red suit.

'Cool,' Bennie whispered. 'CLAW FIGHT!'

'Hurry all you want,' the giant turkey snarled. 'It won't make any difference. You will never—'

Suddenly, Captain Claw was blasted into the air and hurled twenty feet across the room. He crashed into a comfortable-looking swivel chair and rolled another twenty feet, spinning around and around like a hypersonic merry-go-round before finally coming to a standstill, smouldering from head to toe.

The Princess lowered her smoking ray gun.

'Or we could just SHOOT HIM, I suppose,' Santa muttered, raising his bushy eyebrows. 'Blimey, those turkey guns really do pack a punch. He's out for the count!'

'I bet he wished he'd brought his magic sceptre to the fight,' Ravi scoffed.

'If he's anything like my grandad, it'll probably be propped beside the toilet,' Boris said. 'Not that my grandad owns a magic sceptre, but that's what he does with his walking stick.'

Alice sighed. 'Be quiet, Boris. Nobody wants to hear about your grandfather's dickie BLADDER.'

Mabel sniggered. 'You're not going to believe this,' she said, pointing to a side door, which just happened to be the thirty-seventh floor's restroom.

Propped up against the wall outside was the sceptre.

Boris grinned. 'Just like my GRANDAD!'

'Well, I never,' Santa said. 'It looks like we caught Captain Claw with his trousers down.'

Bennie danced past the snoring bird and claimed the sceptre. 'It's rude not to borrow the thing,' he said. *You never can tell when you might need a magic turkey wand.*

Holding her ray gun ready, Princess Cluckety mounted the stairs. At the top, she pushed open the tower's final door and stepped onto the rooftop. The snow thundered. It was impossible to see anything beyond their own noses.

'DOWN!' Santa cried as red laser beams flew at them. 'They know we're here, but they won't be able to target us in this blizzard.'

Mabel nodded. 'We can use the storm to our advantage,' she shouted into the wind. 'We need to disorientate the enemy even more.'

'But *HOW?*' Alice yelled.

Santa's eyes lit up. 'I know just the thing!'

Santa stuck his fingers in his mouth, puffed out his cheeks, and blew as hard as he could. A shrill, brain-numbing whistle screamed across the tower's storm-ravaged summit. The gang clapped their hands over their heads.

'MAKE IT STOP!' Boris groaned. 'I think my ears are *BLEEDING!*'

The piercing sound quickly subsided, replaced once more by the thundering blizzard and the enemy's crackling laser beams.

'What was that FOR?' Bennie asked, his ears ringing.

Santa held a hand up. 'Wait for it… Any second… Wait for it… Wait for it… NOW!'

An instant later, an elf and a dog banged through the doors behind them and stormed out onto the rooftop.

It was Keith and Maggie.

'Oh, it's you two,' Santa said, looking surprised and disappointed at the same time. 'Never mind. Beggars can't be choosers, I suppose. Now that you're here, I need you both to run around for a bit. You know, confuse the birds while we slip in and pull the plug on Gobble-Gobble's doom ray.'

Maggie growled. 'We've just climbed eight-hundred and forty-two steps in under four minutes, and now you want us to worry a flock of mutant turkeys while getting SHOT AT?'

'YES, THAT'S THE SPIRIT!'

Keith shook her head. 'No point arguing with Bearded One. He always right.'

'Can't we wait for reinforcements? A battalion of badgers are on their way up, and they look ready for anything.'

'I'm sure they do.' Badgers were feisty in a tight spot. 'But there's no time.'

Santa huddled the gang together in the snow. 'Is everyone ready? Yes? Good. Split up, run about like headless chickens—excuse the pun, Princess—and when the turkeys don't know if they're coming or going, we charge in to save the day! Oh, and please try not to fall off the tower. You'll make a nasty mess on the pavement if you do. Any questions?'

Mabel put her hand up.

'Yes, little lady?'

'Can I have a grenade, pretty please?' she asked, presenting the old man with her best smile. If you don't ask, you don't get. 'Just a LITTLE TEENY one, that's all.'

Santa scratched the remnants of his beard. 'As it's Christmas, yes, you can,' he replied jovially, tossing Mabel a bomb like it was nothing but an apple. 'You mustn't make a habit of blowing things up, mind. It can be surprisingly addictive.' He was already missing his machine gun pistols.

Mabel stood there grinning like she had just won the lottery.

Suddenly, a red laser zipped past Santa's face so close it made his hair stand on end. His bushy eyebrows were instantly transformed into a pair of electrocuted albino caterpillars, and his beard a petrified pufferfish.

'That was a CLOSE SHAVE!' And he had experienced enough of those recently. 'I think we should make a start before these turkeys get lucky. Good fortune, everyone. Ready? On the count of three!'

The gang narrowed their eyes, gritted their teeth, and nodded their bobble-hatted heads. Then, just as Santa hollered, 'ONE!' something whooshed overhead.

'AH, HA! HERE THEY COME. BETTER LATE THAN NEVER, MY BEAUTIES!' Santa's reindeer flew low over the summit. 'You know what to do!'

Sweeping around the tower's central mast, the formation split apart. Below them, Gobble-Gobble's turkeys opened fire, shooting into the snow-laden sky.

Completely missing out two, Santa shouted, *'THREE!'* and despatched the gang into the blizzard like a pack of howling wolves.

It was chaos. Within seconds, Bennie lost sight of the others. Red lasers pulsed everywhere, illuminating the tower top in a spooky light show. Oddly, Bennie didn't feel scared. There wasn't time. A reindeer raced past him. Then, there was an explosion of orange followed by a jolting bang. Bennie ducked. He carried on running, zig-zagging through the snow.

A giant turkey materialised from the storm, jerking its ray gun at him. Bennie quickly jabbed his fingers at the strange symbols on the sceptre. He hadn't a clue what any of them did and was pleasantly surprised when a bolt of blue shot from the end. Before he knew it, the turkey soldier was sleeping like a babe on a bed of fluffy white snow. 'AWESOME!'

Bennie wondered why the creature wore a tin hat on its warty head. *It probably passes as fashion in Future Earth.*

Bennie headed for the giant mast. He could see its red and green lights gleaming through the falling snow. He found the gang gathered at its base, staring into the sky with horrified expressions on their faces.

Following their gaze, Bennie glanced upwards.

'MABEL!'

'One false move and the girl falls, understand?' Gobble-Gobble warned, shrieking his ultimatum into the blizzard. He gripped Mabel with a leathery arm wrapped around her neck, holding her over the very edge of a metal platform halfway up the mast.

Alice wasn't impressed. 'IF YOU HARM SO MUCH AS A HAIR ON HER HEAD, *I'LL STUFF YOUR BOTTOM SO FULL OF SAGE AND ONION IT'LL STILL BE COMING OUT OF YOUR EARS ON NEW YEAR'S DAY!!!*'

Santa's blue eyes bulged. He didn't think Alice was capable of such an offensive threat. 'It's always the unassuming, well-mannered types,' he mumbled into his beard.

Bennie noticed the Emperor wore a tin hat like his soldiers. *It must have something to do with the doom ray?* Perhaps it protected them from its effects?

Bennie raised his eyes. Wired to the tower's metal prism that rose high above them into the clouds was Gobble-Gobble's machine—a giant cube swirling with yellow energy.

'Father, stop this madness!' Princess Cluckety pleaded. 'We have a chance to make a new home here.'

Gobble-Gobble fumed. 'Foolish hen! Is that what they promised you? How can you trust these savages? They are the root of our suffering, or have you forgotten? Our Earth is dying. It teeters on the brink of destruction all because of their greed and lack of empathy. They are locusts, stripping the planet of its resources without considering the consequences. As soon as your guard is lowered, they will betray you. At all costs, they must be stopped!'

'Not like this, Father. They must be educated, not subjugated.'

Gobble-Gobble hissed. 'It's too late. The ray is ready. Your pathetic rebellion has failed, Daughter!'

While father and daughter argued, Santa and the gang plotted. They noticed what Mabel clasped between her fingers.

'Do not fret,' Gobble-Gobble continued. 'The de-evolution process is relatively painless. Say goodbye to your brain cells!'

'Excuse me, Mr Turkey Emperor,' Mabel interrupted, 'but would you be so kind as to hold *THIS* for me?'

Gobble-Gobble craned his long neck toward the girl. 'What on Earth are you gibbering about, you retched child?' And then he saw what she balanced in the middle of her outstretched hand. Like a big red and green Christmas bauble, a grenade rocked back and forth on her palm, and it was ready to blow.

'NEVER TAKE A RISK CHAMPION HOSTAGE,' Mabel said in a dangerously low voice.

Gobble-Gobble gulped, and his feathered frill quivered nervously. 'Erm... be careful with that, my pretty.'

Tilting her hand, the bomb slowly rolled off Mabel's open palm, dropping between the Emperor's clawed feet with a thud. 'Oh, silly me. BUTTERFINGERS!'

Gobble-Gobble leapt backwards, immediately releasing his hold on the girl.

Now free, Mabel stepped off the platform into thin air. 'MERRY CHRISTMAS!' she yelled, plummeting into nothingness. 'AND A HAPPY NEW YEAR!'

A millisecond before resembling strawberry jam, Mabel was plucked from the sky by Alice and Mockbeggar.

'NOW!' Santa bellowed.

Boris grabbed Bennie under the armpits and launched him onto Grafty Green just as the reindeer flew past. Armed with the stolen sceptre and Ravi's improvised shield, he soared into the night sky like a hero of legend from a fairytale.

Meanwhile, atop the platform, Gobble-Gobble eyed the unexploded bomb with suspicion. 'It's a fake!' he screeched, cautiously nudging the grenade with a clawed toe. 'I should have expected human treachery! Savages!'

Swooping from below, Bennie aimed the sceptre, but the Emperor was ready for him. 'I don't think so, boy!' he hissed, firing his ray gun first.

In the nick of time, Bennie thrust Ravi's window shield in front of his face, blocking the blast. Gobble-Gobble's red laser deflected back the way it had come, pinged off the Emperor's tin hat—knocking the thing clean off his bald head—and smashed straight into the glowing yellow cube halfway up the mast.

The Emperor seethed with rage, shrieking and yelling. 'My beautiful machine! You fools! Look at what you have done!'

One hundred feet below, Ravi danced a jig. 'MIRRORED GLASS! The only material capable of reflecting lasers. IN YOUR FACE, TURKEY TECH!' he roared gleefully as the Emperor's de-evolution machine burst into flames.

Dropping the shield, Bennie pointed the sceptre… and fired! This time, distracted by the destruction of his doom ray, Gobble-Gobble wasn't fast enough to respond. What's more, the laser beam blasting from the sceptre held in Bennie's hands wasn't blue; it was green.

'OOPS.'

Bennie had pressed the wrong button.

The bolt struck Gobble-Gobble right between the eyes, bathing him in shimmering green energy. He began jerking and twitching like… well, like an electrocuted turkey.

The smell wafting from above reminded the gang of Christmas dinner. 'Mmmm… Roasted turkey,' Boris muttered. 'So wrong, but so right.'

Gradually, the emerald glow faded. Gobble-Gobble made a strange mewling noise followed by a series of short, sharp yelps.

'Oh, my,' Gobble-Gobble whispered, admiring the falling snowflakes as they danced playfully in front of his face like fairies. 'I've suddenly become preposterously intelligent!'

He stared down at his daughter, standing beside Santa and the others. 'What have I done? My actions have been deplorably short-sighted and ludicrously illogical. I see that now. I see everything.' And then, with steam billowing from his ears, he collapsed into the snow in a heap.

'IT'S OVER! And all wrapped up by supper and charades. Well done, everyone!' Santa proclaimed merrily. 'How did you know I'd given you a dud grenade?' he asked Mabel once they were all safe and sound at the bottom of the tower.

Mabel grinned. 'Come on, Santa. Nobody in their right mind is going to hand a REAL bomb to an eleven-year-old, are they? Not even you.'

Santa chuckled. 'Well, EXACTLY... Yes, of course... I mean, I wouldn't... THEY wouldn't... As you say, nobody in their RIGHT MIND,' he mumbled, looking decidedly hedgehogish. 'Anyway, what you did up there was very brave, little lady. Very brave indeed.'

'Thanks,' Mabel replied. 'I could see Alice and Mockbeggar coming. It was just a matter of timing.'

'I'm so proud of you all,' Santa gushed. 'Teamwork, hey? You all played your part: Boris tossing Bennie onto Duddleswell like HERCULES, Ravi's ingenious WINDOW SHIELD, Mabel and her nerves of STEEL, Alice flying to the rescue like a BLOOMING VALKYRIE, and good old Bennie with the decisive blow—POW! BRILLIANT!'

'What happens next?' Bennie asked.

'Next, you go home and celebrate Christmas with your families. You've just saved the world, FOR GOODNESS SAKE! I think you deserve a rest. You can leave the grownups to smooth things out. Don't worry; I'll stick around. It looks like I might be needed for a while yet. They'll undoubtedly be one or two heads that'll require banging together in the coming days, and I'm just the sort of cantankerous old so-and-so to do it!'

Princess Cluckety bobbed her head up and down. 'Yes, children, you have earned your rest. I am in your debt. We all are,' she said, gesturing toward the animals and humans gathered in London's snow-covered streets celebrating the victory, including Farmer Grindle.

'Well done, nippers,' the farmer praised, bursting with pride. 'Earth's future is in safe hands.'

Maggie barked her approval. 'You're an example to us all.'

Keith shook the children's hands. 'You surprise Keith,' she said. 'Even geeky one.'

Ravi grinned. 'Thanks, *I GUESS?*'

'I'm sorry about your father, Princess,' Bennie added. 'Do you think he'll be okay?'

'He will live. Our brains can only take so much, evolve so far. My father's, I fear, is ready to burst. Time will tell. Do not blame yourself. His fate is of his own making as it is for us all whether we live in the future or the past.'

Epilogue

Good Tidings

The following Christmas, Bennie's mum and dad had a full house.

It was late. Most guests had either gone home or were snoozing in front of the fire. Hedgehog and Miss Fluff-Face discussed politics with Bennie's gran. Farmer Grindle was snoring his head off in an armchair with Maggie curled at his feet. Morticia, the crow, pecked at the buttons on the TV remote, channel surfing like a pro. Bennie and his friends played board games while their parents played charades with the animals.

'I win again,' Mabel said, smirking.

'That's four in a row, isn't it?' Boris moaned, shaking his head.

Ravi stuffed a toffee into his mouth. 'You've got to be CHEATING!'

'Mabel would NEVER CHEAT!' Alice said, defending her best friend fiercely. 'WOULD YOU?'

Mabel gasped. 'Of course not! I can't believe you would THINK IT!'

The game in question *was* Mabel's favourite: Risk. It was the new 'End of the World!' edition. Players could choose to command armies of humans, bad Meleagris, nice Meleagris, elves, or animals. Mabel had yet to lose.

'One last game?' Mabel asked merrily.

The day, like the year before it, hadn't been easy. Keeping everyone happy was a balancing act. Bennie's mum and dad had felt the strain. Accommodating the relatives over the festive period is challenging enough, but hosting Christmas for a dozen or more species, all with significantly different dietary requirements and *habits*, was something else entirely.

The bathroom, in particular, had taken some hefty punishment. The mighty bull, hero of *Thundersnow Charge* who, incidentally, had decided to be called Kevin, hadn't quite got the hang of, well, *hanging* his substantial posterior over the pan. As for the

Christmas dinner, the expression, 'Feeding time at the zoo', doesn't begin to do the experience justice. Needless to say, the aftermath required more than a mop and bucket to resolve.

Like the world they now lived in, it was all about give and take, compromise and conciliation. After the revelations last Christmas, change was swift. Virtually everyone and everything on the planet became vegan overnight. Nobody wanted to eat food that talked back. It just felt wrong. Of course, it wasn't all plain sailing. There were complications and disagreements: *The Siege of Asda, the Storming of Camden Market, the Bacon Bap Riots, and the Hoof Tax Rebellion*, to name but a few.

Bennie and his friends had returned to school as heroes. Even Mrs Crispwhistle and the Ricky Kittens Gang were nice to them.

Mrs Grindle eloped with a giant turkey to… yes, you guessed it, Turkey, while Farmer Grindle remarried a lovely sow called Sue from, believe it not, Shadoxhurst. As for the farm, they bestowed half to the animals and the other to grow crops and vegetables to feed them.

Bennie and his parents planted a Horse Chestnut sapling in their garden, and even though it would be another fifty years before the tree grew to be half the size of the original, it was the thought that counted. Morticia and her family were grateful.

Having survived his brain's evolution, former Meleagris ruler, Emperor Gobble-Gobble, now the cleverest lifeform on the planet, dedicated his time to uniting Earth's peoples and using his brilliant mind to help the planet's food shortages—at least he did when he wasn't attending therapy sessions and community service. You don't get to walk away scot-free after attempting to take over the world.

Princess Cluckety became Empress of the Meleagris and never had a giant turkey ruled with such devotion and understanding. Professor Wattle-Pluck was named her chief advisor. Under their leadership, Future Earth was successfully evacuated, and the populace safely rehomed in Norfolk.

All in all, things were working themselves out for the better.

'Five-nil to me,' Mabel said with a giant yawn.

'Can we play something different next year?' Boris said. He decided he didn't like Risk, not anymore. No matter which army he picked, he lost regardless.

Suddenly, there was a bang and a crash outside.

Alice stared wide-eyed.

Farmer Grindle sat bolt upright in a panic. 'SHOOT 'EM, GERTRUDE! SHOOT 'EM!'

'Who's GERTRUDE?' Sue demanded with a suspicious grunt.

'Erm… No one important, my lovely,' Farmer Grindle mumbled sleepily. 'What's goin' on, nippers?'

'I don't know,' Bennie replied. 'Wait… There's someone in the HALLWAY!'

Just as Bennie sprung to his feet, sending the board game flying, the door burst open. An old man in a red suit blundered into the living room, coughing, 'HO! HO! HO!' at the top of his lungs.

After hurtling straight into the Christmas tree, the old man turned his rosy face toward the bewildered children and grinned like a Cheshire cat.

'WHO'S READY FOR ANOTHER ADVENTURE?'

~ The End ~

Begin the Timothy Williams Saga!

When Timothy's school becomes the subject of a demon takeover, he and his two friends, Rupert and George, must unmask their foe. Timothy is forced into a battle for survival, not only in the real world but in his very dreams, where he must fight his nemesis to prevent Hell on Earth.

Blood-thirsty battles, monstrous demons, dodgy haircuts and enough possessed wildlife to fill a Satanic zoo!

'A full-on teenage adventure. Original, humorous, and highly imaginative. A rip-roaring read!' **BookViral**

Hell on Earth? Not if Timothy can help it.

Timothy Williams 3

Hellfire & Angel Light

Coming 2024!

Black
Knight

THE AUTHOR

Iestyn Long lives with his family in the historic village of Lavenham, in the Suffolk countryside. He is reasonably tall and narrow but desperately running out of hair, and although English, he has a Welsh name that is a constant confusion to one and all.

While listening to the tunes of Sir Cliff, Iestyn enjoys observing ants, stroking sparrows, drinking copious amounts of tea, and breathing—all of which he likes to practice on a regular basis.

Iestyn writes Young Adult fiction. Expect high-adventure, monstrous demons, epic battles, and dark humour.

For loads of extra demon-hunting stuff, visit these websites:
https://www.demon-hunter.co.uk
https://www.demonhuntersupplies.co.uk

Printed in Great Britain
by Amazon